JUSTICE DENIED

To Marilynn –
A better sister I could not have.
my love, prayers + best wishes
always
Darrell
2010

A NOVEL

JUSTICE DENIED

CARROLL MULTZ

TATE PUBLISHING & Enterprises

Published by Tate Publishing & Enterprises, LLC
127 E. Trade Center Terrace | Mustang, Oklahoma 73064 USA
1.888.361.9473 | www.tatepublishing.com

Tate Publishing is committed to excellence in the publishing industry. The company reflects the philosophy established by the founders, based on Psalm 68:11,
"The Lord gave the word and great was the company of those who published it."

Published in the United States of America
ISBN: 978-1-61739-017-3
1. Fiction / Legal   2. Fiction / Suspense
10.08.04

DEDICATION

This book is dedicated to my wife, Rhonda,
my helpmate, my soul mate, my inspiration.

ACKNOWLEDGMENTS

Writing a novel is like living a fairy tale. Despite life's many trials and tribulations, all the windmills are turned right side up by chapter's end, and everyone goes on to live happily forevermore. With a stroke of the pen, the characters' destinies are forged and are limited only by the author's imagination.

If it had not been for my life experiences, I would have been unable to paint the picture of the lives of the characters I have created herein. My life experiences have been enriched by those with whom I have come in close contact and those whom I have observed from afar. To all of them I am grateful for the walk together.

In a novel about the law, how it functions, and our whole system of justice, I would be remiss in not recognizing those who encouraged me to embark upon my legal journey and coaxed me along the way. At the fore were my parents, who taught me values, observance, and respect for the law and who never gave up.

To my father, the first attorney I knew and admired, and my mother, whose love and inspiration will be with me always, I owe everything. To Associate Justices John C. Harrison and Hugh Adair of the Montana Supreme Court, for whom I law clerked, their belief in my writing skills have brought me to this point, and without their patience, this book and the others would never have been written.

The trial scenes depicted in *Justice Denied: A Novel* were the product of forty-plus years in court and were due in no small measure to the mentoring and encouragement of my father, Edwin Multz, and to Richard Beacom, Larry Long, Robert Russel, Donna Salmon, and Len Chesler. My thanks to them for helping me along the way and for making me look good.

This novel would not be what it is had it not been for family, friends, and associates. First to my wife, Rhonda, for her technical assistance as the family's resident banker and great skill in preparation of the manuscript, and my daughter, Lisa, a therapist who acquired a lot of experience at home with her father; for her editorial assistance, as well as that of my assistant, Sherri Davis, I am most grateful. But for them and my daughter Natalie's prodding, this novel would have gone unwritten.

I am immensely grateful to longtime family friend and former editor of *The Colorado Lawyer*, Arlene Abady. Arlene, who is familiar with my writing, having edited over twenty of my articles for that publication, painstakingly edited my first attempt at fictionalization. She cannot be thanked enough for her efforts, which are reflected herein.

Three of my fellow professors at Mesa State College, Drs. Don Carpenter and Jerry Moorman of the department of business and Dr. Dan Flenniken of the department of mass communications, provided invaluable insights and perspectives in reviewing the manuscript, for which I am most grateful.

To two of my former students and authors of *Magna Sententia*, Annette and Katherine Stadelman, whose *noms de plume* are Anna and Ellie Sherise, I congratulate for their literary successes and express my sincere gratitude for their encouragement and suggestions for *Justice Denied: A Novel.*

And last but not least, a special thanks to my editor, Hannah Tranberg, and the wonderful staff at Tate Publishing for taking a diamond in the rough and making it sparkle.

Cursed is the man who withholds justice.

Deuteronomy 27:19

TABLE OF CONTENTS

PART THREE: THE ORDEAL IS OVER

INTRODUCTION

From the time I can remember, I was offended by injustice. Watching a fellow grade school classmate being suspended for fighting during recess while the aggressor went unpunished was the type of thing that offended me. Even today, when I see the referee eject the player who threw the last punch in retaliation, I am appalled and offended. My heart has always leapt for the underdog, especially the one who has been falsely accused.

Likewise, when I see the guilty escape the clutches of the law, I am offended by that injustice. The wrongdoer should be the one to be punished, not the other way around. That is why I spent almost a dozen years as a prosecuting attorney. Most of the rest of my career, I spent defending the innocent.

The most spectacular spot in Colorado I could choose to be the setting for the courtroom dramas and the events leading to and from the civil and criminal trials in *Justice Denied: A Novel* was Steamboat Springs, Colorado. I practiced law there in the mid-1960s and was a two-term district attorney there from the early 1970s to the early 1980s. I love the geography, the people, and the atmosphere. That is where my passion for skiing was born and my passion for trial work grew.

The juries in Routt County were suited for my taste. I don't recall ever having lost a jury trial as either a defense attorney or a prosecutor in Routt County, and I have nothing but respect and admiration for this law-abiding community and for those connected with and to the judicial system. If there is any hint to the contrary in this novel, chalk it up to rhetorical hyperbole.

Justice Denied: A Novel is a work of fiction. The general geographical data of Routt County, and in particular the Steamboat Springs area is factual. The account of the cowboys versus the college boys was taken from an actual incident in which I was involved as defense counsel, but I embellished to fit the characters and storyline of *Justice Denied: A Novel.*

The occurrence of the ordeal described herein as well as its cast of characters is pure fiction. The incident never occurred and the people never existed. Any resemblance to real people and events is purely coincidental. The notion that there is no such thing as justice is an aberration, and the fact that justice didn't prevail here doesn't mean that some day somewhere it won't.

PART ONE:
PREPARING FOR
THE FINAL CHAPTER

BY A TWIST OF FATE

Wild and crazy thoughts were racing through his head even before he began the journey to Steamboat Springs, Colorado.

Even though he had trained himself to think of the positive rather than dwelling on the negative, his mind was taking him in that other direction. Forgive and forget, he had been teaching his Bible school students, and now he found himself doing just the opposite.

The ordeal had left some deep emotional scars, some that had required professional help. He thought of a time before the ordeal when life was *the* ideal. He could count the ways his life and that of his family had been changed and how their lives had been turned upside down by a twist of fate.

God had a destiny in store for him and to revisit disappointments was an emotional detour he did not need and, especially at this time in his life, could not afford to take.

As his plane descended through the intermittent fluffy cloud cover, he could not help but think of the lazy summer afternoons of Steamboat when his childhood musings were inspired by the heavenly transformation of the floating powder puffs and cotton balls into giant polar bears, poodles, and snowmen that materialized for the moment and then were lost forever.

As a child, his much deeper concentrations found him daydreaming about superhuman feats, the beginning of the universe, its Creator, and the most perplexing, infinity. So deep and serious was his pondering that his consternation would be marked by crying episodes, requiring the consolation of his mother and father.

He had many dreams and visions about events that had not yet happened but did ultimately come to fruition. His dreams were spiritual and philosophical, and he heard music he would later play and, when he became older, would copyright. He was frightened about things that happened that, only days before, he had seen in a vision.

A therapist he saw as a child told his parents he was clairvoyant. It was only after he told his parents of a dream he had about a cousin in a distant state being involved in a swimming accident that they believed. That, however, was only after they were notified by relatives a week or so later that the boy had drowned.

Max didn't want to get his hopes up too high about what the late-night call from his father's former attorney was about. He had been at this stage before only to be turned away disappointed. Hopefully things would be different this time, but he had no false expectations.

It was a drab, dismal day when the 747 landed at Denver International Airport. The runway was no smoother than the airways from the time the plane began its descent until it landed. It was obvious that the winter freeze had taken its toll.

Max was never much of a fan of bumper cars, roller coasters, or his daughter's favorite carnival ride, "The Whip." At the thought of returning to Steamboat, his stomach was churning. Now, he was doing everything he could to keep from using the "convenience" bag provided by the unusually striking and attentive airline stewardess, who had witnessed his sudden and ghastly change of complexion. With the two elderly passengers seated on each side of him enduring the turbulence rather well, Max felt like a wimp.

You never know what to expect in the wintertime in Denver. Max had been in Denver clothed only in running shorts and a tank top the day before Christmas, trimming trees and the next day shoveling snow. He also remembered the terrible winter storm they had in May the year he moved from there. This February winter day was no different from that which he was hoping to escape when he left O'Hare International Airport earlier that morning. The de-icing procedures in Chicago accounted for an almost two-hour delay.

Max was not a very patient man, and every time he flew was dumfounded by the inefficiency of the airline industry. With the screening process, he thought the industry had taken ten giant steps backward. He marveled at the elderly and the single moms with babes in one arm and an oversize travel bag in the other, dragging small children behind them while trying to traverse the airport maze.

This would be the first time Max had flown into DIA. It was a fairly new airport. The terminal building was built to resemble snow-capped mountains, and its rising, ivory-white, canvas, inverted cones stretched heavenward, making travelers think they had landed in the Alps. DIA was located some distance from the downtown area, accounting for the thriving economy now being enjoyed by the shuttle, limousine, taxicab, and bus industries. He liked the old Stapleton International Airport (named after a former Denver mayor), which was closer to the center of town and easier to negotiate.

So much for his whining. His only concern now was to reach the gate that would take him to his final destination, Steamboat Springs, Colorado.

A TIME TO THINK

The weather delay in Chicago and late arrival in Denver, as it turned out, caused Max to miss his connecting flight. The concourse designation and gate number provided by the stewardess upon his arrival at DIA proved to be faulty. Apparently, the change was made after the announcement. Had he checked the monitor, he might have made the flight on time. As it was, he was looking at a six-hour wait for the next available flight. This gave him much too much thinking time.

Having checked in at the posted gate and receiving his seating assignment, he felt more confident now about the anticipated departure. Though almost six hours early and being only one of three in the seating area, he staked out a seat closest to what he anticipated would assure him first-in-line status.

Partly as a diversion, partly for information, and mainly as a way to kill time, he picked up the Wednesday, February 4 edition of *The Denver Post*. Face up was a photograph of one of the most recognized athletes of the time, Michael Phelps. The winner of an unprecedented eight gold medals in the swimming events at the 2008 Summer Olympic Games in Beijing was not pictured with his patented victory sign or with medals draped around his neck or endorsing a product.

Instead, the American idol and sport icon whose photograph was on the front of the Wheaties cereal box, promoting the "breakfast of champions," was pictured smoking a bong purportedly containing marijuana. Max was shocked. *What? It can't be! Probably a trick photograph or a spoof.* Yet this wasn't the *National Enquirer.* The role model that Wheaties eaters attempted to emulate wouldn't do such a thing and certainly wouldn't be stupid enough to allow the incident to be memorialized, let alone disseminated to the public at large.

Max had always been intrigued, if that is the proper word, by those who risked so much for so little. For the moment, he was putting the speculation of the emotions he would be experiencing upon his arrival in Steamboat on the back burner. His mind wandered to Paul Horning, who was a quarterback and a Heisman trophy winner at Notre Dame and was suspended for betting on NFL games while playing for the Super Bowl champions, Green Bay Packers. He also thought of "Charlie Hustle," Pete Rose, a major league baseball player who had not been inducted into the baseball hall of fame because of his gambling exploits. Or how about the NBA referee whose questionable calls were called into play when he was connected to a gambling scandal? If each had done a cost-benefit analysis, none would have opted for the low road.

Max remembered that over the years several Olympic gold medal winners were required to surrender their medals because of the use of steroids or performance-enhancing drugs. Jim Thorpe had to forfeit his Olympic medals because he had received payments for playing semipro baseball. *Great athletes all,* Max thought, *if only they had weighed the probable consequences of their actions.* Max wondered whether their ill-advised decisions were based on inadvertence, ignorance, or blatant disregard for the rules of the game.

Max thought there were some actions not quite so innocuous. One couldn't be as understanding or sympathetic when the action taken is egregious, deliberate, and premeditated. A case in point was the O.J. Simpson case. O.J.'s deliberate and premeditated acts reportedly cost the lives of two people and caused an emotional upheaval to the loved ones who survived. Worse yet, if true, O.J. deprived his own daughters of growing up with a mother.

For every cause, there is an effect—even when the cause is unintended. And in no way did Max intend to minimize the effects of self-destruction on the destroyer. *I guess in some respects the inevitable consequence to the destroyer is deserved,* he thought. Turnabout is fair play! Eh? At least the destroyer is in charge of his or her own destiny. Too bad the victims aren't afforded the same privilege.

Max believed his venting might be viewed as self-realization or self-fulfillment. It was important to him at this juncture even if it served no moral, political, or societal purpose whatsoever. It did bring to the fore the massive and pervasive effect the ordeal had on him and continued to have on all those he cared about.

THE MAIN CHARACTER

If it had not been for Max's father, there would have been no ordeal or at least not *the* ordeal. The second of five boys, James Curtis Cooper was born on July 15, 1938, just outside Steamboat Springs, Colorado, in Routt County, to G. Forrest Cooper and his wife, Bessie.

The Cooper Ranch, as it became known, was acquired by U.S. patent number 501005 dated the "Twenty-seventh day of November, in the year of our Lord, One Thousand Nine Hundred and Fifteen" and signed by the secretary of the general land office on behalf of Woodrow Wilson, then the President of the United States. The land, consisting of 319 and 61/100 acres, to be exact, was homesteaded by Max's great grandfather, Joseph Michael Cooper, born in 1876 and thirty-nine years of age at the time of the grant. Max's grandfather was born in 1908 and would have been seven years of age at the time. The original grant deed was given to Max by his grandfather and hangs proudly on Max's law office wall.

Max's father, whose nickname was Jamie, was the largest of the boys and, save for his father, was the strongest and hardest worker in the family. Since he was the smartest, according to his mother, he was the only one to attend and graduate from college. He obtained his Bachelor of Science degree in business administration in 1959, graduating with honors from Colorado State University in Fort Collins. He lettered in football and basketball all four years.

Max's father would return to Steamboat in the summers during his college years, dividing his time between the Cooper Ranch and the Steamboat Bank and Trust Co. The night processing job at the bank was financially rewarding and not only accommodated his ranching duties but provided him with skills and training he was only too eager to learn. During the summer vacation between his junior and senior years and the Christmas vacation his last college year, he was given responsibilities usually reserved to the full-timers. Upon graduation from CSU, he was offered and accepted a position with the SB&T Co. as a loan officer and, within a short period of time, also held the title of chief operations officer, and later, first vice president.

While attending high school in Steamboat Springs, as Max's father would tell it, he met an attractive and talented cheerleader and track star who had just transferred to his school by the name of Jennifer Mae Carpenter, the daughter of a prominent physician who later became the Steamboat mayor. They were inseparable, and "Jennie," as she was fondly called, and Max's father married during Christmas vacation his senior year at CSU. The new Mrs. Cooper, who had been working in her father's clinic since high school, resigned and resided with her new husband in a small apartment near the CSU campus until spring graduation. Fifteen months later, Max, christened Maxwell Deven Cooper was born on February 21, 1960. His sister, Collette, Max's only sibling, was born on March 23, 1963.

Alden E. Stillwell, the son of the president of Steamboat Bank and Trust Co., went to school with Max's father and mother. In fact, he had a mad crush on Max's mother to such an extent that Dr. Carpenter had hired a local attorney for the purpose of obtaining an injunction to prohibit what Dr. Carpenter's attorney described as stalking and harassing. Alden had been vying for Max's mother's affections since grade school days. The bespectacled nerd, as Alden was referred to by his classmates, was the classic pest and an annoyance to the Carpenter household. The Carpenters believed if Alden was Jamie's competition, there was no contest.

Max always wondered if the genesis of the ordeal was sparked by the perceived grade school rejection. If that were true, then the ordeal was ignited by the high school pairing and ultimately fueled by his mother's marriage to his father. After all, his father, grandfather, and great-grandfather were all servants of the soil and toiled to raise the crops that fed the cattle that kept the banking Stillwell family fattened.

During the Great Depression, farmers and ranchers who could not keep up their loan payments to SB&T Co. shuddered when they heard the Stillwell name. Alden's father, Brandon, and grandfather, *the* Wellington D. Stillwell, had been presidents of the bank and were directly responsible not only for the community's success but also for its very survival, at least according to them. Unless you said "amen," you could end up on the bank's short list. Many a proud farmer or rancher with hat in hand and bended knee was humbled by the ritual required to obtain even a small loan from SB&T Co.

The only decent Stillwell, according to local folklore, was Brandon, who had taken a liking to Max's father. Brandon was noticeably disappointed in Alden, even though Alden was the heir apparent to the Stillwell dynasty. Although Alden said nothing and in fact congratulated Jamie upon his appointment as first vice president of SB&T Co., a move relegating Alden to a position inferior to that of Max's father, Alden showed no outward jealousy. But the sting of depriving Alden of what he considered the ultimate put-down, and by his own father, must have been more than he could bear. Was that the crowning blow that led to the ordeal?

INTO THE WILD BLUE YONDER

The six hours of wait at DIA were more painless than Max expected. Max amused himself with a plethora of reading material. *The Denver Post* was not as substantively charged as he had remembered, and he was disappointed at how much copy consisted of circulars of various descriptions—none of which interested him. He apparently was not the only one of same mind as the pile of discarded inserts was prevalent throughout the airport seating areas.

Hoping to keep from dwelling too much on the ordeal, Max had brought some reading material with him. Although he had packed the new text for the ethics course he was to teach that coming fall, he had also brought Bernard Goldberg's latest book, *Crazies to the Left of Me/Wimps to the Right*. Before he left Chicago, he had finished reading another of his books, *Arrogance—Rescuing America from the Media Elite*. Teaching the Journalism Law and Ethics class at a local community college, he was only too eager to obtain Bernie's slant.

Although he wasn't hungry, Max indulged in a hamburger with the works, fries, and a soda, which he purchased at one of the many "hurry and wait" stands at DIA. It was almost as expensive as lunch at his favorite deli in Chicago. Though billed as "the mother of all hamburgers," it still tasted like cardboard. His stomach was churning as much from anticipation as the hamburger and fries he had just devoured. *They don't serve much food on flights these days, and the muffin, fruit cup, and orange juice didn't go far.*

The waiting area filled and spilled out into the aisle. The scripture declaring "the first shall be the last and the last shall be first" certainly applied at the gate for the departing passengers on the Steamboat flight. The gatecrashers boldly crowded forward and stood in the first-in-line slots ahead of those who had been courteously waiting to form the appropriate lines when called. Patience was not one of Max's virtues, and scorn for gatecrashers, even the pretty young ones, was not something he could easily mask. In any case, with seating assignments, the offenders didn't really gain an advantage; they still had to wait for the rest.

The flight attendants on this flight were picked from a different pool than those on the Chicago to Denver fight. Observing the one assigned to Max's section, it was obvious to him she had been a prison guard in her previous life. Pretty enough, she was gruff, and as the gentleman next to Max was heard to comment, "It's too bad she didn't finish the Dale Carnegie course." She did her job. The ski bunnies and playboys bound for the ski slopes stylish in their bright after-ski (or was it pre-ski) wear were kept in check.

Max had always had a problem with too little legroom, but other than that was comfortably seated in a window seat that was not positioned over the wing. He saw a lot of white ground cover on the mountains west of Denver, and once they passed through those large white cotton balls in the sky and reached their cruising altitude, he saw the rich blue skies over Colorado. Not quite the blue sky country of Montana, but almost.

Once the captain announced his permission, Max adjusted his seat, closed his eyes, and drifted into the wild blue yonder. As if a time machine had turned back the time, Max watched himself as a small boy. He was with his sister and parents on an outing, hiking the steep trails near Fish Creek Falls just outside Steamboat.

The panoramic scene from one of the trails was just as breathtaking as ever. It was as if he had never left that place. There was a serenity he experienced there that was not equaled anywhere else he had ever been. He always had felt safe and free and the freshness of the air was still and friendly. As he was watching the clouds go by, he ventured too close to a cliff's edge. He heard his father yell, "Watch out!" Just then he tripped, and as he was tumbling over the edge, his father grabbed him by the hand.

This surprised Max because his father had been some distance away, and it was implausible to him that his father could have been at his side instantaneously with his fall. His father was pleading with him to hold on tight and give him his other hand so his father could pull him to safety. Impulsively, Max jerked the hand that was in his way, causing him to cascade uncontrollably into the black abyss below. It was as if Max was not actually falling but floating and felt he had the power to float back into his father's waiting hands. It was as if two energies were tugging at him from opposite sides. One voice was begging him to go back; the other was telling him no. Max's consternation was vivid, and his indecisiveness rankled him. It was as if he were paralyzed in time.

In the midst of Max's quandary, he felt a tugging at his arm. His startled look brought a smirk across the face of the peacekeeper assigned to his section of the aircraft. With a tray in one hand and a mini pack of pretzels in the poking hand, she asked what he wanted to drink. Irked by the interruption of his dream as much as the interrupter, he flippantly said, "Something strong and a lot of it." With the salmonella outbreak in the news, it was reassuring she did not try feeding him peanuts and "a lot of them."

Sipping on a cup of hot black coffee and his irritation over the interruption fading, interpretation of the strange dream became all consuming. Did it have a meaning? If so, what was it? Was Max's father speaking from the grave? Max had been bombarded by meaningless dreams on a nightly basis. Maybe it was just one of those. Maybe his subconscious was just playing games and the dream was not a blueprint designed to chart his course or lead him in any particular direction. Yet it was so real, and the invitation for him to break its code was irresistible.

Max never felt that the ordeal was his father's fault and certainly nothing over which he had control. His father had not orchestrated the ordeal and had never intended it to be a subterfuge or guise to abandon Max or his sister or their mother. The ordeal was not his father's great escape. Then why did Max withdraw from his father as his father reached for him? Why did he reject his father and in doing so reject life itself? Didn't the dream demonstrate that even though he didn't think his father was right there beside him and at the ready, he was?

Maybe Max's father experienced great guilt over the ordeal perhaps unnecessarily blaming himself for the hurt that was and still is the constant companion of his loved ones. Maybe he was reaching out for Max's hand, begging that Max might find it within his heart to forgive him and by taking his hand symbolize Max's acceptance of his father's apology. His father was begging for reconciliation, and Max, by withdrawing his hand, conveyed his unequivocal rejection. That must have been disappointing to his father. Max thought, *If only when he reached out I had given him my hand. Yet when I looked into his face and our eyes met for what seemed like an eternity, I did not see or sense contentment or peace. He conveyed instead a longing, an anxiety, and an anticipation that I could have fulfilled; yet, for whatever reason, did not do so.*

When Max had slipped away in the darkness, he did not fall. His rejection was not irretrievable. Max had the power within him to retract his rejection and return to his father's waiting hands and arms. Since he had not hit bottom and the issue was still in doubt, it was probably not too late. He wondered, *How do I convey my love, acceptance, and unconditional forgiveness? How do I obtain forgiveness in return? If I've been a disappointment to my father and my family in general, how do I reverse that? My dream tells me it's not too late!*

All this had been overwhelming, starting with the ordeal in 1972 and all that followed the late-night telephone call Max received from his father's former attorney, Lawrence Whittaker, prompting his having booked this flight and now this disturbing dream. Max had always operated under the assumption that there was a reason for everything. His wife of thirty-four years, Pam, had always said, "God didn't create us to torture or punish us but to bless us, and we must put faith in him and trust that he will do just that." This was his litmus test. Max prayed, "Dear gracious heavenly Father, I place my trust in you, and in the name of your Son, Jesus, I fervently pray that you write the final chapter on the ordeal, and that in doing so, justice finally be done. Amen."

PART TWO:
RELIVING THE ORDEAL

THE ARREST

The stillness of that July morning in 1972 was broken by the sound of sirens groaning from two police cruisers pulling up to the front of the Steamboat Bank and Trust Co., located on the main drag of Steamboat Springs, Colorado. Their abrupt stop was signaled by the screech of brakes. Two officers from each cruiser bolted to the door of SB&T Co., which was opened by an all too eager Alden Stillwell, the thirty-four-year-old son of its president, Brandon Stillwell.

With guns drawn and one set of handcuffs jingling and flashing, they were ushered into the office of one of its vice presidents, James Curtis Cooper, also known as Jamie Cooper. Assistant to the president, Jamie had worked for the bank since graduating from college in 1963. He had risen up from the ranks and was Brandon Stillwell's right-hand man, much to the chagrin of Alden Stillwell, Brandon's son. Jamie and Alden were the same age, had gone to school together, and worked at SB&T Co. the same length of time.

It was almost with glee, as one of the officers was later to testify, that Alden led the officers to Jamie's office and, pointing at Jamie, shouted, "That's the thief who stole $30,000 from the bank." With that he threw $1,000 of fifty-dollar bills strapped together bearing the Federal Reserve Bank of Denver stamp on the desk separating Alden and Jamie. In doing so the strap tore, and the bills scattered on the desk and floor. Within seconds, Jamie was thrown to the floor, his hands were cuffed behind him, and he was jerked to a standing position. Despite his cooperation, Jamie sported a torn shirt, split pants, a large bruise on his forehead from being slammed to the ground, and a bloody nose. The dripping blood made his shirt look as if it had come from a slaughterhouse.

Without saying a word or protesting or offering any resistance, Jamie was advised he was under arrest for a felony: the embezzlement of $30,000 of bank funds. The officers left as quickly as they had arrived, only this time with a prisoner in tow. Jamie had been put into the back seat of a cruiser that had no door handles on the inside and a meshed steel curtain that separated him from the officers in the front seat. During the ride to the police station, one of the officers read from a card, "You have the right to remain silent. Anything you say can and will be used against you in court of law. You have a right to an attorney. If you cannot afford an attorney, one will be appointed for you."

When asked if he understood his rights, Jamie nodded.

Once at the station, he was put in a small room with a small table and three chairs. He was placed in one of the chairs still handcuffed and with blood dripping from his nose, which he surmised had been broken. The lights were so bright, he could not look up. He could hear shuffling behind a large mirror on the wall. He correctly concluded that there was a gallery assembling back there which no doubt included the Stillwell father-son team. "Blood is certainly thicker than water," he mumbled to himself. *How soon they forget,* he thought, lamenting the callous treatment he was receiving, despite his seven years of dedicated service to SB&T Co.

Jamie didn't know what he was in for specifically. He hadn't seen the strapped stack of fifties until they were thrown on his desk. The $30,000 that Alden accused him of taking was a complete mystery. When he asked for a clarification, he was told by the officers that he was being uncooperative and that that would work unfavorably in the setting of the bond, disposition of his case, and in sentencing. He was confused, dejected, and, with a broken nose, was having trouble breathing.

After several relays of officers attempted unsuccessfully to elicit a confession and his repeated request for an attorney, he was finally allowed to make one call. He had worked with Lawrence Whittaker and his partner Gordon Brownell on some trust matters. He knew Mr. Whittaker had done some criminal defense work, so he called Larry. When Larry was allowed to visit his client the next day at the jail located in the basement of the Routt County Courthouse, he agreed to represent Jamie but needed $1,000 up front.

Later that day, Larry met with Jennie Cooper, Jamie's wife, at the family residence. Larry was not able to get there until late afternoon. The Cooper children, Maxwell (twelve) and Collette (ten) were helping their mother prepare dinner. It was evident that all had been crying and were upset. While Larry was outlining the various criminal procedures, Jamie's father, G. Forrest Cooper arrived from the Cooper Ranch. He had ten $100-dollar bills rolled in a bundle and handed them to Larry. He was assured that that would be sufficient for Larry to get started on Jamie's case.

Jamie had been arrested on July 11, hired defense counsel on the twelfth, and would make his first appearance before the Routt County Judge, William Dearborn, on the fourteenth at ten a.m. Larry advised Jamie that bond would be set at that time and that the judge could grant a P.R. Bond. The "P.R.," he explained, stood for Personal Recognizance, meaning that he could be released without having to post a cash, property, or surety bond. He told Jamie that since he had no prior criminal history and was not a flight risk his chances of being released on a P.R. bond were fair to good.

Because of a medical emergency in the Dearborn household, the judge continued Jamie's first appearance, advisement of rights, formal filing of charges, appearance of defense counsel, and bond hearing until July 14 at the originally scheduled time, ten a.m. This meant Jamie would be spending three nights in jail before he would be taken before a judge.

MAKING BOND

Jamie awoke to an eerie gloom on that Wednesday July day. His first night in the "slammer" was fitful at best. He could not remember the last time he had not awakened next to his wife. He knew the call of morning was Jennie resting her head on his chest, long blonde hair spilling across him, and that scent that was uniquely hers. This morning was different in more ways than he could describe.

Although the jail doctor had reset and taped his broken nose, it still throbbed, a sensation he had first experienced on the school grounds in the sixth grade and later on the football field and basketball court. He was not surprised when he woke up and looked in the small metal mirror affixed to the cell wall and saw what appeared to be a raccoon staring back. The two black eyes came with the territory. They were the inescapable result of the nose trauma he'd sustained at the hands of the overzealous arresting officers the previous day.

He had already been fitted in jailhouse garb. The jumpsuit was the color of his orange hunter parka he wore during deer season, only more faded. It was tight, and he felt like 100 pounds of potatoes being squeezed into a ten-pound bag. At six-foot-five, he couldn't expect the jail to keep in stock jumpsuits his size. Besides, he was not going to church or a wedding; he was only going to court.

Jamie was not happy with the continuance, and when he commiserated with Larry, who visited him each day, the two concluded that the delay might actually be a blessing in disguise. The wrath of the Stillwells might diminish, public opinion might soften, law enforcement aggression might subside, and the prosecuting attorney might reconsider filing charges in light of the scanty evidence. At least the rationale, faulty or otherwise, made the stay at the "county hotel" more bearable. Still, being without Jennie and the kids was more problematic than his legal woes.

When Jamie awoke early that Friday morning, and although he could not see the sun rising bright in the eastern sky, he could feel the prayers of his family and friends, and a new optimism permeated his being. *This is the day made by the Lord*, he thought. *The day I will be allowed to return to be with Jennie and my family.*

Although Larry had brought a fresh set of clothes the night before for Jamie to wear to court this day, the jailer refused the tender, citing, "Jailhouse rules." Jamie would be wearing his orange hunter jumpsuit, white socks, and lace-less tennis shoes. *Not fitting attire for a bank officer and president-elect of the Steamboat Springs Chamber of Commerce,* he thought, shaking his head in disgust.

It was nine forty-five a.m. on the fourteenth day of July when Larry arrived at the Routt County Courthouse. Townsfolk were already assembling and scurrying down the hallway to get the best seats in the courtroom where Jamie was to appear. The lights were blazing from the ornate chandeliers that adorned the walls as well as the ceiling. No dark proceedings here.

The Routt County Courthouse had been built in 1922 at a cost of $122,000. It was a stately building standing two and one half stories above ground. There was another half story underground. This was where the sheriff's office and county jail were situated. The district attorney's office was also housed in the half-basement. The first floor was dedicated to the county offices such as the county clerk and reorder, county assessor and county treasurer. The top floor was the regal floor: the two courtrooms and judges' chambers were the government offices located closest to the heavens.

"Actually," as Larry was telling Jamie while they sat together in the holding cell, "Steamboat Springs was not the first county seat. Hayden was.

"In fact," he told Jamie, "the first meeting of the county commissioners was held in 1879 in a log cabin on the Walker Ranch near Hayden." Jamie was visibly agitated, and Larry thought the chitchat might calm him down.

Jamie was ushered into the courtroom by the deputy jailer, whose green uniform resembled a Christmas tree with decorations consisting of badge, patches, two-way radio, keys, and other official paraphernalia that ballooned his otherwise frail frame. In jail house orange, Jamie resembled an elongated pumpkin with cuffs.

At the sight of Jamie, the spectators gasped. There were about sixty of them in number. In unison they made the strange sounds of a dying mule followed by a deafening hush. It was so bizarre that the bailiff could not get his gavel untangled to bang order to the courtroom. The bailiff, mouth wide open, glaring at the packed courtroom, seemed frozen in time. His gavel kept missing the table, though he made several desperate attempts. By the time he made contact, a harsh bang that startled everyone, order had already been restored.

Everyone sat in stone silence, awaiting entry of Judge Dearborn. Larry was positioned at the defense table next to Jamie with open casebooks and the Colorado statutes. The yellow legal pad with scribbles and various clips marking important passages was at the ready. Larry had no more than taken off his glasses and set them on the table when the bailiff again banged his gavel, this time hitting the target and ordering all to stand. "Hear, ye, hear, ye," he announced, apparently having regained his composure, "The county court in and for the county of Routt, state of Colorado, is hereby in session, the Honorable William Dearborn presiding."

Amidst all the fanfare, Judge Dearborn pranced in wearing a black robe much too long for his miniature frame. The judge had black horn-rimmed glasses and a mustache that barely covered his upper lip. In a high squeaky voice, he said, "All right, you may all be seated. Before the court is the matter of James Curtis Cooper, also known as Jamie Cooper."

Peering over his glasses, he asked Jamie, "Are you he?"

Jamie, prompted to stand by Larry, stood erect and said, "Yes."

"Very well," said Judge Dearborn, and facing in the direction of the prosecution's table (which is always positioned closest to the jury box though empty this day) queried, "Bob, is the district attorney's office prepared to formally charge Mr. Cooper at this time?"

"We are, Your Honor," Corbett responded. Larry then asked the judge if Jamie's handcuffs could be removed for the remainder of the proceedings. The judge instructed the deputy sheriff, who was seated behind Jamie to do so, and the deputy readily complied.

Corbett was soon to became one of the key players in the drama that was about to unfold. Robert or "Bob," as he was sometimes called, was first elected district attorney in 1964 and was currently completing his second four-year term. In November 1972, he would run for his third consecutive four-year term. If elected, his third term would commence in January 1973.

Bob was in his forties, was sturdily built, and had sported a crew cut since his days at Penn State, where he played linebacker. He had no facial hair and dressed conservatively, usually in tweeds and never without a tie. His word was his bond, and even his detractors said he was honest. His competitive spirit sometimes got in the way of his better judgment. Once he made up his mind to do something, it was difficult to persuade him otherwise.

The Colorado legislature had divided its sixty-three counties into twenty-two districts and had designated Bob Corbett's district as the fourteenth judicial district, which is comprised of Grand, Moffat, and Routt Counties. Geographically, it was one of the largest districts in the state taking up the better part of northwestern Colorado. It was bordered on the north by the state of Wyoming and on the west by the state of Utah. It was a rough and tumble district with few cattle rustling cases requiring governmental intervention. Corbett was stationed in the heart of the district (Routt County). He had one deputy D.A. stationed in each of the other two counties. One investigator, Dennis Hinton, a retired Los Angeles police detective, divided his time between the three counties.

At the hearing, Jamie could see Larry was bracing himself to make the much-anticipated objection to the district attorney's request to file the complaint. His moment came right after Bob handed the charge form to the bailiff, who in turn handed it to the judge while Bob simultaneously deposited a copy in front of Larry. Larry, barely looking at the tendered complaint, with copy in hand, said, "Your Honor, we object to the filing of this document."

"What?" said Judge Dearborn incredulously.

"I know it's elemental and that Your Honor has already considered it, but Mr. Cooper was arrested on Tuesday without an arrest warrant, and today is already Friday. This is the first that an attempt has been made to file criminal charges. Colorado law frowns on arrests without a warrant and allows that to be done only under very unusual circumstances such as exigent or emergency circumstances." Larry was just getting started.

"Colorado law familiar to Your Honor, specifically rule five, requires that when an arrest is made either with or without a warrant, 'the arrested person shall be taken without unnecessary delay before the nearest available county or district court.' The rule doesn't say 'may,' it specifically says 'shall,' which means 'must!' Again, Mr. Cooper was arrested early Tuesday morning, and today is already Friday, and the time, according to the courtroom clock, is ten eighteen a.m."

The judge interrupted Larry to say, "The court will take judicial notice of the date and time, Mr. Whittaker." *There he goes again,* Larry thought. *He calls me by my last name and the prosecutor not by his last name or even his first name but by his nickname.* Taking a sip of water from the glass placed at the defense table, Larry mused, *That tells everybody who is the "favored son" in this courtroom.*

Larry was now shifting into high gear. "Rule five then goes on to mandate that after a defendant has been taken 'without unnecessary delay before the nearest available county or district court ... a felony complaint, information, or indictment shall be filed, if it has not already been filed, without unnecessary delay in the proper court and a copy thereof given to the defendant.' Judge, it doesn't say 'two, three, or four days later,' and the choice is not up to the district attorney.

"The prosecution," Larry continued, "has not advanced any reason whatsoever, let alone any 'cogent reason' to justify Mr. Cooper's arrest without a warrant or the delay in his being taken before a judge or the delay in the filing a felony complaint. Also, my client was precluded from calling either his family or an attorney for almost ten hours after his arrest. Again, a violation of Colorado law and his constitutional rights."

The judge interrupted Larry and said sternly, "Your client's constitutional rights are not for this court at this time, but for another court at another time." *This was another of Judge Dearborn's canned rulings,* Larry thought. *He must have learned it at judge's school.* Judge Dearborn, noticing Larry's long pause, said, "I'm sorry, I didn't mean to interrupt you. Please proceed and please hurry this along as we have other matters to address."

"Justice cries out for denial of the prosecutor's tendered filing of criminal charges in this case. Because of the delay in the three respects mentioned, inadvertence would hardly be an acceptable legal excuse. Even the attempt to proffer a filing impugns the integrity of the court. To allow the filing would fly in the face of the letter and spirit of the law in Colorado." With that, Larry sat and, bowing his head and closing his eyes, said a quick prayer.

Now it was Corbett's turn. Turning to the DA, Judge Dearborn said, "Bob, do you desire to respond?" Before the DA could even respond, the judge said apologetically, "Part of the delay here was due in no small measure to my unilateral continuance for medical reasons. Somehow I don't see how that should be imputed to the prosecution, do you, Mr. Whittaker?"

"Judge, even if we lop off one day, our argument still appertains," Larry quipped.

Continuing, he said, "Even if you weren't available, Judge Tibbits was. I know because I had a matter before him on Thursday. And I know you were available both Tuesday and Wednesday because I was on your docket. Regardless of whether it was your fault, the fault of the DA or the police, or all of you, an unnecessary delay resulted in Mr. Cooper's being denied his rights. Rejection of the filing is the only proper remedy."

Without Corbett having to say anything, the judge categorically denied the defense motion. The judge ruled, "Even though the prosecution hasn't shown exigent circumstances to circumvent the arrest warrant requirements, the court can and does take judicial notice of the substantial amount of money involved and how law enforcement might have been justifiably concerned about Mr. Cooper's fleeing the jurisdiction to avoid prosecution."

He paused and added, "Especially since the bulk of the money has not been located and is presumably in Mr. Cooper's possession or control."

With a puzzled look, Larry whispered in Jamie's ear, "How does he know all that? We don't even know that. Who in the hell is bending his ear?"

Noticing the side bar and Larry's inability to conceal his chagrin, the judge, bent on justifying his decision, added, "Mr. Whittaker, now just what would the fine folks in our community think if I were to dismiss this case on a mere technicality?"

"They would have applauded your having the courage to do the right thing," Larry wanted to say. *What a sorry excuse for a judge,* Larry thought to himself. "Dearborn's maladroit ruling typified his cowardly nature," Larry would later tell Jamie.

Judge Dearborn then began reading the complaint to himself but loud enough for those seated at the two counsel tables to discern, alternatively, "Um," "Hum," and "Aha." Finally, addressing Jamie, he said, "Young man, please stand while I read the charge against you." Obligingly, Jamie slowly rose to face the judge. "The complaint filed with this court alleges that, 'On or about the tenth day of July, 1972, James Curtis Cooper also known as Jamie Cooper, in the county of Routt, state of Colorado, did then and there knowingly, feloniously, and without authorization obtain control over a thing of value, to-wit: $30,000 in cash, without authorization of its true owner, to-wit: Steamboat Bank and Trust Co. with intent to permanently deprive the aforesaid Steamboat Bank and Trust Co. of the use or benefit of the aforesaid property in violation of C.R.S. 18–4-401, entitled theft, a class four felony carrying a possible penalty of one to ten years in the Colorado State Penitentiary and/or a fine of from $2,000 to $30,000.'"

Judge Dearborn then asked Jamie if he understood the nature of the charge brought against him and the possible penalties in the event of a conviction. Jamie nodded affirmatively. The judge scolded him, telling him the court reporter, who was recording the proceedings on a stenographic machine, could only record that which was audible, not nods. Jamie then quickly and loud enough for all to hear said, "Yes, Your Honor, I understand."

Larry said that later in the day he would be filing a formal entry of appearance in behalf of Jamie, a written request for a preliminary hearing and the usual discovery motions. He then requested that bond be set since theft was a bondable offense. The judge asked the district attorney what amount he was requesting, and Corbett said, "Fifty thousand dollars." Larry stood up and said that such amount would be acceptable if the judge would grant a personal recognizance bond. He also indicated that Jamie's father was present in the courtroom and had agreed to cosign with Jamie if a cosigner was required. "What say you?" the judge asked Corbett. Corbett said he "opposed a P.R. bond because he didn't think it was appropriate, considering the circumstances and all." Judge Dearborn said he was "inclined to agree."

Another setback for the defense: Prosecution 2; defense 0. Larry then asked for a reduction in bond, citing Jamie's age, marital status, length of time in the community, and lack of any criminal record. Corbett graciously said he would leave the matter "up to the sound discretion of the court." The judge reduced the bail to $30,000 announcing "cash, property, or surety." With that, the judge took off his glasses, raised his eyebrows, and looked at the Stillwell family sitting in the front row immediately behind the prosecution table. He said, "Unless...unless the $30,000 mysteriously reappears, then the court might...just might consider a further reduction."

Impulsively, Larry said to the judge, "You're presupposing Jamie took the money."

"Charges don't equate to guilt," he quickly added. Larry could feel the anger swell within him. *Better leave well enough alone*, he thought. The judge surprisingly said nothing and stood, smiling wryly at Larry. "The attorneys will please schedule the preliminary hearing with my clerk before leaving here today." With that he briskly announced, "This court is adjourned."

Larry was grateful that the judge had not taken exception to his remarks. The judge was known for his short fuse and was particularly impatient with attorneys. By instilling fear, he had made attorneys afraid to challenge or embarrass him because of his lack of legal knowledge or common sense, a good ploy practiced by many a judge.

Jamie's father, G. Forrest Cooper, owned Cooper Ranch outright. Since it was unencumbered, a property bond in the amount of $30,000 could be and was posted. Upon Jamie's return to the Routt County Jail, he was processed and released.

Although they had a lot to discuss, Larry knew Jamie was desperate to be with his family and distance himself from the ordeal. Larry couldn't blame him, and after he and Corbett met with the clerk and the preliminary hearing had been set, Larry made a beeline home to the waiting arms of his wife.

Jamie went to Larry's office promptly at eleven a.m. the following Saturday morning, July 15. The handshake turned into a bear hug, and the two toasted a brandy that Larry had placed on a tray with two antique crystal glasses reserved just for such an occasion. Jamie was free for the moment at least. Had they known that the worst of the ordeal was yet to come, there would not have been such a celebration.

Jamie was advised that the preliminary hearing was scheduled for Monday, July 31 at nine a.m., because Judge Dearborn would be spending the whole month of August attending a family reunion at the Shellden Resort on the shores of Pelican Lake in western Minnesota. The judge didn't want to delay the preliminary hearing "longer than necessary."

On his way out the door, Larry handed Jamie a small beautifully wrapped box and said, "By the way, happy birthday number thirty-four!"

Taken by surprise, Jamie queried "How did you know?"

"That's my secret. I know more about you than you think," Larry quickly responded.

"But you haven't asked whether or not I stole that money," Jamie said with a frown.

"Don't have to, but if you want to tell me, now is your chance," Larry said.

"You know I didn't," Jamie said emphatically. Larry knew he didn't, and so did Bobby Dean, nicknamed "Bodean" (pronounced Bow-Dean), the investigator Larry had hired to work on the case right after his first visit with the Coopers.

ESTABLISHING THE ATTORNEY-CLIENT RELATIONSHIP

Anxious, both Jamie and Larry had moved up Jamie's appointment one hour. When Jamie arrived at the offices of Whittaker and Brownell, attorneys at law, at eight a.m. that paradisiacal Monday morning, typical of Steamboat Springs that time of year, he was greeted by Verna Weager, Larry's confident and highly competent legal secretary of over ten years. Jamie guessed Verna, who had never married, to be in her late fifties. She was tall and slender with long, naturally flowing, streaked gray hair. With gold rimmed glasses and neatly attired, every bit the school marm, her eyes and smile engaging, she led Jamie into Larry's office. Standing and quickly rounding the desk, Larry shook Jamie's hand with zeal. They were glad to see each other after Sunday's welcomed interruption of the ordeal.

As Larry led Jamie into the conference room with his left arm draped around him in a fatherly gesture, Jamie asked Larry what the *r* stood for in his name.

"So you observed the shingle too. I seldom use the initial and certainly not my middle name. It's Reginald," he whispered to Jamie, looking around to see if anyone else heard. "I was named after my mother's father, Reginald Pipfer Conahay." With that he directed Jamie's attention to the small serving table on which had sat the brandy decanter and crystal glasses the previous Saturday.

Perking its last chugs and burps was an elegant electric coffee pot emitting that coffee aroma that had stimulated Jamie's senses even before he walked into the room. There was a silver creamer with fresh cream and a small silver bowl filled with sugar cubes. *No country bumpkin he,* Jamie thought.

Verna brought in a tray containing birds of paradise–patterned china saucers and plates, cloth napkins with a fleur-de-lis design, and eighteenth-century silverware—two of each. While they were filling their cups, Verna reentered, this time carrying a large silver tray with an assortment of various French pastries. Although the maple sticks and heavily frosted glazed doughnuts were his health food favorites, Jamie selected one of the large, decadent chocolate éclairs that was begging to be devoured. So as not to disappoint the alluring maple stick, he promised himself that that would be next.

As Jamie and Larry comforted themselves at the large conference table facing each other, Jamie was the first to speak. "In what has been a very painful week, I have gone from the dungeon to the palace. My family and I can't begin to thank you enough. You have provided us with hope once again and confidence that by placing our trust in you, we will not be disappointed." Jamie had not planned to be so dramatic or open. Although he did not want to be vulnerable, he felt he had a moral duty to be frank with Larry and reveal everything he knew about the charges.

Larry was taken aback. "Don't thank me yet," he said. "You don't know anything about me. I may prove to be a dismal failure. The challenges your case presents are not beyond me. I am fully capable. The only unknown is the unknown. That is to say, I don't know if 'effort equals results.' We can do everything correct and the stars may be aligned in our favor, but that doesn't ensure that justice will be done. I can, however, promise you that I will do everything within my power to uncover the truth and, if that truth is your innocence, to fight for your acquittal and exoneration with every fiber of my heart, mind, and soul." *That was quite a promise,* Jamie thought as the two stared at each other.

Larry was just getting warmed up. Though only twelve years older than Jamie, Larry seemed much older and wiser than that dozen-year spread. Jamie was most impressed by Larry's caring and sensitivity.

Verna stuck her head through the conference room door and after apologizing announced that Bob Corbett was on the telephone and was anxious to speak to Larry. Larry said, "Okay, I'll take it, but please continue to hold my calls.

"Hello, Bob, what's so important that you needed to interrupt my morning nap?" With that, laughter. "Uh huh," Larry repeated several times, nodding. "How does two thirty this afternoon sound? Um, okay, see you then."

After he hung up, he told Jamie that Corbett had some discovery to give him and that he thought the two should touch base and see if some of the evidence to be presented at the preliminary hearing could be stipulated to, or if the defense might consider just waiving the preliminary hearing and allow the case to be transferred to district court. He said he agreed to meet Corbett at two thirty to pick up whatever information the district attorney had, as well as explore the possibility of streamlining the preliminary hearing or, depending on what the district attorney offered in exchange, waiving the preliminary hearing altogether.

"Whatever you think," Jamie said. Larry just shrugged his shoulders and repositioned himself.

Jamie had known Larry since 1959 when Jamie returned from CSU. Larry was a frequent bank customer, and both were active together in the chamber. However, they really didn't socialize together or run in the same crowd. Larry defended some high profile defendants and did mostly criminal work. Probably one of the most publicized cases that Larry handled since practicing in Steamboat was one that ended up in the *New York Times*.

When Jamie asked about Larry's representation of four students at Yampa Valley College, one whose father was a famous television personality, Larry was only too eager to relate one of his favorite "war stories." Larry dialed Verna with instructions to bring in the Brian Allen file (1966–002). In less than a minute, Verna had the *Town of Steamboat Springs v. Brian Allen et al.* file sitting on the conference table in front of Larry. Actually, the so-called file consisted of a large, tattered, reddish-brown accordion folder bulging from trying to accommodate six to eight legal-size manila file folders with two-prong file fasteners holding miscellaneous court documents, witness statements, offense reports, clasp envelopes, and newspaper clippings. *Much too much to squeeze into that poor accordion folder,* Jamie thought.

Larry explained that a feud had been brewing between the students who were attending Yampa Valley College and the local cowboys. The two groups met head-on on March 23, 1966, at the Steinkeller Café, a local hangout for college students. At approximately eleven thirty p.m., a group of local cowboys came in and sat at a table. Around eleven forty-five p.m., noticing that one of the students was wearing a cowboy hat and singing what the cowboys considered an unpatriotic song, several of the cowboys, seeking to vindicate the dignity of "cowboyhood" and that of their country, took the matter into their own hands.

Larry said that according to eyewitnesses, all hell broke loose. Apparently, the owner, Dale Jones, stood in horror as his establishment was torn apart. One witness described it as a scene from a Wild West movie. Tables, benches, and chairs were upended and debris was strewn from one end to the other. At least one student was hospitalized. Brian Allen and several others, along with the owner, attempting to restore order, were caught in the melee.

"Needless to say," Larry said, "the police were called, and numerous arrests were made. Four of the cowboys were charged with disturbing the peace and went to trial. The jury ultimately found them guilty, and the police magistrate fined each twenty-five dollars.

"Similar charges were brought against four of the college students, including Brian Allen, the nineteen-year-old son of television personality Steve Allen." Larry showed Jamie newspaper articles chronicling the events at various stages of the tangled legal battles. These Jamie read with great interest, having been a resident of Steamboat Springs at that perilous time.

Larry had Verna come in and find the photographs that memorialized the devastation to poor Mr. Jones's café. "Take a look at these," Larry said, sliding the corroborative photographs Jamie's way. "And these. One sustained a broken wrist, another had been knocked unconscious, suffering a concussion and spending a week in the hospital." Larry shook his head.

"Were any of the cowboys worse for wear?" Jamie asked.

"Other than bruised knuckles and a scuffed toe of at least one kicking boot, I believe the cowboys came through virtually unscathed," Larry replied. "The final score for casualties was students, four; cowboys, zero."

"As I remember, you were successful in obtaining a dismissal for Brian and the others, correct?"

"Yes," Larry replied, "and I hope we can do the same for you."

After court was adjourned on Friday, July 14, Larry kept Verna busy typing a formal entry of appearance of counsel, a motion for discovery, a motion to preserve law enforcement notes and tapes, and a request for preliminary hearing. Larry was always bragging that Verna "was a tachygrapher of the first order." Before day's end, the documents had been filed with the clerk of the county court and copies duly hand delivered to the district attorney's office. Larry was already thinking about the preliminary hearing and its importance.

As he would explain later to Jamie, the preliminary hearing, or simply P.H. was the screening phase designed to weed out the cases that, reviewed in the light most favorable to the prosecution, would be unlikely to succeed. "Why take a case that is a dud to trial when there are so many worthwhile cases standing in line? In other words, if there isn't probable cause or reasonable grounds to believe that a crime was committed and that that crime was committed by the defendant, the case is dismissed. Why waste everyone's time and the taxpayers' money when the effort would be futile?"

"Normally, a D.A. will not file a case he does not expect to win. For that reason, most cases survive the P.H. stage." Even though Larry was not optimistic, he felt the P.H. was an opportunity to showcase the inherent weakness of the case, as well as get a peek at the prosecution's evidence. "Because the P.H. is so matter-of-fact and the outcome is so predictable, the prosecution witnesses are not so well rehearsed. This gives the defense the opportunity to seal their testimony in concrete so that statements they've already made are difficult to later recant. Impeachment by prior inconsistent statements is one of the defense's most effective weapons.

"The defense does not have to call any witnesses but sometimes does depending upon the type of evidence sought to be elicited. Seldom, if ever, does the defendant testify at a P.H." Would Larry chance it in this case? He had entertained the idea but immediately erased the thought for fear of its potentially dangerous consequences. How about calling Alden Stillwell to the stand as a defense witness? It might backfire, yet it was a possibility.

Patience was not one of Larry's long suits, and though anxious, he knew he must await receipt and review of the offense and investigative reports, prosecution witness statements, inspection of the physical evidence and, as importantly, Bodean's investigative results. The P.H. would require some research, and Larry fortunately kept current the library he obtained from Judge Cameron when he purchased the practice.

Larry had tried to dissipate the doom and gloom surrounding this case and bolster his client's morale. Hopefully, Jamie was gaining some confidence and absorbing some of the optimism Larry was trying to emit.

Jamie had not read the newspaper accounts that had appeared in Thursday's newspaper. His wife had been shielding him from the negative press since his arrest. He told Larry that his wife had withheld the negative communications sent through the mail as well, again so as not to depress him any further than he was already. Jennie had also been screening most of the telephone calls since not all were friendly.

Larry asked Jamie if there was any other fallout and if he could detect the mood of the community with which he was associated. Jamie said he and the family attended the eleven a.m. service at the Hayden Congregational United Church of Christ and found everyone most cordial and sympathetic. The minister had said a prayer asking for God's hand and grace in Jamie's court case, and nearly all told him after the service they would be praying for him.

Jamie, Jennie, Max, and Collette had lived for years at the Cooper Ranch in a house originally belonging to his grandfather. When Max had started grade school, they had moved to Steamboat Springs. They purchased an old stately house, which they remodeled, that was close to the bank, schools, hospital, and shopping. They continued their membership in the Hayden Congregational United Church of Christ, despite having moved from the community. Jamie and Jennie were married in the church in 1958. "Our ties to the church and the community date back to 1915 when my great-grandfather, Joseph Michael Cooper, first homesteaded the area," Jamie said proudly. "No wonder they didn't tar and feather me," he said, managing a smile.

Larry knew Jamie had history in Routt County and that the family had been pillars in the community. Larry was counting on a sympathetic jury and hoped the prospective jurors had long memories. Larry was shocked to learn of the animosity Jamie related and hoped it wouldn't divide the community into the "for" and "against" Jamie camps and generate a "letter to the editor" war in the local newspaper. "In a small community like ours," he told Jamie, "everyone knows everyone else, and you don't always know who's related to whom. Everyone knows everyone's deep dark secrets."

He pushed Thursday's newspaper across the conference table to Jamie. "Here, read this," he said, pointing to the front page. "You might just as well get used to it."

Jamie took a deep breath and read:

Banker Busted
The community was still buzzing and shocked at press time over the arrest of prominent bank employee and lifetime native, Jamie Cooper. Cooper was arrested on Tuesday morning shortly after he reported for work at Steamboat Bank and Trust Co. where he held the title of first vice president.

According to a reliable source, it took four armed police officers to subdue the six-foot-five inch, 245-pound former high school and college football and basketball star. Several customers at the bank watched as Cooper, showing the effects of the struggle, was ushered into the parking lot and loaded into a waiting squad car.

Cooper, according to deputy jailer, Dick Towner, was booked into the Routt County Jail about three thirty p.m., Tuesday, July 11, without incident. He was fingerprinted, photographed, and issued a set of jail coveralls.

Apparently, although it has not been confirmed, from the time of his arrest shortly after eight a.m. until three thirty p.m., he was being interviewed by the arresting officers at the police station.

Although criminal charges have not yet been filed against Cooper, it is expected that that will take place later today. No bond has been set by the court, and according to court sources, that will take place at the bond hearing scheduled for ten a.m. on Friday, July 14. The case has been assigned to county Judge, William Dearborn.

Jamie read the article stoically at first. It wasn't long, however, before Larry could see anger building. His face flushed, Jamie said in indignation, "How do they have the audacity to suggest that I resisted arrest and had to be restrained?" It was more of a statement than a question. "When the police first arrived and told me I was under arrest, I thought it was some kind of joke or stunt. I was having a birthday in a couple of days and sensed some kind of surprise but not this. I smiled and stood when the police entered. I never at any time said or did anything or made any furtive gestures."

He paused. "The pummeling I took was totally unjustified. It came out of the blue, and, believe it or not, one of the arresting officers was like kin. Clint Coleman had helped me repair fence at the Cooper Ranch the weekend before."

In resignation Jamie said, "Larry, I can't believe this is happening to me."

Larry didn't know what to say. Fumbling for words and wanting to calm Jamie, he blustered, "I guess we don't know who our true friends are, do we? But it's not a bad article, and the reporter was only reporting what she was told. It's obvious the 'reliable source' was the police department. She'll be hounding you for a statement if she hasn't already. And, of course, you will have to decline comment."

"I guess the reporter was just doing her job and the nasty happenings in the community are newsworthy," Jamie said. "As you said a few minutes ago, I might just as well get used to it. Things aren't going to get any better, are they?"

"No, probably not," Larry replied. With that, Larry turned to the editorial page of the same issue. "This won't make your day either." With that, he slapped the newspaper onto the table in front of Jamie.

Jamie began reading the editorial with some curiosity, not knowing what to expect. Its editor, Corbin Sweeney, was a former classmate and was still one of Jamie's closest friends.

Editorial: Can't Judge a Book by Its Cover
No matter how well you think you know someone, you probably don't know them well enough. Appearances are deceiving, and if you think someone is too good to be true, they probably are.

It pains me to write an editorial about someone I have admired and respected over the years. That someone is James Curtis Cooper, or known to those of us who have been fond of him as "Jamie" Cooper.

I grew up with Jamie. We attended grade school and high school together. He was the valedictorian of our high school class and captain of both our football and basketball teams. He had the lead in most of our plays starting with *The Little Dutch Boy* in the second grade. He dated and married the prettiest and most popular girl in our class.

Jamie's sister was my date for our senior prom. Many a summer I spent at the Cooper Ranch working alongside Jamie and his father, G. Forrest Cooper, the son of Joseph Michael Cooper, who homesteaded the land that was the start of the 1,000-acre Cooper Ranch and was a longtime county commissioner and mayor of our fair city.

Tuesday was a day my heart stood still. When one of our reporters swung open the door to my office without knocking and informed me of Jamie's arrest for embezzlement of funds from our town bank, I experienced that same sick feeling in the pit of my stomach that I experienced upon learning of the death of John F. Kennedy.

Jamie certainly has the presumption of innocence and we would be ill advised to rush to judgment without knowing all the facts, but things don't look good for him. For his sake, I hope all of this has a plausible explanation. Only time will tell!

Larry could tell the editorial had a frigorific effect and that Jamie was fighting the stream of frustration The tears that he had been storing since his boyhood days began to flow, and then all the sadness, frustration, disappointment, regret, and guilt gushed forth. Larry turned his head away.

When both retained some semblance of composure and looked into the other's eyes, a bond formed between them stronger than that between brothers. This was a bond that never would be broken and one that would carry them through the perilous course of the ordeal and beyond.

"You need to have a bucket ready for me the next time this happens," Jamie said, managing a smile. Both began to chuckle.

Jamie pulled a small box from his pocket. It was the box that contained the birthday gift Larry had given him the previous Saturday. He removed the solid silver medal and chain. "I can't possibly accept this."

"Is it against your religion, or you don't like it?"

"Oh, no," Jamie replied. "It looks like something that has been in your family for a long period of time and has sentimental value."

"The medal," said Larry, taking it from Jamie, "has indeed been in the family for a long time, actually for over a century, according to my father. As you no doubt noticed, the crucifix on this side and the Blessed Virgin Mary on the other," he said, pointing to each side of the half dollar-sized silver medal, "are quite worn. It was worn by my grandfather during World War I and later by my father in World War II. I wore it until several years ago when the circular attachment wore through. While it was being repaired and the chain replaced with a more durable solid silver one, my wife presented me with a solid gold medal and chain that I dare not wear.

"There is a lot of history connected with this medal," he said while still holding it and waving it in the air. "It was given to my grandfather by his father and to my father by his father. It was worn during many a battle, including legal battles. We all wore it at different times, not only because of the religious implications, but, and I hate to admit, as a talisman of sorts. It was meant to and did in fact bring us good fortune."

Handing the medal and chain back to Jamie, he said, "I have no son to pass this on to, and I want you to have it. By wearing this, you will show your faith in the Lord, and, while you wear it, it will be a symbol that Jesus and his Blessed Mother are always with you and that no harm will come to you. They will always be at your side."

Jamie hesitated then put the medal and chain around his neck. There it would remain throughout the whole ordeal and beyond.

A POST MORTEM OF JAMIE'S
FIRST COURT APPEARANCE

After all the tears that could be shed were shed, the attorney-client fee agreement and authorization forms signed, all éclairs and parfaits sampled, and maple sticks consumed, the real work began. Almost on cue, Larry and Jamie rolled up their sleeves, sharpened their pencils, and licked their fingers. The bell for round one had rung.

Larry began by handing Jamie a copy of the criminal complaint. They read and studied it together, as well as a copy of the Colorado statute Larry had duplicated for Jamie. Larry explained that not only was the wrongful act required to be proven but the culpable mental state as well. "Here," Larry explained, "the prosecution has to prove that if and when you did it, you had the intent, the specific intent, to permanently deprive the bank of the money." Jamie nodded.

"By the way, we can still raise our objection to the filing of the complaint in district court if it goes that far. Also, and don't you dare breathe a word of this, there is a law in Colorado that says where there is a specific statute covering the same wrongful act as a general one, the district attorney is required to charge under the specific or risk dismissal. In your case, Corbett charged under the general theft statute instead of embezzlement under the banking code. If I make the objection prematurely, the court has the discretion to allow the charge to be amended. Otherwise, it is fatal."

"So *hush* is the word," Jamie said, putting a finger to his lips. What about the police denying me the right to make a telephone call and questioning me for seven hours despite my request for an attorney? Is that really 'for another court at another time' as Judge Dearborn said?"

"Yes," said Larry, "but our time will come. By the way, Jamie, did you see J. Henry Ross, the bank's attorney, present at the bond hearing?"

JH, as he was known, was Brandon Stillwell's yes man. Both knew him as "the weasel." He would do anything for a buck. He was built like a bull with a thick short neck, heavy features, and thick black hair. People speculated that he did a full-body shave every morning before leaving for work. The weasel had stayed behind and was speaking with Corbett when Jamie was led out of the courtroom.

"Yes, what was that all about?"

"Well, the present action is a criminal action for which the state seeks its pound of flesh mainly to punish you for what it perceives is a wrong committed against society. Its purpose is not to collect the thirty thousand dollars; that must be done through a private 'civil' action pursued by the bank. That is why the weasel was there."

"You mean I can anticipate a civil action that I will have to defend as well? It's too bad you don't have children, Larry, because I have a feeling I will be paying enough before this is over to send two sets of twins to college."

Larry laughed. "The answer is yes to your question. And, as to your comment, your contribution to the Whittaker fund for the needy is much appreciated."

"Do you have any other questions…or comments?" Larry asked sarcastically. "You no doubt noticed the Stillwells sitting all prim and proper in the front row on the prosecution's side of the courtroom, of course. All in Sunday attire; Alden with his wife, Debbie, and Brandon with Alden's mother, Laura. Some of the other members of the Stillwell family were seated in the second row directly behind them. I only caught a glimpse, but Debbie didn't seem very happy to be there."

"I didn't look at any of them," Jamie said. "I didn't want to give them that satisfaction. Also I was having blurred vision and trouble breathing. You were wise in advising Jennie and the kids to stay away. I didn't see my father until the bond phase when he emerged from the crowd, bless his soul."

"Court proceedings are like weddings, "Larry commented. "The community invariably takes sides. You can tell whose side they're on by where they sit. Those favoring the prosecution usually sit on the side where the prosecution sits; those favoring the defense sit on the side where the defendant and his counsel sit."

"Sometimes you don't know who your friends are," Jamie said, "or what side they are on. I guess all I have to do is look to see where they are seated."

Larry went over the statements Jamie might have made to the police and what questions were asked. The long and the short of what was a fairly long interrogation, considering the attorney request, was Jamie's denial of all allegations. Larry suggested that they wait until after he received copies of the police reports and the transcribed interrogation. Jamie agreed and stated that, as far as he knew, however, the interrogation was not recorded. "Very unusual," Larry said. "I guess they can fabricate whatever story they want now without having to worry about measuring it against a tape recording."

It was approaching noon, and Larry was scheduled to have lunch with his law partner, Gordon Brownell, who was driving in from Denver. Gordon had been on vacation with his wife and two teenage sons the past two weeks, and Larry was anxious to discuss the Cooper case with this former federal prosecutor. Jamie had planned to drive his family out to the Cooper Ranch to meet with his father to arrange a loan and working arrangements so that he could support his family and pay for the legal fees that certainly would be an integral part of the ordeal.

Larry hoped Gordie, as his law partner was called, would not be late as Larry had an important meeting with Corbett at two thirty p.m. at the district attorney's office. He had scheduled an appointment with Jamie for the following morning to review with Jamie whatever discovery and information he obtained from Corbett, Corbett's mind-set, disposition overtures, and anything else helpful to Jamie's case. Also, Larry would be introducing Bodean to Jamie, and the three would review and discuss the results of Bodean's investigative efforts. Depending on Gordie's schedule, Larry was hoping to introduce Gordie to the case and to Jamie.

Gordie arrived with his family at eleven forty-five a.m. charged and raring to get back into the groove. Marilynn was a fine specimen of a woman. The boys, Taran, fifteen, and Trenton, seventeen, were on summer break and were headed for their sophomore and senior years respectively at Steamboat High School.

After exchanging the usual greetings, pleasantries, and relating the highlights of the trip along the West Coast of the United States and visits with relatives along the way, Gordie's family departed for home, leaving Gordie with Larry. After lunch at one of their favorite spots at River Bend and catch-up talk, Larry introduced him to the ordeal. Gordie had a lot of questions Larry couldn't yet answer.

On the way back to the office, Gordie said he wanted a piece of the action. He had turned a few windmills right side up in his day and, though he had not practiced law as long as Larry, had insight and court sense beyond his years. Gordie was a welcome addition to the defense team, subject to Jamie's approval.

When Larry went to meet with Corbett, he took Gordie with him. Gordie and Corbett were good friends and went to the same church. Their sons were about the same age and had learned to ski together. That wasn't the reason Larry took Gordie. He wanted Gordie to hear directly from the horse's mouth what the people's case against Jamie Cooper consisted of; its strengths and weaknesses. Larry didn't want his biases to slant his version of the case.

Corbett was cordial and greeted Larry and Gordie with handshakes and smiles. He offered them their choice of cold sodas or ice tea. All three had ice tea in genuine glasses with cubes clanking in rhythm to sips. Not contentious here. Corbett had a prepared packet of discovery with acknowledgement of receipt attached by paper clip. Handed to Larry, he signed, returned the executed receipt to Corbett, and proceeded to unfasten and open the folder. The first sheet to greet him was the mug shot of Jamie, front and side, and copy of the fingerprint card. Next was the National Crime Information Center (NCIC) and Colorado Crime Information Center (CCIC) summary sheets. Neither indicated any contact with the law not even traffic violations. *Good news so far,* Larry thought, passing the documents to Gordie.

There was more to the offense report and witnesses' statements than Larry had imagined. Impressed, Larry said, "Your boys have been doing their homework on this one."

"They must want this one pretty bad," Gordie chimed in.

At that moment, Dennis Hinton, Bob's investigator, walked in with a packet of photographs taken at the bank, including Jamie's old office and the offending desk drawer, fresh from the developer. Greetings and handshakes completed, the business at hand resumed.

"Let's see what you have, Dennis," Corbett said, reaching for the packet. As he examined each photograph, he passed it on to Larry, who in turn passed it on to Gordie.

In addition to the photographs of Jamie's desk and office, there were pictures of the main safe, the safe door, the timing mechanism, and a money drawer half full of fifty-dollar bills strapped in $1,000 bundles. There was also a close-up of the Federal Reserve stamps, and a torn strap next to twenty fifty-dollar bills strewn on the top of a desk Larry presumed had been Jamie's. Yellow crime-scene tape was seen in the background encircling Jamie's old desk with the lower right-hand desk drawer pictured ajar and its contents clearly visible. No other desk drawers were ajar or pictured open. There were other bank photographs, the significance of which Larry had no clue.

"Dennis, is this set for the defense?" Corbett asked. Dennis nodded, and the film envelope and all the photographs were given to Larry and Gordie.

"I would suggest you two review the discovery at your leisure. After you've done so, we can regroup and discuss where we go from here." Corbett paused and then said, "There is no easy resolution of this case. It doesn't appear there is any middle ground. In the eyes of a certain segment of the public, we're damned if we plea bargain the case; and in the eyes of another segment, we're damned if we don't. By letting a jury decide, the jury will take the heat."

Another coward's way out, Larry thought. "Why didn't you call a county grand jury on this one? That could have been accomplished in a half day and saved all of us the time and expense of perhaps months and maybe years of hearings, trials, and appeals and perhaps retrials."

"I considered that," Corbett said, resting his chin on his left fist. "I opted to go this route for a number of reasons. As you know, the grand jury is a secret proceeding that takes the place of the preliminary hearing, the later being a public hearing. I feel the public has a right to know, and I believe in transparency. It might have been politically expedient for me to have taken it before a grand jury, but then that would have deprived you of the sneak preview the preliminary hearing provides, and maybe you will be able to convince the court there is no probable cause. That way, you and Gordie can be the heroes and I will be the goat."

"With a preliminary hearing, if the case is dismissed, you can always blame the judge, right?" Gordie queried in a satirical tone punctuated by a wink.

"I guess Gordie's right. Either way, the determination will be the judge's, not mine," Corbett agreed. "I don't have an axe to grind either way. I'm not out to get Jamie, nor am I in the hip pocket of the bank. My job is to see that justice is done—not to convict or acquit. What better way to do that than let Jamie's peers in the community make that decision should Judge Dearborn find probable cause? For now, I'll raise the flag with the evidence at the P.H. and see if the judge salutes."

Corbett was implacable. Larry knew that, without ammunition, any argument he might advance for dismissal would fall on deaf ears. He must wait for the proper time, and that time was not now.

All agreed that plea discussions were premature, and after review of discovery negotiations could ensue, and also there was still time to consider how to streamline the preliminary hearing.

Walking Larry and Gordie to the door, Corbett took a parting shot. "Your client's returning the bank money would go a long way in allowing us to make a sentencing concession. Admission, contrition, and a firm purpose of amendment would certainly sway the court in your client's behalf. Otherwise, denial, lack of regret or remorse, and failing to make restitution will be considered aggravating factors."

"It sounds like you have already made up your mind as to our client's guilt," Gordie said.

"And that you have an *open and shut* case," Larry added.

Unblinking, Corbett responded, "You never know what a jury will do. You lose the cases you think are the strongest and win the ones you think are the weakest."

"If that adage holds up, then according to your assessment, the defense will win this one," Larry said.

Larry and Gordie had plenty of reading material for the night. Their favorite novels would have to wait. They knew that the prosecution's blueprint of the ordeal awaited them and all they had to do was decode it. They hoped the evidence would not get in the way of an acquittal.

PREVIEW OF COMING
ATTRACTIONS

It was one of those rare overcast July Steamboat days, the air heavy as the spirits dampened in the hallowed halls of Whittaker and Brownell, attorneys at law. Larry and Gordie had both reviewed the discovery the previous night and sitting in Gordie's office with cups of the day's brew were already discussing Jamie's case when Verna arrived at seven thirty a.m. With hot banana bread slices served on porcelain plates, she approached her pensive bosses.

"Who died?" she said with her usual sarcasm.

"Who's asking?" Gordie retorted.

Larry, taking his appointed banana bread, hot to the touch and aromatically inviting, licked his lips and said, "Verna, your banana bread is a welcomed respite from an otherwise sleepless night for Gordie and me. Reviewing the dismal discovery in the *Cooper* case has created a maelstrom of confusion for the two of us and we will need rescuing."

"If you could toss us a lifeline," Gordie added, "you'd be our friend forever."

"Isn't it a little premature to be jumping to conclusions?" she asked as she departed, shaking her head and closing the door behind her.

"She's right you know," Gordie said to Larry. "We've been here before. There are two sides to every story. As one of my law professors used to say 'All is not as it appears.'"

Larry knew they were both right. Jamie would no doubt have a plausible explanation for all those calls to the Las Vegas Casino the past two months. Just because Jamie and Jennie had been there in June didn't mean they were serious gamblers or that Steamboat Bank and Trust Co. was "bank rolling" their trip or gambling losses "if any." As his father and grandfather used to say, "Rhetoric is not reason and emotion is not evidence!" Larry was now feeling guilty about doubting Jamie's innocence.

Sensing what Larry was thinking, Gordie said, "It is obvious that Corbett thinks he has found a motive and that the calls and trips to Vegas equate to gambling and gambling equates to losses and losses lead to bank loans, whether approved by the bank or not. I can hear Corbett's final argument now. In his eloquent style he will say, 'Ladies and gentlemen of the jury, the downfall of this once honest and respectable banker was his compulsive gambling and need to borrow money from the nearest available source, the Steamboat Bank and Trust Co. Unfortunately, the bank didn't know about *the loan* until after they found their money missing!'"

"Bravo," Verna said, as she reentered Gordie's office to refill their coffee cups.

"Exactly right," Larry said. "And Corbett will have the telephone toll records they obtained from Ma Bell to prove it as well as the credit manager from Tobiasis Casino in Las Vegas, whom they will no doubt subpoena along with his records."

"Although the records account for only twelve hundred of the thirty thousand alleged missing plus the one thousand claimed recovered by Alden, Corbett will claim the other twenty-seven thousand eight hundred was the cash belonging to the bank that was left on the gambling tables in Las Vegas," Gordie offered. "No wonder Corbett thinks he has a slam-dunk case."

"Let's not fall into that defeatist trap Bob has set for us," Larry said, not just trying to convince Gordie, but himself as well.

Just then there was a buzz on the intercom. Verna announced Bodean had just arrived. "Send him back," Gordie yelled into the speaker. Bodean entered carrying a brown leather briefcase in one hand and holding a cup of steaming coffee in the other. His black leather vest, jeans, and Western boots, long reddish-blond windblown hair, and matching mustache belied his meticulous and truculent reputation as an investigator.

"Hey, Bobby Joe," Gordie said. "Would you like to borrow my comb? You look like you've been caught in the cross winds."

"At least I can change my looks," Bodean jibbed. "By the way, Gordie, did you ever talk to that plastic surgeon I recommended last time we saw each other?"

"Whew," Larry said, "I'm not getting in the middle of this one."

About that time the intercom buzzed again; this time announcing the arrival of Jamie—the main focus of the summit meeting, as Larry had billed it.

"Take him into the conference room," Gordie said. "We'll all go in there."

Verna came in before they got started and made sure they all had a full cup of coffee and brought in the rest of the sliced banana bread, which disappeared quickly.

Jamie looked tired and not his chipper self. It was obvious he'd had the same fitful night as Larry and Gordie. *And he hasn't even reviewed the discovery yet!* Larry thought.

"I gave the check to Verna as per the fee agreement," he said to Larry as Gordie and Bodean were helping themselves to the rest of the banana bread.

"Thank you," Larry replied.

Verna had placed on the conference table four complete copies of the discovery. She knew she was always to keep a clean copy for future use. The clean copy had already been placed in Larry's file. Extra pens and pencils sat in a small box on the table alongside the stack of discovery documents. Larry and Gordie already had their copies containing evidence of review, highlighting, tabs, and other devices to allow for easy and speedy retrieval. Jamie and Bodean were given copies that were in the stack. They each took a pen, and soon their copies were beginning to look like Larry's and Gordie's.

When Jamie started to react to the contents, Larry said, "Please, everybody, just read through the whole thing, and we will dissect each and every bit, paragraph by paragraph, sentence by sentence." Although he showed some reaction, Jamie was restrained and followed Larry's instructions. Jamie's face turned white and red and everything in between. *And for good cause,* Larry thought. *I would be upset too if I were him,* Larry thought.

The journey through the discovery was long and arduous. The plan was to save the photographs for last. Page by page, paragraph by paragraph, line by line, and sometimes word by word, the four plowed through the discovery.

It was only when Verna brought in the prearranged meat and veggie tray, a variety of bread and spreads, condiments, dried fruit, and soft drinks did those assembled realize it was lunchtime. Although one or the other took pit stops from time to time, there was no morning break. Jamie was getting his money's worth today.

Taking time to custom build their sandwiches and pour drinks of choice in ice-filled glasses, everyone began to relax. They made small talk between bites and sips at first; then the counter-offensive began, not heated or vituperative, but emphatic.

Jamie would have made a good attorney, the others thought to themselves, not realizing until after Jamie had left that their observations were shared. Jamie zeroed in on the most damaging evidence and, surprisingly dispassionate, discussed the erroneous inferences that were drawn from the facts. Appearances indeed were deceiving, Larry and Gordie were beginning to realize.

Jamie started out by saying the Las Vegas calls and June trip were all true. However, he "was not much of a gambler," and he and Jennie "usually went to Las Vegas for rest and relaxation and to see the shows." He said he was surprised that the authorities had obtained such private information in such a short time.

In June, Jamie related, he and Jennie met his uncle Matt, his father's youngest brother, Matthew Thomas Cooper, at Caesar's Palace, where they usually stayed. "Uncle Matt's middle daughter, my cousin Patty, had been incurring gambling debts at a rapid rate at various casinos there. She was a high school math teacher living in Vegas and had convinced herself that she had developed a foolproof system of playing blackjack and could beat the odds. The system hadn't worked, and Uncle Matt was picking up the pieces

"To make a long story short, Uncle Matt couldn't keep up with Patty's trail of losses or cover her IOUs, and he called my father. Dad sent Jennie and me out to Vegas with twelve hundred dollars to pick up a chit at the Tobiasis Casino. He paid for our airline tickets and other expenses. Virtually everything was done in cash, as Tobiasis would only accept cash.

"The dozen or so calls we made to Tobiasis were to first ascertain how much was owed and then help Patty make arrangements for payment and to renegotiate when she was delinquent or incurring new losses. I guess Uncle Matt was losing credibility and making too many empty promises. He was becoming 'tapped out' as well. Anyway, Tobiasis was threatening legal action as well as a criminal prosecution. The calls were to stave them off long enough for Patty and her father to cover the losses and redeem the chits. The problem is that Patty was continuing to sink deeper in debt. She said the reason was because she had been doubling up on her bets expecting her luck would change and with the winnings would pay off all her debts and ultimately reimburse her father.

"So the calls that preceded the June trip were to negotiate payment and then settlement and to forestall civil and criminal action. The twelve hundred dollars delivered to Tobiasis was accepted as full payment. Thinking that the crisis was over, Jennie and I returned to Steamboat, only to find that Patty was up to her old tricks. Hence the reasons for the calls after the June trip."

"Was the roundtrip airline ticket to Vegas paid in cash or by credit card?" Gordie asked.

Before Jamie could answer, Bodean chimed in, "By credit card, and I have the credit card receipt provided by Jamie's father." With that Bodean produced a photocopy of a credit card receipt showing that G. Forrest Cooper had indeed purchased a pair of airline tickets on June 9, 1978.

Confidence was beginning to build as Jamie went on analyzing the so-called evidence in a methodical and almost lawyer-like fashion. "The main vault," he said, "had a time clock that was set when the tellers completed their balancing and placed the cash in the vault. The head teller, Rita Baker, counted *all* the cash in the vault in the presence of Alden in accordance with bank policy, which required 'dual control.'

"On the night preceding my arrest, Rita and Alden closed the vault and set the timer for seven a.m. the next morning. I know because I had the closest office to the vault. While talking on the telephone, I watched Rita check off the various rituals she was performing, and I saw Alden initial the closing checklist and hand it back to Rita.

"No one could open the vault until seven a.m. the next morning. And, only the officers, such as Alden and myself, had the combination. Even though I was the last one, other than the cleaning people, to leave the bank Monday night and had the combination, it would have been impossible for me or anyone to open it.

"When I arrived at the bank the next morning, it was almost eight a.m., and Alden and, I can't remember who else, was already there. I know Rita was there and one of the bookkeepers because I saw the light on in the bookkeeping department and I heard noise. Alden was already there with his office door closed. His office was next to mine, and he had full view of the vault through the glass windows on the front of his office.

"Normally, I am there at seven thirty a.m., but that morning I had a breakfast chamber meeting at the Tomahawk Cafe at the

Cross-Bow that started at six thirty a.m. By the time I walked from there to the bank, it was almost eight a.m."

"You walked?" Bodean asked.

"Yes, I had parked at the bank and just walked the half block to the restaurant and walked back. It, of course, is not far. I guess nothing is in Steamboat. I had hardly settled into my office when the police arrived," Jamie continued.

"Did you have any money in your desk drawers that you know of?" Bodean asked.

"None that I know of, no," Jamie said. "The first that I had seen of the fifty-dollar bills was after the police arrived and Alden scattered them on my desk."

Jamie was bombarded by questions on all fronts. When asked how long he stayed at the bank the night before the arrest he said, "Approximately six fifteen p.m." Then he answered no to each of the following questions: Did he ever send money to Tobiasis? Did anyone other than Brandon, Alden, and himself have a combination to the main vault? Did he see who set the timer on the vault? Did he ever call Las Vegas from the bank? Did he know why Alden turned on him? Did he know where the twenty-nine thousand dollars were? Did he ever take money from the bank without authorization? On and on they inquired, and to all such questions, he continued to answer no.

When they showed him the photographs, he identified his office, desk, and drawer. He said the bottom desk drawer was not open at any time he was there, so he didn't know why a picture was taken of it open. The files pictured in the drawer appeared the way they always did. The photographs of the inside of the vault and the inside and outside of the vault door were reasonable representations. The photograph of the cash drawer in the main vault half full of strapped currency looked contrived and would ordinarily have filled the front half of the drawer and not the back half. The other photographs merely showed the layout of the bank, and he saw nothing unusual about them.

Jamie said he would like to review the witnesses' statements more thoroughly and asked if he could take them home. Larry replied that he could take the whole packet of discovery; that was his to keep.

When asked about the accuracy of his so-called interview, Jamie said it wasn't an "interview," it was an "interrogation." He said the four police officers played "bad cop" and "good cop" and did everything they could to get him to incriminate himself. He answered everything truthfully. They made much out of the fact that he was the last bank employee to leave the bank the night before his arrest and hounded him about where the money came from that Alden found in his desk drawer. They told him things would go easier for him if he just confessed and told them where he hid the money. When persuasion didn't work, he said they made veiled threats concerning him, his family, and his property.

Jamie's attention was drawn to page seventeen of the discovery, entitled "Interview of Defendant" and asked to re-read it.

Interview of Defendant
Name: James Curtis Cooper alias Jamie Cooper
Date: July 11, 1972
Place: Routt County Jail
Charge: Theft F-4

Defendant had been advised of his Miranda rights upon his arrest at the Steamboat Bank and Trust Co., county of Routt, state of Colorado, by Officer Gary Boyle, in the presence of Officer's Michael Heath, Lloyd Kinsey, and Clinton Coleman.

During the booking process, defendant appeared uncooperative and kept asking why he had been arrested and what he was accused of having done. No statement was reported.

At approximately 0900 hours, he was questioned by Officers Boyle, Heath, Kinsey, and Clinton. Each attempted to interview him separately, and he was uncooperative each time, refusing to answer any questions.

When he requested to talk to an attorney, the interviews ceased, and he was placed in his cell.

"What the report indicates and what you told us are diametrically opposed," Larry said. "Unless they claim you made statements later, it won't make much difference. But you are certain you made no statements or admissions of any kind, correct?"

"Yes," Jamie said. "But might my version, which is the truth, have a bearing not only in this case but in a civil action we might bring for false arrest, false imprisonment, malicious prosecution, and violation of my rights?"

"Possibly," Larry said, surprised at how astute he was for someone who had no legal training.

"Let's take a break before Bodean takes his turn in the barrel," Larry said.

After they stretched, freshened up their glasses, and had their sidebars, Bodean took center stage. Bodean said he was not allowed by Alden to take any photographs in the bank and that upon advice of the bank attorney no one would be allowed to make any statements.

Bodean, who had been a broncobuster and former rodeo bull rider and used to taking the bull by the horns, continued, "I was banking, excuse the pun, on being able to interview the officers and employees who had been at the bank either on the tenth or eleventh of July. Their testimony would be critical in ascertaining who might have had access to the money and whether the money even ever existed. When I ran into Brandon at Lions' Club yesterday, he appeared willing to talk but said he had left for Salt Lake City on the Saturday before all the fireworks started and didn't return until the following Wednesday. He said he knew nothing about what took place other than what Alden had told him. He said Alden was now the bank's first vice president."

Bodean thumbed through his notes. "I've talked to the cleaning people, and they said when they came to clean on Monday, July 10 at six p.m., Jamie was busy working in his office, the main vault door was closed, and everything appeared secure. They said Jamie left shortly after they arrived. When asked, they said they noticed nothing out of the ordinary. They said they checked all the outside doors before they left and all were locked. When I asked them if while cleaning they noticed any loose stacks of currency anywhere, they said 'no.'"

Larry asked the names of the cleaning people, and Bodean replied "Ron and Betty Skyler." Bodean said he had their names, address, and telephone number in his report.

Next Bodean said he interviewed the owner of the title company across the street from the bank, Ursula Russell. "Ursula faces the front of the bank and has an unobstructed view of the bank. She remembered the day of Jamie's arrest and said she had arrived at work about six thirty a.m. and noticed, about that time, Jamie, who she knows through her chamber membership, drive into the parking lot in his Ford Galaxie and walk directly down the street.

"She said that the chamber monthly meeting is usually held on the second Tuesday of each month starting at six thirty a.m.

She said she was updating an abstract with a deadline she was rushing to meet and didn't attend the meeting that morning. She saw Alden drive into the lot in his Cadillac sedan around six forty-five a.m. She thought that was unusual because he didn't usually arrive at the bank until seven thirty a.m.

"When asked about Monday night, she said she had left work about six thirty p.m. and the only vehicle in the bank parking lot was Skyler Cleaning Service's panel truck. She said she saw no other cars.

"In light of Jamie's narrative, it is more imperative than ever that I interview Rita Baker to determine who set the timer on the vault door."

"The only way," Gordie said, "was if the bank brought a civil action against Jamie; then they could take her deposition. Larry said they could always subpoena her as their witness at the preliminary hearing. The only thing she could do is plead the Fifth to avoid testifying. And if that happens, bingo, we have an alternate suspect.

"We still have plenty of time before the preliminary hearing," Gordie said. "I think we need to regroup and schedule another strategy session."

"Unfortunately," Larry said, "I will be tied up in court the next several days and won't be available until Friday. Would Friday work?" That was convenient for all, and the next summit conference was scheduled for July 21 at eight a.m.

Bodean said he would type up his report and have it ready on Friday. "Happy hunting," Gordie yelled as Bodean headed for his car. Jamie was right behind him, looking forward to spending the rest of the afternoon with Jennie, Max, Collette, and the family pet, Maya.

THE CLOAK OF ANONYMITY

When Jennie returned from the post office with the mail and newspaper Thursday, July 20, Jamie, Max and Collette were playing badminton in the yard along with one of Collette's neighborhood friends. Their dog, Maya, a four-year-old bichon frise, was stealing the shuttlecock every time it became errant.

Maya had arrived at the Cooper home in a shoebox when she was less than two weeks old. She had been one of a litter of four that Jennie's parents were getting rid of in anticipation of their move to Florida upon Dr. Millard Carpenter's retirement. Maya's mother, Nola, would be moving with them "without the pups," Fran, Jennie's mother told her husband. Max and Collette welcomed the new addition and would have taken the whole litter if their parents had allowed.

The challenge of the badminton game was trying to retrieve the shuttlecock as Maya exhibited the speed of a greyhound and the dexterity and leaping ability of a flying squirrel. If you were lucky enough to get the shuttlecock back, she would be poised, waiting for the next opportunity to steal it again and resume her game of keep away. "When you played hide and seek in the snow with her, you couldn't find her," Max used to say, "even though she was right there in front of you."

Jamie's fun in the sun was short lived when he opened the weekly local that Jennie had just brought home. He had never liked anonymous letters to the editor. He thought such letters were nothing more than upgraded gossip. He had been exposed to the laws on defamation, libel, and slander in his Journalism Law and Ethics class at CSU. There he learned from his professor, a retired lawyer, that he who republishes or repeats actionable defamation is as liable as the originator. Besides, he thought the nameless and faceless hate mongers were cowards. If they were unwilling to reveal their identities, their letters should not be printed. *It was a dangerous practice for Steamboat's weekly to print them,* he thought.

He was shocked to see a whole page of editorials in this issue. "Normally they are lucky to have one or two," he said to himself. It didn't take long to realize they were all about him. He read with dread one letter after another. The tone of the letters ran the full gamut, everything ranging from love and kisses to lock him up and throw away the key!" The bulk of the letters were vitriolic and venomous. Jamie could go no further. In a fit of rage, he tore the newspaper into a thousand pieces. *The very thing Larry feared would happen happened,* Jamie thought, *I am being tried and convicted in the newspaper. And they haven't even heard my side.*

Larry, having just read the newspaper and its anonymous letters to the editor, felt a sickness much like when one of his best friends had died. He telephoned Gordie at home and Gordie had much the same reaction. "In a community of less than ten thousand, there's a pretty good chance that everyone knows of the scandal and has already formed an opinion that probably can't be erased."

"We'll have no choice," Larry said, "but to file a motion for change of venue. There's no way we can pick an impartial jury in Routt County."

Both Larry and Gordie had originally thought that the community would be biased in favor of this deeply entrenched family. But the Cooper name had been tarnished beyond salvaging by this incident, and Jamie's attorneys would have to go to plan B.

Both Larry and Gordie thought one of them should call Jamie as a sign of support.

Larry was surprised Jamie answered. "Cooper residence," Jamie said, picking up the phone. "Hi, Jamie, this is Larry."

"Hi, Larry, I suppose you have read the letters to the editor you hoped wouldn't appear."

"Yes, they made me sick to my stomach."

"Me too, only worse," Jamie said.

"We're considering a change of venue. What do you think?"

"Don't think we have a choice. Have you talked to Gordie?"

"He feels the same way."

"We can't get a fair trial in Routt County. The cloak of anonymity has shielded the authors of those letters, and I'm afraid, Larry, that some of those authors may end up surreptitiously on our jury if the trial is held here."

"That's a strong possibility. However, we have to think where the trial might be moved. The last time I made such a motion and it was granted, the judge was willing to remove it only to one of the adjoining counties in our district. That means the choice is either Moffat County or Grand County."

"That doesn't sound like much of an option," Jamie said. "Word of mouth doesn't stop at the county line. I'm sure everyone has heard by now about all the sordid details and is willing to supply the rope as one letter writer has already volunteered."

"What got me was the letter that said the theft was 'generational,' whatever that means," Larry said.

"Definitely a shot below the belt, particularly with all that our family has done for western Colorado since they settled here over half a century ago," Jamie said. "To curse me is one thing, but to curse my ancestry is going much too far. I guess they're blaming the tree for the bad fruit, eh?"

"Well, we'll be seeing you tomorrow anyway. Sorry this happened. Anymore crank calls?" Larry asked.

"Not been paying attention to those anymore. Figure it comes with the territory. I just hang up quickly and let them talk to themselves. I did, however, have a happening. I went into Castle's Hardware Store to purchase some sprinkler supplies, and when I came back out, someone had spat gooey chewing tobacco on the driver's window of my father's pickup."

"Good thing you had the window up," Larry said with a slight chuckle.

PREPARING FOR THE COUNTEROFFENSIVE

When Jamie arrived at the law offices at Whittaker and Brownell that fresh Steamboat July morning, Verna greeted him with "Thank God it's Friday," and "Come on, they're waiting for you." She then led him down the short hall to the conference room, with which he was becoming all too familiar. With its western exposure to Mount Werner and the large windows framing the remnants of the ski trails now lonely without snow, the room was inviting and exhilarating.

Larry and Gordie were already there and had been since seven a.m. Coffee mugs and partially eaten cinnamon rolls had been pushed to the side to make way for the notebooks Verna had assembled. Jamie noticed there were two other notebooks sitting on the glass-covered conference table. They were properly positioned containing the extra sets of discovery appropriately punched and separated by dividers with multicolored tabs. All four of the notebooks had black covers and were oversized but containing name tags for easy identification. One was placed in the spot where Jamie usually sat, and the tag bore his name.

"We made reservations for you," Larry said with a smile while pointing to Jamie's place.

"We've got to quit meeting like this," Jamie said, returning the smile.

Gordie, head buried in notebook, said, "We're going on the offensive, or should I say we're going to *be* offensive."

At that moment, Bodean made his presence known by loud clatter of boots on the tile hallway leading to the conference room and banging open his briefcase on the glass table top boldly as he entered. "Howdy," he said in a contrived Western drawl.

"Did you hear something?" Larry asked, looking at Jamie.

"Didn't hear a thing," Jamie said, deliberately not looking at Bodean. Gordie looked up and, sizing up Bodean's appearance, said, "While you were at Goodwill selecting that outfit, you should have bought a comb. If you don't have the money, I can loan you a couple bucks."

Bodean with Chiclets-white teeth exposed and grin from ear to ear said, "I didn't know they still made clothes out of recycled Teflon and rubber tires; do you want the name of a tailor who can make them fit? Oh, by the way, is that a paisley tie, or one that has soup souvenirs from last week's meals?"

Even with all the worries generated by the ordeal, the bantering between Gordie and Bodean generated a laughter Verna characterized as "boisterous" as she brought in cinnamon rolls for Jamie and Bodean and coffee all around. "I see you resurrected those old clay mugs I had been hiding. What's the matter? Doesn't the coffee taste as good in the china cups?" she said, directing her remarks primarily at Larry.

"These are the tough man's badge of courage—no more sissy stuff. We're tired of having sand kicked in our face," Larry said, gritting his teeth and snarling.

"I think he means it," Gordie said. That set the tone for the remainder of the day.

The first item on the agenda was the matter of the editorials. What to do about them. Gordie had said he thought they had tainted the jury pool and that even if a prospective juror had not already judged Jamie, he might succumb to peer pressure and vote for conviction for fear of alienating his neighbors or some paranoid fear of reprisal. What if they filed a motion for change of venue and it didn't succeed? Wouldn't that engender public resentment? Suggesting an accused would not receive a fair trial in Routt County would be perceived as an insult. But that was not as urgent a matter now as finding a way to stifle all the "hate speech."

Larry was convinced that a letter should go out immediately to the newspaper, attention Corbin Sweeney its editor, objecting to the libelous nature of the letters to the editor and demanding that the newspaper immediately cease and desist from printing any further such letters. The threat would be a lawsuit and/or the obtaining of a court order or injunction. All that the adverse pre-trial publicity was accomplishing was an excuse for the court to grant a change of venue. They all agreed it was probably already too late to counteract the negative public opinion of Jamie.

What about the libel aspect? Although truth is a defense, much of what was contained in the letters was false. It was not only what was said but was not said. The implications, innuendos, and double entendres were libelous as well. Although it was not technical hate speech under the law because it was not directed at ethnicity, for example, it was hate speech nonetheless.

The newspaper was propagating this questionable activity by providing the vehicle of dissemination and allowing anonymous comments. They doubted the letters would have been submitted had they required signatures.

They felt the newspaper would not risk a libel suit and certainly would opt ethically to take the high road. The same number of newspapers would be sold regardless of whether future letters were printed, and Corbin had the reputation of doing the right thing.

Discussing the legal aspects of a potential libel action was something Larry and Gordie had a responsibility to do with their client. They explained that Colorado was somewhat unique in certain respects inasmuch as the person defamed had a difficult burden in a suit against a newspaper.

The standard of proof was higher for public figures than for private persons, unless the matter involved was one of great public interest and concern. If that were the case, the private person would be morphed into the same category as the public figure.

Certainly, they pointed out, Jamie's situation was one involving a matter of great public interest and concern. Therefore, in order to succeed in a libel suit against the newspaper and unknown defendants, Jamie would have to prove not only that the offending statements were false but that the defendants *acted with malice*. "That means," Gordie said, "the defamers knew at the time they made the statements they were false or that they acted 'with reckless disregard of the truth.' And unlike the burden of proof in ordinary civil cases, which required only proof by a preponderance or greater weight of the evidence, Jamie would have to prove his case by 'clear and convincing evidence.'"

In response to Jamie's question concerning the burden of proof in an ordinary civil case, Gordon and Larry asked if he was familiar with the icon of the lady of justice blindfolded, holding scales in one hand and a sword in the other. He was. They then explained that if the scales tipped, even slightly to one side or the other, the side to which it tipped won. The burden of proof in a libel action was even more onerous than in a criminal case, where the burden of proof was "proof beyond a reasonable doubt," they told him.

Since a libel action could be brought at any time within one year after the publication of the false defamatory statement, all agreed further consideration should be tabled. However, the letter to Corbin Sweeney should proceed as proposed. After they adjourned this day, Larry said he would draft and have hand delivered such a letter.

Treating the summit conference as a board meeting, Jamie said he didn't want to take matters out of order but he was worried about the bank filing the contemplated civil action. He asked if Larry or Gordie would explain. Larry took the lead and said that the bank had really one choice if it decided to proceed and that was to file a conversion action. That meant that they would seek to recover money damages for the lost funds, attorney's fees, and court costs. Ordinarily, the interest would run on the $29,000 from the date of judgment, and it would be unlikely that the court would award attorney fees.

Having been in the banking business until ten days ago, Jamie was aware that because the bank was federally insured, there might be federal action. Gordie said even though the state and federal governments both had jurisdiction, the feds would relegate to the state and let them do their thing. He said it was good that Jamie was aware of the possibility but that it was highly improbable that the feds would step in.

Everyone seemed willing to allow Jamie to direct the course of the meeting at least for now. They knew Jamie's emotions were fragile and that he needed time to heal some of the wounds opened by the letters to the editor. They were willing to give him space and address all his concerns before delving into the tedious P.H. preparation.

Jamie could tell the defense team, as they were beginning to refer to themselves, was indulging him. He wanted to discuss, even though it might be premature, the possibility of bringing a civil action against the police department, the jail, and maybe even the district attorney's office. He said that he had been falsely arrested. During the arrest they searched him and did a strip search at the jail, all without a search warrant. At the time of his arrest, they also searched his desk and briefcase. While one searched his office, another took his car keys and entered his locked vehicle that was parked in the bank parking lot. In fact, the second officer was searching the trunk as the other two officers drove him out of the parking lot on the way to the police station.

Jennie had told him that on the afternoon of his arrest, she spotted a marked police cruiser parked in the driveway of their home, and when she went to investigate, two uniformed officers exited the side door of the garage and walked across the yard and through the gate to their cruiser. She said the double bay doors facing the street had been closed and locked and that the officers would have to have entered through the door they exited.

Obviously, the officers detained him against his will at the bank, police station, and jail. When he was not in his cell, he was handcuffed and accompanied by at least one officer.

The officers mistreated him at the time of his arrest and assaulted him at the bank and again at the police station. When he was put in the police cruiser in the bank parking lot, one of the officers shoved the end of his baton into his ribcage and tried to slam the cruiser door on his leg. "It still hurts," he said. They denied him medical attention for his broken nose for over twelve hours. At the booking, they twisted and sprained his index finger on his right hand while fingerprinting him. They used excessive force even if the arrest were legal.

They apparently were having comic relief during his interrogation, as he could hear laughter behind the two-way mirror throughout the whole ordeal. He didn't know who was back there, but there were several. When he was led out, he saw the chief of police, Jarred Hammerville, and one of the arresting officers, Clinton Coleman, exit the room immediately behind the mirrored interrogation room. Both were laughing, and the chief was patting Clinton on the shoulder in a congratulatory gesture.

They harassed him during the arrest while being transported to the police station, at the police station, during booking, and while he was being placed in his cell. Actually the jailers were civil and were the ones who ultimately called the jailhouse doctor.

He noticed the police had been following him in their cruiser since his release, and his father reported that they had been on his land without his permission "snooping around." Periodically he would see a strange vehicle parked down the street with someone sitting in it. The other day Max, his son, while riding his bicycle, came upon the strange vehicle with a man in the front driver's seat looking through binoculars in the direction of Jamie's home.

When Jamie paused and put his hand to his forehead with his elbow rested on the conference table, Bodean, who had been writing feverishly, said, "As a retired police officer myself and having been through the police academy, I can tell you they did all the things we were taught *not* to do. As you talked, I listed ten crimes they committed: (1) false arrest, (2) false imprisonment, (3) malicious prosecution, (4) assault and battery, (5) official misconduct, (6) abuse of official position, (7) harassment, (8) stalking, (9) invasion of privacy, and, (10) criminal trespass."

"Wow," Gordie said, "I'm impressed—here I thought you were just another pretty face."

"Jamie, the three of us have been in law enforcement," Larry said, "and have great respect for those who lay their lives on the line to protect society. For the most part, I have found police officers to be a conscientious, dedicated, and an honorable lot. What concerns me, is why the police officers, one of whom you described as being like kin, did all these terrible things to you."

"I was thinking the same thing," Gordie said. "I can understand Alden's motives, but I can't understand what motives Clinton Coleman and the others, particularly the chief, would have. Have you done something you haven't told us about?"

Before Jamie could respond, Bodean said, "I've always considered myself one of them and socialized with most of the Steamboat officers. As an alumnus, I am usually invited to the Police Officers' Association annual meetings and banquets. Now, after my involvement in your case, I am a *persona non grata*. They go out of their way to avoid speaking to me if they can. Back when I broke up with a high school girlfriend, her friends treated me like that. I was bothered by it then, and I am bothered by it now."

"My father called me last night after he had read the weekly scandal sheet to provide a little encouragement and to let me know that both he and Mom were praying for me," Jamie said. "Dad told me he had been trying to figure the whole thing out for days and particularly after reading the scathing letters to the editor. He said he was in a quandary and, after discussing it with Mom, was able to connect the dots."

Leaning forward, Larry, Gordie, and Bodean listened in anxious anticipation as Jamie continued. "Some years ago when my uncle Lewis was still alive, he and my father found signs of poaching and butchered cattle on the far rocky reaches of Cooper Ranch. Apparently this had been going on for several years. So when they found fresh slaughter hanging from a tree ready to be retrieved, they lay in wait. Sure enough, after it got dark, a four-wheel-drive pickup truck drove down a seldom-used dirt road not much larger than a cow trail and stopped less than twenty yards away. With rifle in hand, a rough, large man emerged with a young boy he guessed to be twelve. In addition to the rifle, they were carrying butchering tools and canvas bags. Both were wearing miner helmets with mounted flashlights. After the large man set down his rifle against a tree, he began finishing his carving project while the boy laid out packaging material for the prey.

"Uncle Lewis and my father, emerging from their hiding place with rifles drawn, approached the game poachers. They caught them in the beams of a large portable spotlight, and the trespassers' crimes were exposed. The large man reached for what turned out to be a loaded .30–30. Just as he was about to take aim, my father shot it out of his hand, permanently injuring him. The young boy was frightened and just froze in his tracks, quivering and unable to move.

"After the man was treated by a medical doctor who lived near the Cooper Ranch, he was transferred by a deputy sheriff to the Routt County Jail. He was charged with cattle rustling and a hunting violation. He pled guilty to both charges and served time at the Colorado State Penitentiary in Canon City."

Jamie stopped and took a drink of his now cold coffee. The suspense, of course, was raising havoc with the three listeners. Like kids, they bombarded Jamie with a myriad of questions, all at the same time. "What happened next? Who were they? What happened to the boy? What's this got to do with your case? When did this happen? Was the boy related to the man? How old was the boy?" Jamie knew how critical this information was to his case, and he deliberately stalled in answering their questions and, in fact, delayed its revelation until nearly the end of the session.

"I now know what it feels like to be cross-examined. How impressive," he said, still toying with them. "I'll try to answer your questions as I remember them. This happened in 1944. The boy was the son of the man. The man was thirty-eight years old at the time having been born in 1906. The son was twelve years old at the time, having been born in 1932; now he would be forty years old. Both still live in Steamboat. The father has a withered right hand." Jamie stood up and handed the weathered news clippings he had been reading to Larry.

"Oh my God," the three said in unison. "The father is Summer Hammerville, and the son is Jarred Hammerville, our chief of police."

"Any other questions, gentlemen?" Jamie asked. Stunned, silent, and shocked, they just sat there staring at each other. Jamie then said, "I rest my case!"

None of them could think of anything clever to say. Finally, Larry said, "This is a good time for a luncheon break."

Verna had deli sandwiches, Larry's favorite hot pastrami on pumpernickel with German potato salad, cabbage slaw, and kosher pickles. "Just like going to Ken's Grill on Copley Square in Boston," Bodean said, corralling his allotment.

"I love kosher food too," Gordie chimed in. Selecting their favorite soft drinks they all settled in for some cozy chitchat.

Taking a bite out of his pickle first, Larry said he had a confession to make. "Call me a doubting Thomas," he said to Jamie. "I feel like I've been on a roller coaster since becoming involved in your case. I did what I have told my juries not to do and that is don't jump to conclusions—listen to all the evidence first before you make a decision—keep an open mind. I learned a very valuable lesson today. Even though I have been leaning your way from the start, I must confess I let some stinkin' thinkin' creep into my mind the past twenty-four hours. You have countered every accusation with a plausible explanation. I guess it's easy when you're telling the truth. And, in my heart, I know you are."

Gordie and Bodean followed suit. Confession, contrition, and a firm purpose of amendment are needed for forgiveness, and they were asking for forgiveness. Jamie said he didn't blame them for how they felt and only hoped he could help them help him.

"How do you keep such a positive attitude, especially after having read the letters to the editor, most of which contained pejorative comments?" Gordie asked. "I think Larry and I and maybe Bodean as well were more traumatized than you. And they weren't even about us."

"Thank you for the compliment. I'm practicing an art I learned from a book I read some years ago about a prisoner of war who had been confined by the enemy to a birdcage of a cell for a number of years. When he was liberated, he was asked by his liberators how he was able to survive. He said in his mind he played golf every day, he lounged at various resorts around the world, and drank mint juleps every afternoon. He called it disassociation. That's what I'm doing. I have to cope because of all the people out there who depend on my strength—especially now."

Larry, still intent on making up for his lack of trust, said to Jamie, "You thanked me for taking on your case. Actually, it is I who should be thanking you. I will certainly be more circumspect."

"Win, lose, or draw," Jamie said, "Ill never be able to adequately thank all of you for your taking on this rebel's cause and, more importantly, for the friendship I sense is developing between all of us." He rose and walked around the table, shaking each man's hand as if he were campaigning for office. Upon returning to his chair, he and the others finished the lunch that had pretty much gone untouched up until that moment.

When Verna cleaned up and collected the leftovers, she said, "What's up with the hungry jacks? Didn't you like the food? You ate like birds. I'll put the extra food in the fridge and you can help yourselves when appetite returns."

Everything seemed to take on a new hue now. With renewed vigor they began to dissect the case against James Curtis Cooper alias Jamie Cooper. They started with the police officers' witness interviews. The first interview was of Alden Stillwell.

Alden told Officer Coleman that he was an officer at the Steamboat Bank and Trust Co. He, the president (Brandon Stillwell) and the first vice president (Jamie Cooper) were the only three who had the combination to the main vault where the bulk of the bank's money was kept. The bank had a system of dual control whereby the head teller (Rita Baker) and one of the three officers, usually himself, would count the money at day's end and set the timer on the vault door for seven a.m. the following morning. One would close the door and spin the combination in the presence of the other. This procedure was followed on July 10. Normally Brandon would open the vault. During the week of July 10 through the 14, however, Brandon was out of town, and so Alden opened the vault on each of those days.

Alden, according to the discovery, told Officer Coleman that he opened the vault door on Tuesday, July 11. He then went to his office to begin work for the day, and when he went to Jamie's office to retrieve a file, he discovered the $1,000 in one of Jamie's desk drawers. He immediately went to the vault, and when he examined one of the cash compartments in the vault, discovered that $30,000 in straps of $1,000, some containing fifty-dollar bills and others containing one-hundred-dollar bills, were missing. Each strap had a stamp on it bearing the Federal Reserve Bank of Denver. He then searched Jamie's other drawers but didn't find the other $29,000. He stated that he was the first to arrive that morning and that Jamie's 1970 Ford Galaxie was in the parking lot when he arrived. He didn't see Jamie. Jamie did not arrive at work until eight a.m. When he left the bank, the previous evening at approximately five forty-five p.m., Jamie was still there.

According to Officer Coleman's report, he next interviewed the bank's head teller, Rita Baker. She stated that she and Alden counted the money in the bank's main vault at day's end on Monday, July 10. She and Alden set the timer on the door of the main vault for seven a.m. the following morning and together closed the vault door, locking it behind them. She double-checked to make sure the vault door was closed and locked. She arrived at work the usual time the following morning July 11, which would have been at seven forty-five a.m. Alden greeted her with the $1,000 strap he said he obtained from Jamie's desk drawer and told her that he checked the vault and discovered $30,000 missing from the main cash compartment. He then looked in

Jamie's office for the other $29,000 but was unable to locate it. He called the police and while waiting for the police to arrive, they searched the rest of the bank in an effort to locate the other $29,000. While they were in the midst of conducting the search, Jamie arrived. Within minutes after Jamie's arrival, the police came in and arrested him. She, Alden, and the rest of the bank's employees searched for the money after the police left but to no avail. Alden then ordered her to have all the bank locks changed, to box up and bring to him all of Jamie's personal effects, and after the police were finished searching Jamie's car, to have it towed away, which she did.

"Officer Coleman has been a very busy man," Larry said somewhat sarcastically.

"Sounds more like an overzealous cop to me," Bodean said emphatically. "He's shooting for rank and more pay, and it's obvious he's trying to curry the chief's favor."

"The chief wants a Cooper's head on a platter," Jamie added wistfully. "With what's happened at the bank, his wish has been granted, and a Cooper's head, namely mine, is just falling into his lap."

"You wonder how many sleepless nights he fantasized about the devastating and painful ways he would exact his family's pound of flesh for what happened to his daddy," Gordie pondered aloud.

Coleman had contacted the custodian of the records at the telephone company, seeking the toll records for the calls made from Jamie's home telephone for the months of June and July 1972. Copies of those records were included in the discovery. Checked off were seven calls made to a Las Vegas number in June and five in July. The numbers, according to Coleman's report, were traced to Tobiasis Casino, a gambling establishment on the strip in Las Vegas, Nevada.

Another page in Coleman's investigative report centered on the verification of a trip Jamie and Jennie made between the telephone calls in June. He had obtained records from United Airlines confirming the issuance of roundtrip airline tickets in Jamie and Jennie's names to Las Vegas with a departure date of June 23. "Hmmm," Jamie said in a huff, "I have the damn tickets sitting on my desk at home as we speak. If they had asked, I would have given them those, the Caesar's Palace hotel receipts, the limousine receipts, and anything else they wanted. Remember our airline tickets were purchased by my father and were put on his credit card. He would, of course, have those records."

Coleman's report noted that he had contacted a Katherine Tilley, a bookkeeper at Caesar's Palace, who verified that a Mr. and Mrs. James Cooper had checked in on June 23 and checked out on June 26. "'Because it was a recent transaction,' the report read, 'Ms. Tilley said she would be able to retrieve and forward a copy of the registration to this investigator.' I can't believe they would just give that information out over the telephone," Gordie said.

"No copy of the registration form is in the discovery, so I assume the police department doesn't have it yet."

"By the way, Jamie," Larry asked, "How did Coleman know to check at Caesar's?"

"Everyone at the bank knows where I stayed. Whenever I went out of town, I made sure they knew where to reach me," Jamie replied.

Perhaps the most damaging piece of discovery was a photocopy of a receipt from Tobiasis Casino for the payment of $1,200 issued to a Jamie Cooper on June 23, 1972, "In full payment of redemption of chit number 72-PD4485." Noted on the bottom of the photocopy was the following handwritten scribble, "Officer Coleman, I assume this is what you wanted. If we can be of further assistance, please feel free to recontact us." The notation bore the signature, Horace Green, Head Bookkeeper, Collections. "The *PD* on the chit number, I assume," Gordie said, "means 'past due.'"

This was the guts of Corbett's case, Larry had said. Although the case was still young, there were already over fifty pages of discovery. When Bodean was spending more time on particular points than the others thought necessary, Larry prodded him along. This would have been the longest of the sessions, and when five and then five thirty passed, it was decided to call it a day. They had accomplished all they had hoped for and more.

"What do you think of Jamie taking a polygraph?" Gordie asked, looking around the room. Jamie said he had no problem with that. Larry said he felt very comfortable that Jamie would pass, especially now that he had heard the rest of the story. Bodean said he thought a lie detector test was a good idea. Who would administer the test and when was Jamie's concern. It was decided that everyone would sleep on it and they would decide later. Jamie was to call Larry or Gordie on Monday to discuss it further and maybe meet again on Wednesday. Larry and Gordie had separate court matters and appointments stacked on Monday and Tuesday. Bodean said he would be available on Wednesday and, in the interim, would scout out a polygrapher who didn't have a prosecution mind-set, someone preferably in the area.

Exchanges of endearment, some kibitzing, and then the good-byes. If this day was but a drop in the bucket of the emotions they would experience on the long journey through the ordeal, they didn't want to know about it—at least not just yet.

THE CLOCK TICKS

When the summit conference was over on Friday, Jamie and Bodean walked to their cars parked on the side of the building. Small talk at first, then Bodean reflecting his ex-cop curiosity said, "Jamie, there is something that has been bothering me all afternoon."

"What is that?" Jamie asked inquisitively.

"Regardless of whether it was you or someone else, how could the money have been removed from the vault from the time the bank vault time lock was set until it expired at seven a.m. the next morning? In other words, even if you or that someone else had the right combination, the door couldn't have been opened. They would have had to wait until the time ran down, right?"

Jamie, throwing his notebook, folder, and legal pad across the driver's seat to the passenger side and pulling his large upper frame out of the car, almost stepping on Bodean's feet, said, "The bank's main vault time lock was an antique, and from time to time we upgraded it. The lock has two movements to provide redundancy in case one fails. The theory behind two is that if there was only one movement and it failed, it would almost take dynamite to gain access. Going in and out of the vault for thirteen years, I've noted that the manufacturer of the time lock was Howard and Co., of Boston, Massachusetts. I do remember that when I first started working at the bank and the door didn't open, even when Brandon had dialed the right combination, he went to his office and called the manufacturer. He was gone for quite a long period of time while the tellers waited anxiously. He finally returned and referring to numbers on a small slip of paper that no one could see dialed a bypass combination, which apparently overrode the time lock. I'm not aware that that ever happened again."

"That's what I wanted to know," Bodean said, nodding his head in understanding. "Up until that time," Bodean said pensively, "no one at SB&T Co. knew the secret combination, not even Brandon. What about you and Alden? You had the regular combination, but did either of you or both have the secret combination?" he asked.

"I didn't," Jamie said. "I don't know about Alden. Someone must have, and the most likely person was Alden because Alden had access to his dad's office."

Speculating, Bodean said, "He could have been looking for something in his dad's office while his dad was in Salt Lake and stumbled on the secret combination."

"Either that," Jamie said, "or Alden had the window of opportunity from seven thirty a.m. when the vault opened until seven forty-five a.m., when the first bank employee arrived, to take and stash the loot."

"It doesn't appear in the discovery or anywhere that anyone ever searched Alden's desk, office, or Cadillac. In fact, it appears that he was assisting and directing everyone else in the search."

Shaking his head, Bodean concluded, "It's like the fox guarding the henhouse."

"It's pretty clear that Alden directed everyone in my direction. For whatever reason, jealousy that his father favored me over him, that I had 'higher rank' if you choose to call it that, that I was the star and he was the nerd through school, that he was rejected by the woman I dated and married, or some other inexplicable reason that's been gnawing on him for three-plus decades. The officers had tunnel vision. I was accused, charged, and convicted all in one quick swoop. All that awaits is the hanging. And flavor the mix with a chief of police and henchmen who want to vindicate the dignity and restore the reputation of the chief's father, who was convicted of a felony and went to prison all because of a Cooper."

Bodean was beginning to feel a respect and admiration for a man who was being wrongfully accused, denied by those he thought were his friends, and sold out for thirty thousand pieces of silver, much like someone he has known in his heart and who lived, suffered, and died almost two thousand years ago.

The case would hinge on who the jury would conclude would be the most likely candidate to have stolen the money—the son who would steal from his own father or really from himself since he was the sole heir or an employee who had a gambling addiction and couldn't cover his losses. Bodean knew he had his work cut out for him.

Bodean told Jamie he had a former roommate at Michigan State whose family had been in the banking business and he would call him to discuss the bank vault time lock (BVTL) aspect of the case. He said he had been thinking of calling him for some time now and this would be a good excuse. Because of the impact of the BVTL aspect of the case, Jamie and Bodean agreed to meet at Larry and Gordie's office on Monday at one p.m.

On Monday, July 24, Jamie called Bodean and said he, Jennie, Max, and Collette were all at the Cooper Ranch and had been since Saturday morning, helping his father mend a fence. He asked if they could postpone their appointment until four p.m. Bodean said that would be better for him as well.

As the clock on the town hall struck four, Jamie and Bodean drove into the parking lot at Whittaker and Brownell, attorneys at law, Jamie in his drab 1971 Ford Galaxie and Bodean in his bright red 1972 Ford Mustang. Having his fence-mending outfit on and not having had time to change, both were similarly dressed. "I see you got the memo," Bodean said as both trotted across the tile floor, *clickity-clack, clickity-clack.* Verna, diverting her attention away from the typewriter while lowering her gold wire-rim glasses down over her nose and peering over the top, was greeted by two unkempt and ruffled ranch hands. Her mouth gaped, and she just stared.

"We just came back from a wedding," Bodean said. "We figured you missed us."

"Can't get rid of a bad penny," Jamie chided. "It's an old banking joke."

"You two are just too funny—funny acting and funny looking," she said with contrived indignity. "Isn't the leash law in effect today?" she asked.

"We know you missed us," Bodean said. "Do you mind if we use the conference room? We need to plot strategy. The walls have ears in all the coffee shops and soda fountains, and we dare not go into the bars. You know how gossip starts."

"Larry and Gordie are still in court and have been all day. The door is open, just set the books aside, and if you close them, set a marker or you'll get me fired. Also help yourselves to the sodas and iced tea in the fridge and ice in the freezer. Just make yourselves at home. But, please do me a favor?"

"What's that?" Bodean boldly asked.

"Don't let anyone know I know you two. If anyone asks, I'll just say you couldn't find your way to the box cars and stopped to ask for directions," Verna quipped.

"Nice, Verna, and we used to like you too," he murmured as the two clicked their way to the all too familiar conference room. Settled in their usual place and drinking their usual drinks, they resumed their usual roles.

"Did you make contact with your former roommate?" Jamie asked.

"I did," Bodean said, retrieving a yellow legal pad with writing from his briefcase. "It was good to talk to Dustin Davies again, and he provided a lot of good information. He has been working at the family bank at a branch in Kalamazoo, Michigan. Apparently, the bank just replaced a dinosaur made sometime in the 1800s with a time lock containing what he called a three-movement, double redundancy time movement, made in Switzerland.

"Dustin said each BVTL was different, depending on year of manufacture, type, model and manufacturer. He said the early locks contained a mechanism that when a special combination was inputted, the time lock would be disengaged. He also referred to the special combination as a bypass or secret combination known only to the manufacturer. The manufacturer would only reveal the secret combination to bank personnel in the event of BVTL failure and the urgent need to open the vault.

"Dustin said the BVTL evolution was marked by two or three movements, providing 'redundancy' in the event one timer malfunctioned. Otherwise, the door could only be opened by what he called extreme and sometimes destructive methods.

"He confirmed what you had already told me about the regular combination needing to be dialed even after the timer runs down. In other words, the vault door does not automatically open at the appointed time.

"He said he would send me copies of whatever he had and could come up with the name of an expert in the field if we intended to call one. He also indicated that such experts were expensive and that they usually wanted their money up front. I told him we would let him know."

About that time, briefcases in hand, books under arm, the "Perry Masons of Steamboat" shuffled their way down the hall, muttering obscenities about the lack of time management and scheduling procedures of both the county court and district court dockets. Peering into the open door of the conference room, they engaged in dialogue about disciplining whoever left the back door to the office unlocked and allowing alley trash access, whether they should call animal control, or whether they should call the exterminator and have the conference room sprayed for fleas.

"Climb down out your ivory towers and see how the working class dresses," Bodean said.

"This is my Superman outfit," Jamie said. "I changed in the telephone booth on the way in."

Once things settled down and Larry and Gordie had deposited their carry-ins in their respective offices, they returned with their *People v. Cooper* files and folders in hand. Both were appreciative of the crash course on BVTLs and having learned a new acronym. They all briefly debated the pros and cons of bringing up the BVTL at the P.H. or saving it for trial. All agreed that it would be them providing the sneak preview at the P.H., and thus, by placing the prosecution on notice, would be allowing the prosecution to arm itself in anticipation. The evidence on the BVTL should be saved for trial.

Larry took a poll of those assembled at this impromptu summit conference to determine what each considered to be the Achilles heel of the defense's case. He told each of them to write it down and not let the others see. The ground rule for this parlor game was that each could only list one item.

When everyone had finished writing, Larry started around the table. "The telephone calls and trip to Las Vegas," they all said without exception.

"It provided the motive," Bodean said.

"Easily explainable," Jamie said.

"Not so easy," Larry and Gordie said in unison.

"Now that we have established the number-one challenge," Larry said, "what are we going to do about it?" The wheels were turning. You could see it in their eyes and, if you listened carefully, you could hear the grinding.

It was Bodean who spoke first. "We need to contact Jamie's uncle Matt and cousin Patty. They will provide the 'alibi,' so to speak."

"Have you spoken to either of them since the beginning of the ordeal?" Gordie asked Jamie.

"No," Jamie said, "I've been too embarrassed."

"Well, they helped get you into this predicament; they can help get you out of it," Gordie said.

Larry interjected, "Even though we wouldn't call them at the P.H., we need to contact them without further delay to insure their availability and cooperation. Bodean, can you do that before our conference on Wednesday?"

Bodean, who was taking notes, asked Jamie if he had their addresses and telephone numbers. He said he did and retrieved a small folded slip of paper from his wallet. He unfolded the slip and handed it to Bodean, who copied the information onto his legal pad and then returned it to Jamie.

"Wouldn't Coleman and the others like to have a copy of that?" Gordie asked, catching himself and adding, "Strike that, I'm sure they have already had a sister agency in Las Vegas interview Cousin Patty and Uncle Matt. That probably was the first information the police found and copied when they rifled through Jamie's wallet upon his arrest."

"That might have been what triggered the Las Vegas connection," Larry mused.

"Shouldn't we have them testify in our behalf?" Jamie inquired.

"Not necessarily," Gordie responded. "The fact that you went to Las Vegas to bail Patty out of her predicament doesn't help our case at this point for a number of reasons. The first is the P.H. is not a trial or even a mini trial. If there is a factual dispute, that's for a jury to decide. A second reason is that it is immaterial what the money was used for, whether to cover *your* gambling losses or Patty's, it was still the bank's money, and you didn't have their permission to take it. So what does their testimony accomplish?"

Bodean said he thought that the statements taken by their sister agency in Las Vegas would be skewed anyway. "All they wanted to document was your trip to Vegas," he said to Jamie. "They didn't know about it, and Patty was not about to divulge her woes. They didn't ask; she didn't tell. So all that Coleman's report incorporated in the discovery indicates is that 'Patty Cooper confirmed that her cousin Jamie Cooper and his wife Jennie were in Las Vegas between the dates of June 23 and June 26, 1972.'"

"Well, doesn't Corbett need to fly them out here to testify at the P.H.? Otherwise, isn't that hearsay?" Jamie asked inquisitively.

"Good questions, both," Larry responded. "No, in answer to your first question and an equivocal yes in answer to your second question. It *is* hearsay when a person testifies as to what someone else told him or her. For Coleman to testify as to what Patty told the Las Vegas cop, who in turn told him is double hearsay. Unfortunately at the P.H., the rules of evidence are tempered, and hearsay is allowed at the sound discretion of the judge."

"Why couldn't Bodean interview Patty and Uncle Matt over the telephone and then relate at the preliminary hearing what they told him? That would only be firsthand hearsay and even more reliable than Coleman's."

"Wow!" Gordie said. "I feel like I'm taking the bar exam all over again. That conceivably could be allowed. But what do you prove? All you do is corroborate that you brought money into Vegas to support their local economy. It is still money and money that inferentially belonged to the bank."

"In law school, we called that a 'circulis extracabulis,' which loosely translated means 'going around in circles,'" Larry said.

Jamie, still confused, asked, "Does that mean that Coleman could be the only witness called by the prosecution and could testify as to what the various witnesses told him?"

"That's a possibility," said Gordie. "Technically, Judge Dearborn has discretion to allow that. However, he would probably rule that the victim, here the bank, through one of its officers, should establish the existence of the funds, its disappearance, Jamie's access, and more importantly the finding of the one thousand dollars in Jamie's desk drawer."

"By the way," Bodean interjected, "the finding of the one thousand dollars in Jamie's desk drawer could have been a close second on my list of weaknesses in our case. If anyone is interested, I'll tell you why." Everyone nodded. "In theft cases, I found when I was in law enforcement that the jury required that the accused be caught with his hand in the proverbial cookie jar in order to convict. Here, if we believe Alden, the 'cookies' were found in Jamie's lower desk drawer."

"I would second that," Gordie said. "Although it won't make any difference at the P.H., at trial everything hinges on Alden's credibility. If the jury questions Alden's credibility seriously enough to rise to the level of reasonable doubt, Jamie is home free. Otherwise, if they believe Alden, Jamie's goose is cooked!"

"It's amazing," Larry exclaimed. "I almost put Alden's claim of discovery of the one thousand dollars in Jamie's desk drawer the 'number one' concern. The only reason I didn't is because the one thousand dollars were never seen by anyone else. The only person who had it in his possession was Alden. When the police arrived, it was not in Jamie's office or on Jamie's desk until Alden, emerging from his own office, with cash in hand, threw the offending bills on Jamie's desk. That was witnessed by everyone, including the officers who had 'bad intentions.'"

"So you think Alden's credibility is the number one prosecution concern?" Jamie asked Larry.

"Yes," Larry said without hesitation. "I think his credibility is the key to the whole case."

"My sentiments exactly," Gordie said.

"Mine too," echoed Bodean.

"I think, and I've thought about this a lot," Larry said, "it was probably a spur of the moment thing for Alden. When he stumbled on the secret combination in his father's drawer the day before, he didn't think much of it. But after he went home and, maybe while he was reclining in his favorite rocker and replaying the day's events in his mind and pausing on the combination discovery, formulated his clandestine plan. After his wife was deep in slumber, he snuck out of the house, drove over to the bank, and, finding that the secret combination worked, removed the thirty thousand, placing one thousand in his desk drawer as Jamie's office was locked, and then drove himself and the twenty-nine thousand home and, after hiding the money, slipped unnoticed back into bed."

"Gosh, Larry," Gordie said, "do you hire out for bedtime stories? My boys have tired of my mundane fables and anecdotes."

Ignoring Gordie because of deep concentration, Larry continued, "As I said, it could have been a spur of the moment thing, something totally impulsive, but I may be wrong. Alden may have been planning the frame-up for a number of years. With his father out of town, the opportunity presented itself, and Alden acted upon it."

"With his parents out of town," Bodean speculated, "Alden could have placed the twenty-nine thousand temporarily in their home or outbuildings. They lived side by side, and Alden undoubtedly had a key."

"If Alden had been caught at the bank that evening," Bodean said, "he could have aborted his plan, at least for the evening, and claimed he was attending to some unfinished business. He had a built-in excuse. All the cards, however, fell into place. Mission accomplished and not a trace."

Larry then asked Jamie, "Do all the officers lock their offices? I guess I'm asking if Alden had a key to yours."

"There would have been a duplicate in Rita's drawer, but I don't think Alden had a key to mine, and I know I didn't have a key to his," Jamie responded. "I think he was in a hurry the night before, didn't want to take the chance of being seen at the bank, and therefore, didn't take the time to hunt for the key."

"I'm sure," Larry said, still deep in thought, "that Alden figured he would be first to arrive at the bank the next morning and would have plenty of time to plant the one thousand in Jamie's office. Unable to find the right key and not expecting the bookkeeper's early arrival, Alden had to improvise. He was probably nervous about having the one thousand still in his possession and, knowing he had to get rid of it, made his dramatic entrance into Jamie's office, scattering the bills in his haste."

"How do we prove all that?" Jamie asked, looking in Larry's direction.

"It's just speculation and conjecture. It's not evidence. Just as the evidence surrounding you is circumstantial, so is Alden's in developing our alternate suspect defense. It is up to us to paint the picture and plant the seeds of doubt. Maybe we'll get lucky, and Alden will make a mistake."

"Since it is just as likely that our version of events occurred as theirs," Gordie said, "the tie is required by law to be resolved in our favor!"

Bodean, not to be outdone said, "We don't have to prove anything. The defense never does. We don't have to prove our theory of the case. We just need to raise reasonable doubt. If the prosecution doesn't prove their case beyond a reasonable doubt, the jury has to return a not guilty verdict."

About that time the telephone rang. On the fourth ring, Larry looked at his watch, and noticing it was after seven p.m. and realizing that Verna and Terry had already left for the day, answered the telephone on the credenza. "Whittaker and Brownell," Larry answered. "Yes, he does … he's on his way. He has been unavoidably detained … I'll tell him to hurry!

"That was your wife," he told Gordie. When the phone rang again, he knew who it was, and when he answered just said he was on the way and hung up.

Jamie looking at his watch asked, "Anyone know a good divorce attorney?"

Bodean said, "Hire me one too."

Like a fire drill, the defense team raced out to their cars, heading for the people who really cared and mattered.

Larry yelled after them, "See you all at eight a.m. on Wednesday. In the interim don't forget your assignments. Class dismissed!"

It was really only a recess as the ordeal would prove, and they were never very far from its grasp.

CAUGHT IN THE CROSSFIRE

Early Tuesday morning, Bodean was on the telephone trying to reach Jamie's uncle Matt and cousin Patty. The number for Patty had been disconnected. He tried Information, but there was no listing for Patty Cooper. Bodean finally reached Uncle Matt after several unsuccessful attempts.

When he identified himself as Jamie's attorney, Uncle Matt was speechless. He was even more stunned when he was informed of the nature of the charges. "I thought that boy would be president some day," he said. Bodean assured him Jamie had been wrongfully charged and that everything would probably be resolved in Jamie's favor.

"I surely hope so," Uncle Matt said. "I would trust that boy with my life."

Bodean explained that the authorities had misconstrued Jamie's Las Vegas telephone calls and trip. "They have alleged Jamie embezzled bank funds to pay gambling debts," Bodean informed him. "They have obtained copies of his airline tickets, hotel registration slip, and receipts for the redemption of a chit at Tobiasis Casino." Bodean then asked Uncle Matt what he knew but first wanted some information about him.

Uncle Matt said his full name was Matthew Thomas Cooper and he was four years younger than Jamie's father, having just turned sixty in May. A widower for two years, he had a daughter, Patty Ann Cooper, who was thirty-two. Patty was unmarried and was a high school math teacher in Las Vegas. She had been married for seven years but had her name changed back to Cooper when she divorced. She has lived in Las Vegas for approximately ten years. She has had a drinking problem at least five of those years and a gambling addiction as well. She is well known on the Vegas strip, and credit has been freely extended to her. Her compulsive gambling has resulted in her losing her teaching position, being evicted from her home, kiting checks, attempting to redeem various chits, defending lawsuits, and on July 19, being arrested and charged with a felony fraud by check charge. She has been unable to make bail, and he is unable and unwilling to obtain a surety bond because of the high premium and the bondsman's requirement that the bond be secured by his home.

Bodean asked if Patty was currently represented by an attorney. He advised Bodean that the court had appointed the public defender to defend her and that they had been involved in plea negotiations that would allow her to plead to one of the felony charges. In return, she would be granted probation and the remaining five felony counts would be dropped. She would also be required to perform one hundred hours of community service, be involved in an alcohol rehab program for a specified period of time, and make restitution.

Uncle Matt stated that he had washed his hands of his daughter. She had placed him on the verge of bankruptcy, and he was on the hook for several notes he cosigned.

Bodean asked why Jamie had made the trip to Vegas in June. Uncle Matt told him it was to help him pay off a chit or marker that Tobiasis was hounding Patty to redeem. When asked if the chit was in any way related to Jamie gambling, Uncle Matt said, "What gambling? That boy is as conservative as a preacher and as straight as an arrow. I'll do anything and everything I can to help him clear up this mess."

Bodean then asked if he knew where Jamie got the money to redeem the chit. "When I called my brother, Forrest, he volunteered Jamie to help since Jamie was a banker and knew what to do. Forrest said he would send Jamie with the money and pay Jamie's travel expenses. I assume that's what he did. I promised Forrest that once we got Patty out of the mess, I would pay him back."

When Bodean had asked if the authorities contacted him, he said he had had several messages on this telephone a week or so back from the Steamboat Springs Police Department, but he never returned the calls. He also was told by his neighbor that a Las Vegas police officer was looking for him, apparently needing to speak to him. He thought it might have to do with Patty, so he was avoiding them.

Bodean next asked if he knew whether or not Patty had been contacted by the Colorado authorities. Uncle Matt said he wasn't sure whether it was the Colorado or local authorities who talked to her, but she mentioned talking to an Officer Coleman and later to another police officer shortly before her arrest on July 17.

As soon as Bodean hung up the telephone, he tried unsuccessfully to reach Jamie at home and ultimately reached him at the Cooper Ranch.

"Did you reach the Las Vegas Coopers?" Jamie asked.

"Do you want the good news or the bad news first?"

"Tell me the good news first. I haven't had any in a while."

"Well, I had a good chat with your uncle Matt. He said he was willing to do anything he could to help you."

"Did he confirm the purpose of my trip and the bailout of Patty at Tobiasis?"

"Everything was consistent with what you told us—in every respect. Do you want the bad news?"

"Should I be seated?" he asked Bodean.

"Patty was apparently contacted by Clinton Coleman the week of your arrest presumably because of her name and Vegas telephone number having been found in your wallet. Anyway, Patty was caught in the crossfire and was arrested on June 17 on six felony fraud by check charges. Your uncle Matt has refused to bail her out, and she's sitting in the clinker as we speak."

Jamie was silent for a long moment and slowly and sorrowfully moaned, "The sniper has taken aim and hit his mark once again. My cousin Patty absolutely was caught in the Hammerville crossfire, as you label it. There is no doubt in my mind now that the chief, bent on vindicating the dignity and restoring the reputation of his dear old dad, will stop at nothing to bring the Coopers to their knees. He wants complete annihilation."

"I remember you telling me that your father has experienced strange sightings at the Cooper Ranch since your arrest with strange cars and people snooping around. I don't think it's just trying to sniff out where you stashed the loot or looking for a stray to butcher or game to poach, but I think it's to find something to pin on your dad. What goes around comes around. Hammerville and friends are looking to return the favor."

"Bodean, you're right on. I don't think the chief is content to settle for a trade on one for one. I think he wants to topple the whole Cooper house of cards. And, frankly, I think Alden for some inexplicable reason is on the same mission."

"Wasn't there something in the Great Book about the generational thing you were discussing in reference to the letters to the editor last week? Something about paying for the sins of the father? What was that?"

"Until my arrest, the term *curse* had no meaning. Now I think someone is sticking pins in a Cooper voodoo doll because the Coopers are starting to feel the pain. Any sins there be were not of my father, but of me. I am responsible for what has happened to the family, including Patty, and it is me and not them who should be punished. I just hope my children don't have to pay for the sins of their father."

Now it was Bodean's time to be quiet. Not knowing quite what to say, he finally got up the courage to offer Jamie some brotherly advice. "They've dug a hole, a deep dark one, to put you in. The only way you're going to end up there is if you let them push you in. You're much too strong and determined to let them do that. You can't give up the good fight or even think about it. If there is a curse, it can be reversed. And I'm going to help you do it."

DISPELLING THE MYTH

"Never waive a preliminary hearing," Jamie could hear Gordie say.

"What the hell did those ivory tower intellectual snobs disguised as law professors know anyway?" Jamie could hear Larry say.

"What's with them?" Jamie asked in a hushed tone to Verna. "They've been doing that ever since I got here," she whispered back.

It was now eight a.m. sharp, and Larry came out of Gordie's office with an empty cup in each hand, looking for refills. Seeing Jamie, he said, "Oh good, you're here. Grab a cup and one of Verna's patented frosted cinnamon rolls."

About that time Bodean arrived and, sniffing in the air like a starved cat, exclaimed, "I smell the scintillating aroma of one of Verna's out of this world creations. Where's mine?"

"Where's your manners, and where did you develop that insatiable appetite?" Verna asked Bodean.

"You have to admit I have good taste," he replied.

They all migrated to the conference room. Set up on a stand was a flip chart with the following appearing on the exposed sheet in dark heavy block letters, obviously in Gordie's printing style:

Purposes of P.H.
1. Screening device
2. Serves as fishing expedition
3. Pins down testimony
4. Criminal version of pretrial discovery
5. Reveals prosecution's weaknesses
6. Showcases the defense of the accused
7. If no PC, case dismissed

"Looks like someone's holding a seminar," Jamie said.

"Sounded more like a barroom brawl," Bodean said. He turned to Larry. "Did Gordie just insult your mother?"

"Call it a discussion," Larry responded.

"When last we met," Larry said, imitating a college professor, "we discussed the nebulous nature of the preliminary hearing, also known as the P.H., and whether we gain anything by having one."

"Or, not having one," Gordie added.

"Oh, yes," Larry continued, "I will be lecturing on why we should waive the P.H., and Professor Gordie will be lecturing on why we shouldn't."

"Before we do that," Larry said, abandoning at least for the moment his pedagogical impersonation, "let's have Bodean brief us on the Las Vegas connection."

Bodean filled Larry and Gordie in on his telephone interview of Jamie's uncle Matt and the precarious position in which cousin Patty had found herself.

"Chances are that she will be convicted of a felony by the time our case goes to trial if it goes that far," Gordie said. "That means she can be impeached with that felony if she testifies, and the jury will be instructed that they can take that into account in determining credibility. In other words, if you are a convicted felon, you are likely a liar as well."

"Wow," said Jamie. "That amounts to a nullification of convicted felons' testimony. They'd be better off not to testify in the first place."

They all agreed the matter was moot at this point, as they had no intentions of calling Patty as a witness at the P.H.

"A P.H. or no P.H.," Gordie said, "that is the question!"

Gordie said he had agonized over the issue and had been vacillating, as had Larry. He said he was leaning in favor of the P.H. Stepping over to the flip chart, he suggested that they analyze the purposes of a P.H. and integrate it in their discussion in attempting to reach a decision.

Since he was in favor of the P.H., Gordie acknowledged that it was only fair that he go first. The first point was screening device. Both he and Larry agreed that the P.H. was indeed a screening device. Its primary purpose was to determine whether there was probable cause or reasonable grounds to believe that a crime was committed and whether the accused committed it. Both also agreed that the prosecution was not required to lie out for inspection and for full examination all witnesses and evidence. Therefore, much latitude would be accorded the prosecution, and the judge would be required to view the evidence in the light most favorable to the prosecution.

Theoretically, the prosecution could call only one witness, Clinton Coleman, and he could testify as to what the witnesses told him. However, all agreed that most likely Alden Stillwell would be called as a witness as well. It was explained to Jamie once again that hearsay and other evidence, which would be incompetent if offered at trial, could constitute the bulk of the evidence at the P.H.

Gordie went on to point two: serves as a fishing expedition. Both agreed that though the defense didn't have a lot of leeway, they could cross-examine in an effort to discover more than what was in the discovery documents.

Point three was: pins down testimony. Again, both Larry and Gordie agreed that the P.H. afforded the defense the opportunity to chisel in granite the testimony of the prosecution's witnesses. And if a witness told a different story at a later hearing or trial, he or she could be impeached by his or her prior inconsistent statements. Both, however, acknowledged that where the officer testified as to what witnesses told him and witnesses testify differently at trial, they could claim that the officer didn't record their statements correctly or took them out of context. The hearsay testimony at the P.H., therefore, had a built-in escape hatch.

Point four: criminal version of pretrial discovery is much like point number two. The discovery in both civil and criminal cases is designed to prevent trial by ambush. They differed in that in criminal cases what the prosecution would be seeking from the defendant would be protected by the Fifth Amendment to the United States Constitution. In other words, as was explained to Jamie, an accused was not required to speak or turn information over to the prosecution if it would tend to incriminate him or her. The prosecution, on the other hand, was required to turn virtually everything over to the defense, with exception of their work product or information that might temporarily jeopardize an ongoing investigation. In civil cases, there were few restrictions. Both Larry and Gordie again agreed that there would be little leeway at the P.H., and the judge would prevent them from going too far afield.

Point five: reveals prosecution's weakness. The prosecuting attorney normally was not going to file a case he couldn't win at trial. Since the P.H. is a screening device and not a trial, the quantity and quality of evidence to bind a defendant over for trial is a little more than a scintilla of evidence. The prosecution, therefore, did not have to show its full hand or put its best face forward. At the same time, the prosecution wanted to show some force to apply pressure to induce a plea. Both Larry and Gordie agreed that by the time all the discovery had been provided and the defense had completed its investigation, they would be aware of any weaknesses. In fact, they already had an idea.

Point six: showcase the defense of the accused. Larry and Gordie were apprehensive about showing too much of their hand at this stage. Sometimes it was the catalyst in convincing the prosecution to take a plea and, in rare cases, a dismissal. However, they didn't feel that would happen in this case. Too much lead time would only give the prosecution the opportunity to plug the holes and block the escape routes. There was no advantage in giving them a sneak preview; they already had a running start.

Point seven: If no PC, case dismissed. Should they be that fortunate and the prosecution failed to establish probable cause (PC), the case is dismissed. Even then there is a chance it could be re-filed. Dismissal was extremely unlikely, due to the low threshold of proof required. The evidence presented must be viewed in the light most favorable to the prosecution, and if the testimony is conflicting, an inference must be drawn in favor of the prosecution. "It's just not going to happen," Larry said, echoed by Gordie and Bodean.

"Too bad," Jamie commented.

Before, making a decision, Jamie wanted to know what would happen if Judge Dearborn found PC. Larry and Gordie told him the judge would bind the case over to the district court. The county court would no longer have jurisdiction. All court appearances, hearings, and trial would henceforth be in district court. Judge Dearborn would set a first appearance date (prearranged with the district judge's clerk) in district court. The good news was that Judge Dearborn would be replaced by District Judge Clayton Tibbits. The defense would request continuance of the bond in the present amount, and the parties would go their separate ways.

"Is it possible the judge could revoke my bond and I would have to post another?" Jamie asked anxiously.

"Possible but not likely," Gordie said.

"A lot less likely if you waive the P.H.," Larry added.

"The P.H. would be a spectacle; better than watching the barber give a haircut," Bodean said, finally having an opportunity. "A hearing and the judge finding PC is a lot more newsworthy than your waiving the P.H.," Bodean said to Jamie. "Getting the word out in advance will prevent a run on the courthouse and afford a little solitude."

"As much as I hate to admit it," Gordie said, "with your help I have talked myself out of a P.H."

"Me too," said Bodean.

"You finally got religion," Larry joked.

"Don't want to agree with you too much," Gordie joked back.

Turning to Jamie, Larry said, "Jamie, the decision is yours. You are going to have to sign a waiver acknowledging that this is a free and voluntary act on your part and that you are irrevocably committed, meaning you cannot later change your mind. Is that what you want do?"

"Absolutely," Jamie said.

"While I have Verna type the waiver form for Jamie to sign, why don't you three figure out where we go from here? Speedy trial requires that trial be held no greater than six months from the date of Jamie's entry of plea in district court." With that Larry left the room.

When he returned with the waiver form, he allowed Jamie time to read and assimilate the various provisions, and then Jamie signed it.

Larry signed the certification of hand delivery on the bottom portion of the waiver form, took the original back to Verna, and returned with three copies. One he gave to Jamie, one he stuck in his file, one he would deliver to Corbett, and the original would be filed with the court. Ordinarily this would be handed to the judge at the time of the P.H., but in this case he wanted it filed early so that everyone knew there would be no P.H. Jamie was told he would still have to appear on Monday, and he was instructed to come to Larry's office at eight thirty a.m.

While the three stayed behind to conclude the summit conference, Larry left with original waiver in hand and a copy for Corbett. He handed the D.A.'s copy directly to Corbett, who was headed for court. As they walked up the two flights of stairs together, Larry advised Corbett of the waiver and obtained Corbett's assurance that he would not oppose continuation of the bond in its present amount. Corbett told Larry that additional discovery was being duplicated and could be picked up possibly later in the day.

Corbett was headed for Judge Dearborn's courtroom, so both stopped long enough to see if the judge was available so they could inform him of the waiver. Standing in the doorway of his chambers was Judge Dearborn at the ready for his grand entrance. Larry handed him the original waiver and asked if he wanted Larry to file it with the clerk. Judge Dearborn said, "No," that he would handle it. The three discussed the bond, and the judge agreed to continue the bond in its current amount, but reminded them all would still have to appear on Monday.

As Larry was returning to his office, Jamie and Bodean were just leaving. He filled them in on his discussions with Corbett and Judge Dearborn and the existence of additional discovery. They agreed to be in touch. Jamie would be at his office no later than eight thirty a.m. on the thirty-first. They wondered what would be in Thursday's newspaper and whether Larry's letter to Sweeney had been taken seriously.

A COMMUNITY DIVIDED

Jamie was anxious to look at Thursday's hot-off-the-press edition of the weekly rag. On the front page, resembling a tombstone ad, was the following:

Preliminary Hearing Vacated

The clerk to Judge Dearborn today announced that the preliminary hearing in the Jamie Cooper bank embezzlement trial has been vacated.

Gloria Fitzsimmons, county court clerk, stated that Cooper, thirty-four, former employee of Steamboat Bank and Trust Co., has waived the preliminary hearing scheduled for Monday, July 31 at nine a.m.

Cooper will still be required to appear, according to Fitzsimmons, to schedule his first appearance before District Judge Clayton Tibbits.

Skipping over the article, Jamie was anxious to see if any of the letters to the editor that his attorney had objected to were included. He was relieved when he found none. His eyes caught Corbin Sweeney's editorial.

"Editorial: A Community Divided"
Because of the derisive nature of the letters to the editor regarding the Cooper embezzlement case, the editorial staff has elected not to print them. A community divided against itself cannot stand. Steamboat Springs is a respected community and its image is tarnished by the letter writing campaign being waged by the two camps. The newspaper feels it would be irresponsible to continue to print letters of this nature for a number of reasons, the least of which is the possibility that they might result in a change of venue not only in the Cooper case but future cases as well.

Effective immediately, the newspaper reserves the right to reject any letters to the editor that do not contain a signature and an address. This editor and this newspaper refuse to be enablers.

Jamie thought the editorial was appropriate, especially the new policy barring unsigned letters to the editor. He had hoped, however, that Corbin would have included language encouraging the citizenry to keep an open mind and not prejudge him. As Larry had said, "The charges are not evidence of guilt; they are mere accusations waiting to be proven."

———

When Jamie first informed Jennie there would not be a preliminary hearing and that he was going to waive it, she appeared upset. "Why?" Jennie asked. "If you're innocent, why would you waive the preliminary hearing? Wasn't that the opportunity you were waiting for?"

Jamie said he told her that even if a preliminary hearing was held, he would not testify. "What about Patty? Wouldn't she testify?" Jennie wanted to know. "Nobody saw you take the money; none was ever found in your possession. Nobody has recovered the money. The vault was locked the night before by Alden and Rita, and Alden is the only one who was there when the vault was opened the next morning. Alden is the one who had the thousand dollars. How could they connect the dots?"

It took Jamie a lot of patience explaining, but ultimately Jennie understood. She loved her husband unconditionally and was suffering for him. She knew he was innocent and was frustrated. She couldn't understand why anyone would believe he did what he was accused of doing. He was not capable of it. He needed to get his story out. She thought the preliminary hearing would have been the time and place to do so, and that because of the scanty evidence, patently contrived, the case would be dismissed. In her heart she felt the ordeal would then have been over once and for all.

They spent the weekend at the Cooper Ranch. Bodean came out with his wife, Natalie, and four-year-old daughter, Katie. Katie rode Flossie, an old pony his father had had when Max and Collette were that age. Flossie was being spared being sent to the glue factory, thanks to Grandpa Cooper's sentimentality and doting attention.

Bodean had really come to interview Jamie's father, primarily to ask about the Las Vegas connection and the Hammerville incident. It was just as Jamie had described to the other members of the defense team. Now he had corroboration. Bodean instantly liked Forrest and Bessie, and the three families enjoyed each other's company from early morning until nightfall.

═══════════════

When the Jamie Cooper family left the eleven a.m. service at the Hayden Congregational United Church of Christ and said good-bye to Grandma and Grandpa Cooper, they stopped by the post office in Steamboat and picked up the mail that had accumulated in their box since Friday.

Jennie noticed a strange envelope addressed to Jamie. *His name and address were typed by someone who should have taken typing lessons,* Jennie thought. A lot of strikeouts; no attempt to erase mistakes, only typeovers. She looked for a return address on the front and on the back. None. "I wonder who this is from," Jennie asked.

"Open it and see," Jamie replied.

Jennie slid her slender finger through the side of the flap and shredded the envelope open. Inside she found a three-fold slip of tablet paper with frayed top. Typed on the paper, not respecting the lines and with strikeouts reminiscent of the envelope was the following:

> You robbed the bank. I ~~se~~ saw you.
> ~~Fore~~ $5,000, I will keep my ~~month~~ mouth shut.
> Otherwise I will ~~tale~~ tell the police.
> I will give you one ~~wek~~ week to pay.
> Wait for my next ~~later~~ letter.

Eyes wide, mouth ajar, hand trembling, Jennie sat numb. "Well," Jamie said, "who's it from?" Stuttering and stammering, Jennie read the note aloud.

"Some cruel joke from some crank," Jamie said. "Don't pay any attention to it. Here, give it to me."

Noticing that Jennie was still shaken, Jamie pulled her close, and, holding onto each other tightly, both dreamed of the day they would be free from the ordeal.

THE MODERN-DAY COLISEUM

On this bright last day of July, Larry and Jamie arrived at the Routt County Courthouse early, but they were not the first ones there. The spectators were scattered, busying themselves with gossip, speculation, and conjecture concerning the Cooper Case—no doubt the story of the year. Shortly after Larry and Jamie positioned themselves, the Stillwell wolf pack arrived with the weasel in tow. "Wouldn't miss it for the world," he overheard Alden tell the elderly couple seated behind the Stillwells.

"The courtroom is the modern-day version of the Coliseum," Larry said to Jamie in a low voice. "The righteous citizens have come to watch the Christians being fed to the lions. But no fight to the death struggle here! At least not this day."

"They'll all want refunds on their tickets," Jamie whispered to Larry. Both were surprised there were as many there and still filtering in, considering that the P.H. had been vacated and the newspaper had so indicated.

Corbett and his investigator, Dennis Hinton, swaggered into the courtroom, big broad smiles for all. Corbett was making the most of his election year presence known and managing to shake every spectator's hand, ingratiating himself, even to the least friendly.

I can't imagine what it would be like if the P.H. had gone as scheduled, Jamie thought. "I'm just glad none of my family is here," he told Larry. Gordie hadn't come because of the perfunctory nature of the proceedings. Besides, the conservative folk might think Jamie was being frivolous with his money, or more to the point, the bank's money. When Gordie entered the picture, both had assured Jamie they were not double billing. When the ordeal was over, Jamie would make it right.

The pounding of a gavel was heard, and the bailiff announced, "The district court in and for the fourteenth judicial district is now in session, the Honorable Clayton Tibbits presiding." Judge Tibbits sat down at the bench while his bailiff commanded everyone to sit.

Judge Tibbits looked and acted as one would expect a district judge to look and act. He stood six feet tall with chiseled features, a medium build, and marshmallow-white hair that belied his fifty-two years. He was learned and much respected by those members of the bar who appeared in front of him. He took more decisions under advisement than the average, which may have accounted for his extremely low rate of reversals. Polite to both sides, he referred to Bob as Mr. Corbett and to Larry as Mr. Whittaker. *No favoritism or perception of favoritism here,* Jamie thought.

"Quite a contrast between Tibbits and Dearborn," Larry wrote on his yellow pad for Jamie to see.

His first appearance or "return date" was over before it began. Jamie was re-advised of his rights, the nature of his charges, and provided an outline of the court process from this point forward and was arraigned on the charge brought against him. When Jamie was asked for his plea, Jamie, standing erect and this time not sporting two black eyes and a broken nose, said, "I plead not guilty to this charge, Your Honor, and I request a jury of twelve."

Judge Tibbits said, "Very well then, let's set a motions hearing date that is convenient to all."

Questioning Larry, he said, "Counselor, I know it is too early to tell, but what motions do you contemplate filing?"

"Judge, the defense has not received the entire discovery yet, but tentatively, we can tell Your Honor that we will be filing a motion for change of venue, and, depending on the discovery, a motion for suppression of evidence and possibly statements. We will also be filing a motion for bill of particulars to ascertain, for example, the exact date and time of the alleged theft, and depending on the specification, a notice of alibi. We may also be filing a motion to strike."

"I'm sure Mr. Corbett has anticipated your filing a motion for bill of particulars and realizes that under Colorado law, he is required to provide a bill of particulars upon your request inasmuch as this is a theft case. Is that correct, Mr. Corbett?"

Corbett stood and said succinctly, "Yes, Your Honor."

"Very well, Counselor," Judge Tibbits replied.

The attorneys were then asked how much time they needed. The change of venue hearing, it was determined, would take the bulk of the time, as much as four hours; the remainder of the motions, about two. The motions hearing was scheduled from eight a.m. until noon and two p.m. until four p.m. on September 15. All agreed that that would be sufficient time. Larry was given the usual twenty days to file defense motions. They would be due on August 21, Judge Tibbits told Larry. Corbett, he said, would have ten days from that date or until August 31 to respond.

Judge Tibbits told Jamie his bond was continued until the motions hearing date. He politely reminded him that his bond would be revoked and he would be rearrested if he failed to appear on that date.

Larry and Jamie didn't have time to discuss the case prior to Jamie's first appearance and arraignment in district court. That was reserved until after their return. Gordie and Bodean were already waiting in the conference room for the two upon their return from court. After obtaining their cold drinks of choice and ice-filled glasses, they exchanged the usual pleasantries and were more somber than might have been expected.

The realization was setting in that they were on a fast track. Even though speedy trial requirements mandated trial no more than six months after arraignment, they knew that Judge Tibbits was prone to moving his cases right along. The motions hearing date and deadlines for defense motions and prosecution matters were shared and recorded in their assorted calendars, as well as the master calendar Verna maintained. She would "tickle" those dates, as she called it, as well as interim check dates.

Gordie said he was surprised that Judge Tibbits had asked for a plea before the motions hearing and rulings thereon, even though the rules seemed to require it. Normally, Judge Tibbits had held the arraignment after the motions hearing. Larry said it probably wouldn't make any difference anyway since the defense could always waive speedy trial and allow a special setting outside the six-month period. All agreed it was a good thing that Larry had prepared Jamie to enter a plea.

Jamie had already pulled from his folder the envelope and letter he and Jennie had received the day before; the one that had all the typing strikeovers. After it had been passed around and all had read, Larry, Gordie, and Bodean sat there with poker faces. Jamie couldn't tell what they were thinking, and they sat there not knowing what to think.

Jamie broke the ice by saying it was just some crazy hoax by a bunch of kids not knowing what to do with themselves. Gordie said it was more than that; it was an extortion threat that needed to be taken seriously. Noticing the postmark, he said it was mailed from Craig at seven thirty a.m. on Friday. The use of the mail was a federal offense. Also, state offenses had been committed in both Moffat and Routt Counties.

Larry pulled the Colorado statutes from the credenza behind him. Turning to the proper statute, Larry stated that extortion was a class four felony and carried a penalty of from one to five years in the Colorado State Penitentiary and/or a fine of from $1,000 to $15,000.

"So, see," Gordie said, "it's more than kid stuff."

"Whoever typed it," Larry said, "needs to retake Typing 101 and hire a good attorney."

The dilemma now was what to do with it. They all agreed that they couldn't trust the police department because the chief was not there to help Jamie. "In fact," Bodean said, "I wouldn't be surprised if this is the chief's doing. His mind has been so obsessed with vengeance that he may think this is a way to sniff out the bank's money."

No one had been careful about the handling of the envelope and extortion note and came to the stark realization that they had obliterated any fingerprints. *How stupid,* they all thought, especially Bodean, who hit his forehead with his palm several times. "The handling at the post office on both ends didn't help either," he murmured.

It was decided that Jamie would immediately notify Bodean of any future suspicious mail and would use his handkerchief to handle it. They would not report it yet and maybe catch the culprit at the "drop," which they expected would be specified in the next anticipated set of instructions.

There was a lot to do before drafting the motions. Had Bodean come up with the name of a reliable polygrapher? A police-annexed polygrapher would be seeking to obtain a confession in his so-called quest for the truth. Or, he would claim "deception" where there was none. What were the options? A voice stress test was not reliable, and Jamie surely wouldn't consent to the intrusive nature of injection of a truth serum. The others knew they wouldn't.

"Who was it that said polygraphs weren't even admissible in court because of their questionable scientific reliability?" Jamie asked. "Any one of us could have told you that," Larry said, "but if you pass it, we will try to get the results admitted or at the very least broadcast that you did."

Bodean pulled an address card from his now famous brown leather briefcase. The card looked like it came from some sort of address spindle. He read the name Dr. Alphonso Lauderback, stating that the doctor was well respected in the law enforcement community and had a Ph.D. in sociology and criminal justice. He had moved from Colorado Springs to Denver and would not charge an arm and a leg. He had been employed as a polygrapher for the police department in Colorado Springs, but now he was doing polygraphs on job applicants, both for the public as well as the private sectors. He was familiar with Dr. Lauderback and his work when he was in law enforcement.

Both Larry and Gordie wanted a polygraph, and Jamie was willing to do it. If Jamie passed it, as expected, he or Gordie would prepare a motion for acceptance of polygraph results, which would be filed with the court.

They brainstormed the types of motions that would be filed. Larry having forgotten to stop by the D.A.'s office to pick up the additional five pages of discovery that had been sitting there since last week said he would do so later that afternoon as he had other matters at the courthouse. They all acknowledged their assignments, as well as the ticking clock. "Keep each other updated; we'll meet again soon." In the interim, Larry and Gordie would be preparing the motions and drafting the memorandum briefs in support thereof. So far, they were surviving the ordeal and attempting to minimize its sting.

SO HELP ME GOD

Even though Larry hadn't sorted through the blizzard of paperwork starting to stack up as a result of his preoccupation with the
Cooper case and was up to his eyeballs in research and drafting,
he insisted on accompanying Jamie to Denver to be polygraphed
by Dr. Lauderback.

Larry had had some bad experiences, not necessarily for him
but several clients who proclaimed to be innocent and, trying to
save a few bucks on attorney fees, declined representation and
submitted to polygraphs administered by law enforcement personnel. They had proved to be disastrous and resulted in the
poor misguided souls providing the pieces of the puzzle needed
to insure a conviction. In other words, they built the gallows for
their own execution.

Jamie said he had been spending little time with Max and
with Max starting back to school soon wondered if his son could
accompany them on the round trip to Denver. Jamie was anxious
for Larry to meet Max and vice versa. Max was looking for yard

work to supplement his allowance, and this would be a good time for Max to start lobbying.

Larry insisted on driving, and at seven thirty a.m. on the first Friday of August, he arrived at Jamie's home in his 1972 Chrysler Town and Country station wagon with Jamie and Max raring to go. Larry was invited in just long enough to meet Jennie, Collette, and Max. Larry would later tell Max how much he liked his family, and they would later tell him how much they liked him. Jennie sent a basket of sandwiches, diced fruits and vegetables, and Max's favorite, Mom-made chocolate chip cookies, and of course, a small ice chest with an assortment of drinks, mostly juices.

Chatting easily, they drove east through the pines over the Continental Divide. They drove east to Vail, through Silverthorne, and through Eisenhower Tunnel into the Mile-High City and on into the traffic maze called the mousetrap.

They arrived a little before noon, and after having scouted out Dr. Lauderback's office, they stopped at a sporting equipment store to browse. Larry purchased a baseball mitt Max had been ogling and an "official" baseball. Larry promised Max he would watch him next time he had a little league game. By coincidence, Larry had played second base also, from Little League through his second year in college. Max's jersey number was two, and so was Larry's. Jamie was starting to feel like the odd man out. However, watching Larry, who had no children, and "Mr. Max" interact generated a contentment inside that defied description. Max looked and acted like Jamie. Every time Jamie looked at him, it was like turning the clock back and looking at himself. Larry, in some ways, was providing a strength that not even a blood brother could have provided.

They arrived at the polygrapher's office a few minutes before one p.m. Dr. Lauderback was not as they had imagined. He was almost as wide as he was tall, and he had a full white beard and long white hair. He presented a release/authorization form that he required Jamie to sign before he would proceed, and Jamie obliged.

Larry had prepped Jamie via the telephone when he realized Max would be joining them. Max's ears were too young and too sensitive to be exposed to the ordeal.

Larry and Al pretty much agreed on what questions would be asked. Of all the questions, Larry only objected to one. That was, "Do you know what happened to the money?" Jamie did know that $1,000 was in the hands of the bank, but he did not know what happened to the remaining $29,000. And since he could only answer yes or no, the question had to be rephrased, and it was. Larry had instructed Jamie to take deep breaths before he answered, even the control questions; otherwise, it might detect deception, even though there was none.

The control questions were to establish a lie pattern. Jamie was given the ace of diamonds from a deck of cards and a mix of five other cards. On each card Al displayed, whether it was the ace of diamonds or not, he was to answer yes. In other words, four out of the five answers would be a lie, thus establishing a lie pattern.

Larry was ushered out of the room but was allowed to watch from behind a two-way mirror, where a speaker was set up so Larry could listen. Max sat in the waiting room reading.

After wires were attached across Jamie's chest and to his right index finger, Al began to ask questions and plot numbers and symbols at various intervals on a graph that simulated an electrocardiogram, only larger and encased in a tabletop console. Before they started, Jamie was once again instructed that he could only answer yes or no.

Q. Is your name James Curtis Cooper?
A. Yes.
Q. Is your nickname Jamie Cooper?
A. Yes.
Q. Do you reside in Steamboat Springs, Colorado?
A. Yes.
Q. Have you been charged with felony theft?
A. Yes.
Q. Did you ever work at Steamboat Bank and Trust Co.?
A. Yes.
Q. Is your wife's name Jennie?
A. Yes.
Q. Do you have a son named Max?
A. Yes.
Q. Do you have a daughter named Collette?
A. Yes.
Q. Have you ever told a lie?
A. Yes.
Q. Have you told me the complete truth?
A. Yes.

Interspersed were questions regarding Jamie's criminal prosecution:

Q. Did you take the money you were accused of taking?
A. No.
Q. Did you ever take money from the bank without permission?

A. No.

Q. On July 10, 1972, did you take any money from the bank vault without permission?

A. No.

Q. On July 11, 1972, did you take any money from the bank vault without permission?

A. No.

Q. From the time the bank vault was closed at five thirty p.m. on July 10, 1972, until seven thirty a.m. on July 11, 1972, did you enter the vault for any reason?

A. No.

Q. Do you know who took the money from the bank?

A. No.

Q. Do you know where the missing $29,000 is?

A. No.

Q. Did you put the $1,000 in your desk drawer?

A. No.

Jamie was then asked to continue to look straight ahead and continue to remain still and not move. Then Al held each of the six cards from the same deck. As he held each card up and asked if each was the ace of diamonds, Jamie was to say yes. His lie pattern was then recorded with respect to the five cards that were *not* the ace of diamonds.

Al repeated the test two more times, varying the order of the questions and each time keeping track. After completion of the third test, he unhooked Jamie and sent him out. He then analyzed each of the three tests and in about thirty minutes joined Jamie, Max, and Larry.

Looking Larry straight in the eye, Al said, "I have found absolutely no deception. If any there be, I would have found it. This man, so help me God, did not steal the bank's money." Jamie just looked at Larry with lips pursed that said, "I told you so!"

Al said his findings and the process he followed in arriving at them would all be incorporated into a formal report, together with his ultimate opinion. Included would be the questions asked and answers given. As soon as it was finalized and typed, it would be in the mail to Larry.

Al said he would send Larry a bill along with the report. When Larry presented Al with a $500 check already prepared for payment in full for all services rendered, Al accepted it, and with handshakes all around, Larry, Jamie, and Max left riding on the peak of that roller coaster ride they called the ordeal.

CAUGHT RED-HANDED

In the mail at the post office on Saturday was a small package wrapped in brown paper containing heavy transparent tape without a return address. Jamie's name and address were in the same typed strikeover format as the suspicious letter. The postmark displayed the following: Craig, Colorado, July 31, 1972, seven thirty a.m.

Lifting it by its corners and carefully sandwiching it between other mail, Jamie transported it home. Opening just one end, he coaxed the small box from its paper encasement. Careful not to obliterate any foreign prints, Jamie opened the box and found an unlocked combination padlock. The exposed hole was taped to prevent it from being accidently locked. The same notebook paper as the other containing the same careless and inept typing read:

In the back of Howard's truck stop in Craig
Near the man men's restroom are six ode old lockers.
Place the $5,000 in the locker closest to the

Door and lock it with the this lock. If it is not
There buy by seven thirty a.m. on Saturday, August 12, I will
Tell the police everything I no know.

With the rest of the weekend full of yard work, family time, and dinner with his wife's sister and family on Sunday, Bodean would prefer to meet with Jamie on Monday at nine a.m. at Larry's office. He had earlier heard about Jamie passing the polygraph and was ecstatic. He had already scheduled a meeting with Larry to go over the additional discovery and assist Larry in obtaining affidavits to attach to the motion for change of venue. That would be a good time to discuss how to foil the extortion plot. Larry's and Gordie's input would be helpful.

It was about eight fifty a.m., ten minutes early, when Jamie arrived at the offices of Whittaker and Brownell, attorneys at law, that clear early August Monday. Birds chirping, air still and sky clear. Jamie was wondering why he was early. *Must be anxious,* he thought.

Verna greeted him with "Congratulations!" and "Everyone is so happy for you! You know where the coffee and blueberry muffins are." Barely a minute after he was seated, Bodean strutted in. He greeted Jamie with a robust lumberjack handshake.

"Hello, good looking," he said, shouting in Verna's direction. Without looking up from her work, she asked Bodean how he was.

"Are you taking my medical history?" he asked, feigning indignation.

"We already know how you are psychologically. I was only asking how you were physiologically. Is that a crime?" she said, mirroring his indignation.

In more of a serious tone, she said, noticing that Bodean had already helped himself to the fresh steaming coffee and still warm-to-the-touch blueberry muffins, "They're waiting for you in the conference room."

When Jamie and Bodean entered the conference room, books and papers strewn around, the legal beagles arose and rushed at Jamie as if he were the prodigal son—first Gordie, then Larry. Bodean then said, "Now I know how the son who stayed home helping his father felt. No fatted calf for me!" With the jubilation having subsided, each had a different idea of where to start.

The most important were the motions, but first Larry wanted to distribute copies of the additional discovery, which consisted mainly of the Las Vegas connection, the telephone call to Cousin Patty, and the local authorities. There was also an entry about the contact and conversation Clint Coleman had with the bank's insurance company. Apparently, the "errors and omissions" policy was going to cover the $30,000, minus the deductible and the $1,000 already recovered. Standard Casualty Insurance Company of Connecticut (SCICC) had already sent an adjuster to verify proof of loss and check the mechanism on the vault door. He was Joseph Michaels out of Hartford.

"Does that mean there won't be a civil action brought against me?" Jamie asked.

"It only means," Larry said, "that if the insurance company pays the loss, they will be the ones bringing the action if there is one. The subrogation clause in the insurance policy says that the bank claim is automatically assigned to SCICC upon payment of the loss."

"In other words," Gordie added, "SCICC stands in the shoes of SB&T Co. as far as the claim against you is concerned."

"What are the chances SCICC will file suit?" Jamie inquired.

"There's probably a pretty good chance that will occur, although now the suit will no doubt follow your criminal trial," Gordie responded.

"Without the insurance payoff," Larry said, "the bank and the weasel figured they would apply the pressure and obtain valuable information from you with pretrial discovery and a trial that would help the state in your prosecution. They figured it was a win-win situation because, even if you invoked your Fifth Amendment rights against self-incrimination, they would basically win their case by default. The weasel is not smart enough to know that the court has the power to stay the proceedings pending the outcome of the criminal proceedings."

"Or, maybe," Bodean volunteered, "the bank had planned all along to let the prosecutors do their dirty work first and piggyback on their work product as SCICC will probably do."

"I think the weasel is more interested in billable hours and would probably have been successful in convincing his bloodthirsty clients to jump the gun and file the civil suit," Jamie said.

Not much more to say about the Las Vegas connection, they all agreed.

Jamie now opened the small brown paper bag he had sitting beside him at the conference table. He poured the contents out, revealing a brown wrapper bearing his typed name and address, the folded typewritten note, and the small box containing the combination padlock.

With Jamie seated, the rest of the defense team gathered around him and, without touching anything, examined the collection. All read the new extortion note with instructions, the address label, and the postmark. They then examined the unlocked padlock, touching it only with the eraser end of a pencil.

Same old strikeovers, no doubt with the same Underwood Standard typewriter and typist, as with the suspicious letter they had previously examined.

The latest in the saga of the extortion plot appeared now to be the most urgent. "D-day" had arrived. A decision and formulation of strategy could wait no longer. This was Bodean's territory, and he was conscripted to "carry the ball."

"In the past I have collaborated with a private investigator in Craig (Moffat County) on several capers, Capp Farley. He thinks that to involve the police at either the Routt or Moffat County end would be a mistake at this juncture because of the animosity toward Jamie. What he would like to do is to have Capp assist him in setting up a surveillance at the drop site starting at least an hour before the deadline drop time set by the extortionist."

"Whoever our extortionist is," Larry said, "is anxious for his money. He doesn't appear to be wasting any time."

"He's obviously an early riser, as both postmarks are at seven thirty a.m.," Gordie said. "If it is like here, the post office opens at seven a.m., and the post office posts only on the half hour. This means that both the first suspicious letter and the latest were deposited between seven a.m. and seven thirty a.m. And the instructions with the lock have a drop deadline of seven thirty a.m."

"The package had the proper postage and a special postal service sticker on it, meaning that it no doubt was weighed at the post office by the clerk who ostensibly sold and affixed the proper postage thereto," Bodean said.

"That would mean that the clerk got a look at our extortionist," Jamie said.

"Are you familiar with Howard's Truck Stop?" Larry asked Bodean. "It is a popular fueling spot for eighteen-wheelers, farm and ranch vehicles, and delivery trucks. They always have piping hot coffee and are famous for their jumbo cinnamon rolls, though not as good as Verna's. They do an unusually high volume of business and have the usual assortment of oil, common truck accessories, work gloves, some hats, clothing items, and such. Actually, it is a typical convenience store, country friendly, and open from five thirty a.m. until eleven thirty p.m. all week long. Howard's is the gathering spot during midmornings and midafternoons for those who don't wear suits and ties. I forgot to mention, they also sell a lot of smokes and chewing tobacco."

"Our extortionist must be a regular," Larry mused. "At least someone who is familiar with the layout and comfortable being there."

"Are there any buildings close by where you and Capp could conduct surveillance or a blind where your presence could go undetected?" Gordie asked Bodean.

"Yes," Bodean said, "there is Cattlemen's Hardware Store right on the side alley separating the two businesses and some buildings across the back alley. I would have to scout out the area to be sure. I know where the restrooms are, but I don't remember any lockers. Could I use your telephone?" Before Larry could respond, Bodean asked if everyone was comfortable with using Capp for this job. All nodded their approval, and Bodean, after first calling his office for Capp's telephone number, called Capp.

Capp was now aboard. Bodean would meet Capp at Capp's office in Craig at four p.m. They would scout out the area and stop off at Cattlemen's Hardware Store and meet the owner,

Capp's fellow Lions' Club compatriot, Ross Jenkins. Then they would make arrangements to use the storeroom with the windows facing the restrooms and lockers at Howard's Truck Stop.

"Wow!" said Larry.

"Couldn't have done better myself," said Gordie.

Jamie was briefed by Larry and Gordie on the motions they would be preparing. Larry gave eight affidavits to Bodean to have signed before a notary public. They will be attached to the motion for change of venue. Since Bodean was a notary, the process would be simple.

"What are the purposes of the affidavits?" Jamie asked.

"Basically," Larry responded, "We want to show that the pool from which your jury will be selected has been tainted by the excessive and widespread adverse pretrial publicity."

Retrieving one of the predrafted affidavits from the stack, Larry summarized, "Under oath, each affiant will swear that he or she is a residence of Routt County and possesses all the qualifications of a juror. He or she will acknowledge that he or she could be called as a juror in your case. Then each will discuss his or her exposure to the pretrial publicity."

"I'm sure everyone has heard about all the sordid details about my case by now," Jamie said morosely.

"You can count on it," Gordie responded. "That's the whole thesis of our motion."

"To continue," Larry said, "each affiant will attest to his or her familiarity with your case through exposure by way of the newspapers, radio accounts, and, of course, television. As a result of that adverse publicity, he or she will state that he or she has formed the opinion that you embezzled funds from the bank where you worked."

"I'm not sure everyone believes I'm guilty," Jamie interrupted.

"Of course not," Larry responded. "We will be obtaining affidavits only from this who have been persuaded to the contrary. Anyway, the critical portions of the affidavit focus on the potential juror's inability to set aside his or her misconceptions. For example, he or she will state that it would be difficult, if indeed impossible, to change his or her opinion even if instructed by the judge to do so."

"Selected jurors are required to have an open mind as they embark upon their service as jurors," Gordie stated. "In other words if they've already made up their minds they cannot be 'fair and impartial.'"

"The key here to having the place of trial changed to another county," Bodean said, "is not only that a juror has been prejudiced but that he or she cannot set aside his or her bias and prejudice despite the evidence to the contrary."

"The affidavits will state that the affiant is prejudiced against you," Larry continued. "Also, he or she will state that he or she has conversed with others in the community who share the same opinion. Ultimately, he or she will state that in his or her opinion you absolutely cannot receive a fair, impartial, and expeditious trial in Routt County."

"How could a judge find otherwise?" Jamie asked.

"Not without risking a reversal," Gordie responded.

Bodean promised he would have the eight affidavits duly executed and returned to Larry by Wednesday. Larry and Gordie continued to work on the motions and tried to keep up with the demands of their other clients. Jamie, Jennie, Max, and Collette would spend the rest of the week at the Cooper Ranch helping Forrest and Bessie generate income that now was required to support two families.

It was Saturday, August 12, 1972. Capp and Bodean had front-row seats for a real-life drama that was about to unfold. Facing the six lockers, in remarkably good condition despite their exposure to the weather, Capp and Bodean riveted their attention on locker number twenty-one, the one closest to the men's restroom door. The lockers were used to store coats and other items by truckers while using the restroom to wash away the dirt and grime from their hands and arms and sweat from their brow. A baptism as it were for once tired truckers emerging fresh and anew.

Capp and Bodean had fashioned newspaper pages into the size and bulk of $5,000 in bills. These were packaged in heavy butcher paper and inserted into a small shoebox that had been modified to accommodate the simulated bills. The box in turn was covered in more butcher paper with extra layers of opaque shipping tape. This was done to dissuade the extortionist from taking the time to inspect the contents. They wanted to catch the culprit red-handed, with package in hand.

They had put the special package in locker number twenty-one, inserted the combination padlock into its mooring, compressed the pivoting inverted U-shaped lock into its base, and spun the dial. Both made sure the door was secure and the lock irrevocably unyielding, at least for now.

With the furtive movement of a fox, they retreated to their place of concealment, waiting for their prey to take their bait. Sure enough, at seven forty-five a.m. they saw a tall, medium-built young man in his late teens dressed in blue jeans and a white grease-stained T-shirt wearing well-worn Western boots come traipsing around the corner and into the men's restroom. Within minutes and after looking both ways, obviously making sure no one was around, "Blue Jeans" approached locker number twenty-one and began dialing admittance.

After a few unsuccessful tries, while Capp snapped photographs at various intervals, Blue Jeans, shaking his head in disgust went back to the front of the truck stop and reappeared with a slip of paper to which he referred in dialing the proper combination. *Snap,* the lock opened, and Blue Jeans retrieved his pot of gold. In his haste and exuberance, he left the opened padlock dangling on the door.

Bodean was already making his way to the front of the hardware store, and Ross Jenkins held it open as Bodean exited. Bodean ran to the edge of the building and, peering around the corner, observed that Blue Jeans had already claimed his prize and was walking with it to the front of the truck stop. While Bodean was exiting through the front, Capp exited through the back. Walking at first as if to go to Howard's, and not appearing to notice Blue Jeans, Bodean blocked the alley just long enough for Capp to grab Blue Jeans from behind.

On the way out the door, Bodean had instructed Ross Jenkins to call the police. Not being far away, two uniformed Craig police officers drove up in their cruiser. Blue Jeans was arrested. The package he was carrying was taken from his arms and placed in evidence but not before Capp had captured the moment on camera. He had taken another photograph of the locker, only this time with the door open and the padlock dangling. The padlock was carefully removed by one of the uniformed police officers. Blue Jeans was handcuffed, searched, and transported to the police station, along with his surprise package and padlock.

Capp and Bodean met the police officers at the station house. They brought with them the two extortion notes, envelope, box, and wrapping. All were marked and placed in evidence envelopes. Capp and Bodean told them all they knew. They had another officer retrieve Blue Jeans's truck parked in front of Howard's Truck Stop. In searching Blue Jeans's truck, they found the notebook from which the paper containing the type-written extortion messages had been torn. They also retrieved tape identical to the tape used on the packaging Jamie had received in the mail. The factory packaging for the combination lock lay on the floorboards of the passenger side of the truck. The price tag showed where it had been purchased: Cattlemen's Hardware Store. These items were also marked and placed in evidence envelopes.

When Blue Jeans was arrested, he was searched, and the fac-tory combination to the padlock was taken from his left, front pants pocket. In his left back pants pocket was his wallet, which was not searched until he reached the station house. While in the cage in the back of the cruiser, Blue Jeans was read his rights. When he was booked, it was determined that his date of birth was May 24, 1954, and his name was Derrick Hammerville, the eighteen-year-old son of Jarred Hammerville, the Chief of Police of Steamboat Springs.

When Bodean saw the impounded pickup, he noticed that it matched the description of one of the suspicious vehicles Jamie's father had seen driving back and forth on the county road bordering the Cooper Ranch. It was an old, faded, light green pickup truck similar in color to those driven by the U.S. Forest Service with a faint logo barely visible.

Blue Jeans, now known to be Derrick Hammerville, was released to the custody of his mother. One of the arresting offi-cers said it was professional courtesy, inasmuch as the Steamboat Police Department was one of its sister agencies. Having been in law enforcement, Capp and Bodean understood this only too well. Derrick had also been allowed to call his employer, a local farmer for whom Derrick had been working the past summer, to let him know he would not be coming to work that day. He did not want to call his father just yet. He was allowed to drive his pickup home with his mother close behind.

Derrick had confessed to the extortionist plot and said it was all his idea and no one had put him up to it. *Sure,* Bodean thought to himself. *Now that he had been caught red-handed, everyone would be distancing themselves from the fatal plot.* Bodean mused, "When you're riding high, everyone's your friend. When you stumble and fall, no one has ever heard of you. Just ask Jamie."

DISPARATE TREATMENT

"It's not what you know; it's who you know," Jamie said to Bodean.

"Especially if that someone is the chief of police," Bodean said.

Jamie and Bodean had been summoned to the offices of Whittaker and Brownell, attorneys at law, to review the first drafts of the motions that Larry and Gordie proposed to file. It had been almost a week since Derek Hammerville had been arrested for extortion. The only thing they knew was what they read in the Craig and Steamboat newspapers. Bodean had clippings of both. The one in the local press was buried in the middle of Thursday's issue.

"Teen Arrested in Shakedown Attempt"
    The Steamboat Police Department would neither confirm nor deny that a local teen had been arrested in an attempt to obtain hush money in the Jamie Cooper embezzlement case.

According to reliable sources, the shakedown was stymied before any money was paid. The newspaper has learned that the alleged scheme occurred in both Moffat and Routt Counties and authorities in both counties are investigating the matter.

The name of the teen was not released. Craig authorities have confirmed that the teen was released to the custody of his mother. "Sounds pretty innocuous," Jamie said. "The Steamboat Police Department has made it sound like a juvenile was involved."

"At age eighteen, he's an adult under the laws of our state, but he's sure not being treated as one," Bodean said in agreement.

"The Craig paper didn't treat the incident much better," Verna said, joining the conversation. Bodean read aloud from the Craig account:

"Extortion Plot Foiled"

The Craig Police Department today issued an official release on the local sting operation just completed. According to local authorities, a teen had been arrested in the alley between Howard's Truck Stop and Cattlemen's Hardware Store. The teen was caught red-handed with what he thought was the extortion money he had demanded but later found to be fake money. The drop was a locker in the rear of the truck stop, and surveillance had been set up in the storeroom of the hardware store. Sources said the incident was filmed. Detective Logan Anthony said as soon as the investigation was completed, the case would be turned over to the Routt County authorities for possible prosecution. Our call to Steamboat Chief of Police, Jarred Hammerville, had not been returned by press time.

"They sure tweaked that one," Jamie said. "If that had been me, they would have had my name and my so-called alias plastered on all the billboards."

"But you're not related to the chief," Verna said. "You need to change your name."

When the client left Larry's office, Larry came out to greet the scalawags. "Come on back to the conference room," he said. Gordie had his door closed and was still with a client.

They could hear the clock on the City Hall chime ten a.m. "We're getting a later start than usual," Larry said.

Before they even sat down, Larry told them about the latest gossip. "The Steamboat Springs Police Department has lost the evidence connected with the extortion plot."

"What?" Jamie said incredulously.

"Apparently," Larry continued, "late yesterday afternoon, Clinton Coleman drove to Craig to pick up the tagged evidence. While driving back with it, he handled a disturbance call at a bar on the outskirts of Steamboat. He apparently left the car unlocked, and when he returned, due to either carelessness or lassitude or both, he found that the evidence had 'disappeared.' Apparently, he was working a double shift. But, anyway, according to him, someone stole the whole shooting match while he was inside."

"And, without any evidence, there is no case against Coleman's boss's son!" Bodean said in resignation.

"Not so fast," Jamie said, "We still have the smoking gun; something the prosecution doesn't have in my case. You have eyewitness accounts. Capp and Bodean witnessed the whole event. You have a confession. Again, something you don't have in my case. Larry kept copies of the extortion notes. You have

Jennie and me. Ross Jenkins may even remember selling the combo lock to Derrick."

"We have a client who makes Sherlock Holmes look like a rookie," Gordie said with glee as he entered the conference room.

"Thank God for the backup," Larry said.

Gordie went on to relate that the word was out that the teen extortionist was the chief's son. "It would be interesting to know who leaked it," Larry said.

"It sure wasn't the chief," Gordie said. "The client I just finished with said that while at breakfast at the Sundowner, he overheard the chief, who was seated at the table next to him, say that it was just a harmless childish prank, no doubt referring to his son's misguided caper."

Bodean said he had talked to Capp earlier in the morning and Capp related what happened when he took a set of the photographs he had had developed and was waiting for the detectives. Apparently, an elderly hulk of a man with a withered hand walked out of the chief's office yelling, "My grandson was only trying to do his civic duty in attempting to recover the stolen money. He should have been given a medal instead of a scolding. That's why nobody has any respect for you guys."

"Guess who?" Larry said.

If they all hadn't been so sickened about the whole thing, they would have laughed. But it wasn't funny. They all knew of the double standard that marked one of the shortcomings of the criminal justice system, and even though this was a fact of life, they believed it was not something society should condone.

"Should we turn it over to the feds?" Bodean asked.

"Not right now," Gordie responded. Had they known there would be no prosecution, they would have considered the alternative.

<hr/>

Copies of the motions and memorandum briefs were passed all around. The first on the stack was a motion for bill of particulars. It requested that the prosecution specify the exact date and time of the alleged offense, the precise manner in which the offense was alleged to have occurred, and the name and address of each person present at the scene of the alleged offense at or about the time the offense was allegedly committed.

The most important information sought to be obtained was the date and time of the alleged offense. This would allow the defense to specify where Jamie was during that critical period, which they presumed would be seven p.m. on July 10 to seven a.m. on July 11. The Skylers were cleaning the office until seven p.m. on the tenth, and Alden had arrived at the bank at seven a.m. the following morning. If that were the case, Jamie's alibi was that he was at home with his wife and kids. There would be four witnesses to establish that.

The next was the motion for change of venue, which stated that Jamie could not receive a fair, impartial, and expeditious trial in Routt County, and that the citizens thereof had been prejudiced because of the adverse, massive, and pervasive pretrial publicity. The pretrial publicity consisted of newspaper articles, editorials, and letters to the editor, and radio and television broadcasts. Attached to the motion were the newspaper articles, editorials, letters to the editor, and the eight affidavits.

Next was the motion to suppress statements and evidence. It targeted any inculpatory statements Jamie may have made and evidence seized at or after his arrest from his person, vehicle, and effects. This would include the slip of paper with Uncle Matt's and Cousin Patty's names, addresses, and telephone numbers taken from his wallet and any evidence derived therefrom, including the whole Las Vegas connection. Since all were the result of an unlawful arrest and thus an unlawful search, they should be suppressed.

"We may want to reconsider suppression of Jamie's statements," Larry said, "considering they were exculpatory in nature and not incriminating in the least."

"Basically all I said was I didn't do it," Jamie said.

It was quickly decided that Larry would have Verna retype the motion to delete all the portions seeking to suppress Jamie's statements. It would only be a motion to suppress evidence.

The most problematic of all the motions was the motion to admit polygraph results. There was a 99.9 percent chance this one would not fly.

"Polygraph results are not deemed to be reliable evidence; they're not scientifically recognized," Gordie said.

"I guess we still need to raise the flag and see if Judge Tibbits salutes it," Larry said.

Also included was another motion for discovery since the case was now in another court. Of lesser note was a motion to strike. This was aimed at Jamie's "alias."

"Including the alias in the caption had no purpose other than to alienate and inflame the minds of the jury," Larry said. "Defendants with aliases are no doubt sinister," he added mockingly.

"Been with me since birth," Jamie said. The motion labeled the alias as "immaterial, impertinent, and scandalous." It was not a life or death motion by any means but one, they all agreed, needed to be made.

The failure to charge under the specific bank embezzlement statute rather than under the general theft statute was not tactically feasible at this time. If the judge agreed, the prosecution would just move to amend which, at this stage, would be granted without argument. They might consider it later, although they concluded it probably would be deemed by the court to be untimely.

The legal authority for the granting of the various motions was included in the respective motions. The motions appeared to pass the strict scrutiny test of the defense team and were filed later that day. Copies were duly served on Corbett, opposing counsel.

Corbett filed his bill of particulars indicating exactly what the defense team had anticipated. "The offense was committed between seven p.m. on July 10 and seven a.m. on July 11, 1972."

Larry filed the notice of alibi, specifying that Jamie was at home during the aforesaid dates and times , with the exception of the last half hour when he was attending the chamber meeting down the street from the bank. Witnesses were Jamie, his family, and his fellow chamber members. The notice also certified that Jamie would be asserting this alibi as a defense at trial. With the exception of the motion for discovery Corbett opposed the other motions, challenging the facts and legal authority and offering countervailing facts and legal authority of his own. At the motions hearing on September 15, all that the parties had to do was to convince Judge Tibbits that he should rule in their favor.

A SEA OF DISCONTENT

On Friday, August 18, while the family was preparing to head for the Cooper Ranch, there was a knock at the door. When Jamie answered, he saw a uniformed Routt County sheriff's deputy standing there with official looking documents in hand. "Are you James Curtis Cooper?" the deputy politely asked.

"I am," Jamie replied.

"I have some papers to serve on you." With that the deputy handed the following documents to Jamie and departed.

DISTRICT COURT, ROUTT COUNTY, COLORADO
Case number 72 CV 98

SUMMONS
Steamboat Bank and Trust Co. (SB&T Co.) and Standard Casualty Insurance Company of Connecticut (SCICC) as Subrogee of SB&T Co., Plaintiffs v. James Curtis Cooper a.k.a. Jamie Cooper, Defendant.

The People of the State of Colorado
to the Defendant(s) named above:

You are summoned and required to file with the clerk of
this court an answer or other response to the attached complaint within twenty (20) days after this summons is served
on you in the state of Colorado, or within thirty (30) days
after this summons is served on you outside the state of
Colorado.

If you fail to file your answer or other response to the
complaint in writing within the applicable time period,
judgment by default may be entered against you by the
court for the relief demanded in the complaint, without any
further notice to you.

Date: August 17, 1972
Elizabeth J. Martin, Clerk

IN THE DISTRICT COURT IN AND
FOR THE COUNTY OF ROUTT
AND STATE OF COLORADO
Civil Action No. 72 CV 98

COMPLAINT
Steamboat Bank and Trust Co. (SB&T Co.) and Standard
Casualty Insurance Company of Connecticut (SCICC) as
Subrogee of SB&T Co., Plaintiffs v. James Curtis Cooper
a.k.a. Jamie Cooper, Defendant.

Come now the plaintiffs above named, by and through
their undersigned attorneys, and state and allege as follows:

1. During all times herein mentioned Defendant was employed by SB&T Co. as a first vice president and had access to SB&T Co.'s vault containing U.S. currency.

2. Between seven p.m. on July 10 and seven a.m. on July 11, 1972, Defendant converted to his own use, without authorization, the sum of $30,000 belonging to SB&T Co.

3. Defendant has refused to return the aforesaid sum although $1,000 thereof has been recovered.

4. Pursuant to an insurance agreement between plaintiffs, SCICC has paid SB&T Co. the sum of $24,000 and has become subrogated to SB&T Co.'s interest in that amount; SB&T Co. has sustained a loss of $5,000 representing the deductible.

Wherefore, plaintiffs demand judgment against defendant in the amount established by the evidence, interest, and costs.

J. Henry Ross, Attorney for SB&T Co.
Richard D. Kuenzi, Attorney for SCICC

Jennie, finishing with the breakfast dishes and with dishtowel still in hand, emerged from the kitchen to see who had come to the door and why Jamie was detained. They both read the court documents, first Jamie and then Jennie. "Better call Larry," Jennie admonished.

Dialing a number he knew as well as his own, he reached Verna, who insisted on interrupting Larry, who was in with a client. If Jamie could come by with the summons and complaint before the Cooper family left for the Cooper Ranch, Larry could squeeze him in.

Not wanting to have to leave his family waiting in the car while he met with Larry, Jamie decided to go now and come back and pick up Jennie, Max, Collette, and Maya, the dog. Max wanted to go with him, so the two, with court documents in hand, went to the all too familiar law offices of Whittaker and Brownell.

Larry dismissed his client, put his arms around his new buddy Max, and ushered him and his dad back into his office. Max marveled at Larry's large desk, all the certificates on the wall and the memorabilia attorneys collect and put on display. He assured Max he had not read all the books in the rather large library and said it was okay if Max wanted to go in and browse.

Jamie handed Larry the summons and complaint that he had just been served. They seemed simple enough. Larry just shrugged his shoulders as he flung them on the desk. "I guess we anticipated these. However, I didn't think it would be now. I thought they would wait to see what happened in the criminal trial."

"Greed," Jamie said. "Alden is just interested in money. Jennie calls him a Shylock, and she's pretty accurate. We think he's been that way all his life. I guess the whole family has been that way, going back to Wellington D. Stillwell."

"Alden is getting some fiendish delight in all this, and that may be the motivation more than the money," Larry said.

"I feel as though I'm adrift in a sea of discontent with the water pouring in on all sides and no life boat," said Jamie.

"When it rains, it pours. I'll bring Verna in after you leave and get an answer typed and filed by lunchtime. What do you think of including a counterclaim for a groundless and frivolous action? That way maybe we can collect attorney fees and court costs if we succeed."

"Speaking of attorney fees, my father has another check that I'll bring in on Monday."

"Don't worry about it. Your credit is good here. I only wish all our clients were as conscientious," Larry said.

"Not all your clients keep you as busy as I do. You should be paid for what you do. Besides, I don't want you to put my case on the back burner. We now have wars on two fronts!"

Gordie emerged from his office and, sticking his head in the door, asked, "Who's the new law clerk busy at it in the law library? He looks officious and familiar."

"Be careful what you say about Max because someday he might be one of your associates," Verna said as she entered the room with a stack of recently typed documents requiring Larry's signature. "He wants to be a lawyer just like Uncle Larry and Uncle Gordie," Jamie chided.

"We wouldn't wish that on anybody," Larry and Gordie said in unison.

Gordie reviewed the latest in the saga of the ordeal. He thought the timing strange as well and wondered if it would be to the defense's benefit in the criminal case to have a civil trial first. They had some Fifth Amendment concerns, but felt Jamie had nothing to hide and the sooner they let the air out of the public's perception balloon the better.

"A verdict in favor of Jamie in the civil case would sure dispel the myth of Jamie's culpability and take some wind out of their sails," Gordie said as he departed. "I need to get back to work."

Max returned from the library with book in hand. "Can I borrow this?" he asked Larry.

"Let me see it." Larry read the title and with a broad acknowledging smile handed it back to Max. "It's yours," he said. Jamie, not fully understanding the significance of Max's selection, read from the cover, "*My Life in Court* by Louis Nizer."

Larry had another appointment waiting. The two men and the boy stood as equals. Jamie and Max shook hands with Larry. On Monday, Max would work around the building, doing chores suitable to a twelve-year-old. Jamie and the rest of the defense team would meet at ten a.m., the soonest Gordie would be available.

Returning home, Jamie and Max picked up the rest of the family and they departed for the Cooper Ranch. Another hurdle to overcome, but just another challenge in a series of strands interwoven in the web of the ordeal.

━━━━━━━━━━━━━━

After his appointment, Larry dictated the answer and counterclaim appearing below. After it was typed and signed, Verna filed the original with the clerk of the district court, paid by check the filing and jury fees, and upon returning to the office, mailed copies to each of the opposing attorneys.

IN THE DISTRICT COURT IN AND FOR THE
COUNTY OF ROUTT
AND STATE OF COLORADO
Civil Action No. 72 CV 98

ANSWER AND COUNTERCLAIM
Steamboat Bank and Trust Co. (SB&T Co.) and Standard
Casualty Insurance Company of Connecticut (SCICC) as

Subrogee of SB&T Co., Plaintiffs v. James Curtis Cooper a.k.a. Jamie Cooper, Defendant.

Comes now the defendant, by and through his undersigned attorneys and answers the Complaint as follows:

1. Defendant admits the allegation in paragraph one.

2. Defendant denies the allegations in paragraph two.

3. Defendant denies taking or owing the money and therefore didn't "return" said sum as alleged in paragraph three. Defendant doesn't contest the allegation that $1,000 was recovered from some source.

4. Defendant is without knowledge as to the allegations of paragraph four and therefore puts plaintiffs on strict proof thereof.

Defenses: defendant states: the losses allegedly sustained by subrogor SB&T Co. were caused as a result of its own actions or inactions, which are imputed to subrogee.

As a counterclaim against plaintiffs, defendant alleges as follows: plaintiff's claims are groundless and frivolous, entitling defendant to attorney fees and court costs in defending this action. The defendant has incurred and will incur attorney fees and court costs in an amount to be proved at trial or by subsequent affidavit.

Wherefore, defendant requests judgment against plaintiffs consistent with this pleading including attorney fees, expert witness fees, costs and such other relief as the court deems just and fair.

Defendant requests a trial to a jury of six (6) persons. Defendant's jury fee has been posted contemporaneously with defendant's filing fee.

Whittaker and Brownell
By Lawrence Whittaker
Attorneys for Defendant

LITTLE CAUSE TO CELEBRATE

It was a cool, overcast August Monday, the twenty-first, the day defense motions were due to be filed. Fortunately, that had been done the week before. Now the defense team could concentrate on the civil case, at least for the moment.

Copies of the summons, complaint, and answer and counterclaim were positioned at the two places expected to be occupied by Jamie and Bodean. Larry and Gordie already had their copies and were looking them over and discussing the advisability of having the civil case precede the criminal case if it was within their power to do so.

There were things the attorneys wanted to discuss among themselves, lawyer talk, that was sometimes best said outside the ears of the client. They had assembled a half hour before Jamie and Bodean were due to arrive just to discuss such things.

Gordie asked Larry about a malicious prosecution suit against SB&T Co. arising out of the criminal action and whether that constituted a compulsory joinder of claims. In other words, was a future malicious prosecution claim required to be joined as a counterclaim in this action or be forever barred? Larry didn't think it was because an acquittal in the criminal action would ordinarily trigger a malicious prosecution claim, and that time had not yet come. Besides, he was not sure the defense could meet its burden of proving that Alden hadn't found the $1,000 in Jamie's drawer or that Alden had intentionally fabricated Jamie's involvement.

It was one thing to successfully defend a suit where the plaintiff had the burden of proof, and another where the defendant had the burden of proof in proving his or her counterclaims. Even if there was an acquittal, that didn't mean that Jamie *ipso facto* would have a malicious prosecution claim that he could successfully pursue. Otherwise, in every criminal case where there wasn't a conviction, there would be the constant fear the acquitted defendant would sue.

Gordie agreed with Larry that malicious prosecution or intentional infliction of emotional distress actions were something that would arise, if at all, sometime in the future and would not be barred by any joinder requirements.

Larry and Gordie then evolved to a discussion of the inherent problems with civil discovery versus criminal discovery. There were no Fifth Amendment shields to hide behind in civil cases. The opposition could delve into any and all matters that may have a tendency to lead to the discovery of admissible evidence, truly labeled a fishing expedition for good reason.

Jamie arrived followed by Bodean. They were caught up to speed and quickly integrated into the discussion. If only there was some way for Jamie to be able to go to trial and not have to strip naked, so to speak, as part of the discovery process. If SCICC was as anxious to go to trial as SB&T Co. and didn't want a stay until after the criminal trial and lengthy appeals, then there might be some wiggle room.

"Surely they don't think that Jamie's refusal to submit to discovery would trigger a default judgment, do they?" Gordie asked Larry.

"I'm sure the SCICC attorney, at least, is sophisticated enough to know that the Constitution of the United States trumps every other law and that to punish a defendant for invoking his Fifth Amendment rights would be doing indirectly what can't be done directly. In other words, the conflict between the result dictated by law and the result dictated by the Constitution will always be resolved in favor of the Constitution."

"Well spoken, Justice Whittaker," Gordie said. "And, for what it's worth, I agree with you."

"Maybe SCICC, since they're the biggest stakeholder on the plaintiffs' side, would be willing to forego discovery on both sides," Larry said, "and convince SB&T Co. to do the same. That would save them a lot of time and expense especially since they already know what each side is going to say."

"I can't imagine," Gordie said, "that they would agree to a unilateral waiver of discovery. But I think you're on the right track. They might consider a mutual waiver."

"It depends on how desperate they are, doesn't it?" Bodean asked.

"Interest doesn't begin to run on the $29,000 until the day of judgment," Larry said. "The longer they wait, the longer it takes before they get that interest clock ticking. And you know how bankers and insurance companies are. They are tortured by idle funds."

Larry agreed to call Richard Kuenzi, SCICC's attorney, and discuss the situation; otherwise, the case would sit in limbo for six months if there were no appeals, and perhaps years if there were. All agreed that that was the end they should start on, although the weasel might be motivated, depending on what his income was this month. And if Alden thought Jamie would be dissipating all his assets to defend the criminal prosecution and there may not be a pot of gold at the end of the rainbow, the bank might be motivated to proceed *posthaste*.

With their arguments being so persuasive, Jamie said on a scale of zero to ten, ten being the highest chance of SCICC and SB&T Co. agreeing to a mutual waiver, he had, in just a few minutes, gone from a zero to a ten. All laughed, feeling an infusion of optimism.

Jamie said, "Let me put this in context. The civil lawsuit ordinarily in a case such as this would not have been filed until after the criminal trial so as to first preview the strengths and weaknesses of the case. Because of the long statute of limitations, there would be no rush to file for either the bank or the insurance company. The only urgency would be if I dissipated all my assets in fighting the criminal case before a judgment could be rendered in the civil case. I can't be forced to waive my right against self-incrimination, and invocation of that right can't result in me being punished for having done so. In all likelihood then, the civil case would be stayed or held in abeyance until the criminal prosecution was complete, and only then would I lose my Fifth Amendment rights.

"At the civil trial, I would have to testify or risk losing the case. If I testified, I would be subject to cross-examination. That would be restricted to my testimony, and the plaintiffs' attorneys could not go beyond the scope of that testimony. Since the burden of proof in the civil case is only the greater weight of the evidence, the plaintiffs have a lesser burden than the prosecution in a criminal case where Corbett, for example, will have to prove my guilt beyond a reasonable doubt. So if I win the civil case, not only do I escape paying the $29,000, but I send a message to the DA that if the weasel and the rest can't win with a lower standard of proof, he better dismiss the criminal prosecution to avoid embarrassment, especially during his election year."

"Very well done, my son," Larry said. "We've taught you well."

"I don't see where Jamie has anything to lose by testifying or going to trial in the civil case," Gordie said. "It gives us a chance to see how he would hold up in the criminal case and also gives us a chance to evaluate the prosecution's witnesses."

"Who would the plaintiffs call beside Alden and Rita Baker?" Jamie asked.

"Maybe Horace Green, the head bookkeeper and custodian of the records at Tobiasis," Bodean said, "to produce the receipt showing payment of the chit."

"We're going to have to make sure Green also produces the chit itself that will prove that it was Patty's and not Jamie's," Gordie said. "We need to have Bodean talk to him ASAP. His telephone number is in the discovery documents." Bodean said he would.

They discussed who would be Jamie's witnesses at the civil trial. Jamie, Jamie's father, uncle Matt, maybe one of the Skylers, Ursula Russell, and Jennie. The defense could call Alden and Rita Baker as well, depending on the type of testimony needed. Hopefully, the defense would be able to elicit the needed testimony on cross-examination. What about one of the arresting officers who could testify that it was Alden who brought the $1,000 into Jamie's office and that it was not found there to begin with?

"Depends on what Alden testifies to," Larry said. "It would be good to corroborate Jamie's testimony on that point."

"I suppose Dr. Lauderback's polygraph testimony is inadmissible in the civil trial because of its lack of reliability and lack of scientific recognition," Jamie said.

"True," Gordie said. "Maybe we should waive a jury trial in the civil case and have it tried before the court. After the motions hearing, Judge Tibbits will know Jamie passed the polygraph."

"I have a feeling Judge Tibbits will be excusing or disqualifying himself since he will be presiding in the criminal case," Larry said. "Otherwise he may hear evidence in the civil case that might not be admissible in the criminal case. Once he's heard it, even if he can segregate it, it can't help but influence his decisions and rulings. It's impossible to un-ring a bell."

═══════════════

On August 25, Verna buzzed Larry, announcing that Richard D. Kuenzi was on the telephone calling on the Cooper civil case. Verna didn't have to bring in the file; Larry had it sitting in front of him.

Richard D. Kuenzi, who said he preferred to be called "RD," seemed pleasant enough. They soon determined they had two important things in common other than being attorneys and liking the outdoors. Both had been members of the same social fraternity, Sigma Chi, and both had been members of the same legal fraternity, Phi Delta Phi. It was unfortunate they were now on opposite sides. It was understood, however, that they could disagree without being disagreeable.

"I received a copy of your answer," RD said. "The counterclaim bothered me, but you know what you're doing."

"You don't know Jamie like I do," Larry said. "Comes from a fine family, and he has been unjustly accused. I don't doubt money is missing, but Jamie didn't take it. If you would like a copy of his polygraph results, I would be glad to send them."

"Do that. Even though they're not accepted in court, I find them helpful. I was a deputy district attorney in Boston for a short period. They can be a valuable tool."

Umm, Larry thought, *RD is just the opposite of his counterpart, J. Henry Ross, Stillwell's attorney, a.k.a. the weasel. We're not going to have trouble telling them apart but the initial similarity. What's with that?*

"Are you still there?" RD asked.

"Just thumbing through the file. Sorry about that."

"I see you requested a jury trial."

"Yes, I usually do on cases like this. I wondered why you didn't request one."

"I didn't want to get hometowned, although I've found the juries in Colorado to be more tolerant and fairer than most. With regard to the Cooper Case, let me lay it all out on the line," Larry said. "The civil case is an obstacle we would like to remove. There doesn't seem to be any room for negotiation. The bank is convinced he did it. Jamie is adamant about his innocence, which is borne out by the polygraph results and his clean record. I don't have any trouble putting him on the stand, but I wouldn't be much of a lawyer if I fed him to the lions by allowing pretrial discovery in a related civil case. If you will waive pretrial discovery, I will do the same. Then we don't have to get a court order to freeze the proceedings and wait months and maybe years to have a civil trial."

"I have complete authority in this case, but I will need at least through the weekend to consider your proposal," RD replied. "I will be frank with you as well. SCICC is afraid that if we wait too long to go to trial and even if we win, there won't be anything left to collect. We understand that your client is now unemployed, and I can imagine the legal fees he is incurring. The people I am responsible for want us to get what we can as quickly as we can. With the Colorado Homestead Exemption and other exemptions afforded to a judgment debtor, there won't be anything left to execute upon."

"Do you have any idea how the bank will react?" Larry asked. "They may be the fly in the ointment."

"Our insurance contract gives us the right to make all trial decisions although we like to respect the bank's wishes as well. However, since we have paid the bulk of the loss, the bank would be hard pressed to be heard to complain. I have spoken with a Mr. J. Henry Ross, who has already, on behalf of his client, given us the green light to proceed in any manner we deem best."

Larry said, "I think through stipulations mutually beneficial to both sides, we can cut down on expensive travel costs for witnesses. I for one am not good at games and am anxious to have this matter resolved in a fair and expeditious manner."

"I agree and always opt for the high road. I look forward to working with you and apologize for not giving you advance warning of my call," RD said.

"No apologies necessary, I was contemplating calling you today myself. I shall await your call on Monday, or is that rushing you?"

"That would be more than enough time. Even though I know what my decision will be, I had better sleep on it. I will call you at, say, eleven a.m. your time if that is convenient."

"It is. Talk to you on Monday."

After hanging up, Larry felt good. Although there may be little cause to celebrate, Larry felt in his heart that to go forward with the civil trial would be the right thing to do.

_____

RD, true to his word, telephoned Larry on Monday, August 26, with his decision. The two agreed that there would be no pretrial discovery as between the parties; that is, no depositions, no interrogatories. Requests for admissions and denials would be elicited from either Jamie or his wife or Alden or his father. RD agreed to draft a stipulation, sign it on behalf of SCICC, and forward it to Mr. Ross (the weasel) for his signature and delivery to Larry. After affixing his signature, Larry would send a conformed copy with his original signature to RD. The original would be filed with the court.

RD said he would send Mr. Ross his available trial dates and he and Larry could attempt to obtain an early trial date. RD gave Larry his telephone number; Larry already had his address.

Larry had looked up RD's attorney Peer Review Rating (PRR) in *Martindale-Hubbell*, a national legal directory. RD's PRR was "AV." The *A* meant his legal ability rating was "very high to preeminent." The *V* meant his general ethical standards rating was "very high." This was the highest possible rating obtainable. If RD had looked up Larry's and Gordie's PRR, he would have found the same. The weasel was unrated.

_____

It was not long before the weasel delivered the stipulation containing the pretrial discovery waiver. Larry added his signature to the original and the three duplicates. One was returned to the weasel, the second sent to RD, and the third Larry retained. The original Larry and the weasel filed with the district court clerk. They also obtained a trial date. It was a tentative date since Judge Tibbits, according to his clerk, was disqualifying himself because of his involvement in the criminal case.

Larry and the weasel were told to wait a minute while the clerk went into Judge Tibbett's chambers. She emerged and said that Judge Cole Black from the Ninth Judicial District, residing in Glenwood Springs, would be presiding in the case and that Judge Black would be available the week of October 16. The attorneys were to meet with him in chambers at eight a.m. on that date with jury selection to commence promptly at nine a.m. So the trial date on the civil case was fixed, the first of the two trials that would mark the ordeal.

VIEW THE SCENE

With permission of RD and the weasel, Dustin and Bodean were allowed to view the scene. Dustin Davies, the banker from Kalamazoo, Michigan, a self-proclaimed expert on bank vault time lock (BVTL) antiques, surprised Bodean with a telephone call from Denver. He was there for a banking seminar, and he and his wife had rented a car to "take a banter or frolic into the mountains of Colorado." Was it okay to spend the weekend in Steamboat? Stay with us, Bodean insisted.

Bodean convinced Dustin to play hooky from the seminar and drive up early on Friday, September 1. That way they would have longer to visit, and anyway, he wanted Dustin to examine the time lock mechanism on the bank vault he had spoken to him about previously. Brandon Stillwell said one thirty p.m. that afternoon would be convenient.

Steamboat was nudging autumn, and the air was a little crisper than in Denver and much welcomed by the longtime strangers to the western slope. Dustin and wife, Sherri, arrived at approximately eleven thirty a.m. and called from a Texaco service station on the eastern edge of Steamboat. He was told to drive to the other edge of town and meet Bodean and Natalie at Riverbend for lunch.

Bodean and Dustin had much to catch up on reminiscing about the good old college days while their wives embarked on a conversational journey of their own. Bodean and Dustin ordered from the sirloin specials; the ladies from the salad specials. With one thirty p.m. quickly approaching and not wanting to be late for their appointment to view the scene, the two old buddies left in the rental car. The women would be driving home in Bodean's Mustang.

Bodean and Dustin arrived on time at the historic Steamboat Bank and Trust Co. It was a stately and stylistic building, bold in its imposing large blocks of granite. Taking up a quarter of the block and standing two stories tall, it might have been mistaken for the courthouse. Positioned on the corner as it was, the imposing structure stood as a sentinel, guarding the business district now for almost three quarters of a century.

The front entrance was carved into the center of where the east and south walls met. In other words, the front was not perpendicular to the two adjoining walls. The solid granite lintel, with stone corbels holding the roof above the second story, had chiseled thereon the building's name, "Sentinel Building." It was clearly visible if one were walking cattycorner in a northwesterly direction from the opposite end. The Roman arch was of solid granite and was labeled, "Steamboat Bank and Trust Co."

The building has been described by the discerning as a mix between Roman and Victorian architecture. For example, the granite, Roman arches above the long slender windows had flowers etched along their semicircle borders. The ornate designs in the interior belied their Victorian influence. Virtually everything had been maintained by the Stillwells in classic mint condition. The copper railings were kept shined, the hardwoods oiled, and the plaster painted. All would pass the military's white glove inspection. Most impressive were the counters, teller cages, and of course, the main vault.

One might mistake the main vault (one of two vaults) as ornamental because the vault door was always open, exposing the gold and silver of its various compartments, bolts, wheels, and intricate mechanisms. But it was used also to store large amounts of cash. Its cash drawers were a little more than an arm's length away from the entrance, though kept locked by a key possessed only by the bank's head teller and the bank president.

With the exception of the office occupied by the bank president, all the offices were fairly small in comparison to the size of the building. The fronts consisted of tinted glass framed by the original hardwoods, and plush carpet covered the office floors.

Bodean and Dustin were greeted by Brandon, who turned the tour over to Alden. Alden appeared gracious, showing the two the various offices including his, with its annex containing his grandfather's old rolltop desk, which he proudly pointed out, as well as the vacant office next to him that was formerly Jamie's. After obtaining Alden's permission, Bodean proceeded to take photographs.

Alden shadowed every move Bodean and Dustin made, especially when they approached the main vault and were examining the door and its time lock. Careful not to touch anything, Dustin confirmed that its manufacturer was Howard and Co. of Boston. He also spotted the name of the patent holder, H. Gross, and the year it was patented, 1876. It was a two-movement lock, used to add redundancy. He copied the movement number (3099) and combination lock bolt number (4072) onto a scrap of paper he was carrying.

Dustin asked Alden if the bank had had any trouble with the vault time lock, and Alden said, "Not that I know of." Pressing his luck, he asked Alden if the bank could bypass or override the time lock. Alden gave the same answer.

Bodean was shown the cash drawer in the vault that contained the deficiency. He couldn't open it or the others because they were locked, and only Rita and his father had a key. "When Rita is not here and your father is gone, what do you do?" Bodean asked.

"Rita has a hidden key in her office that only she, Dad, and I know the whereabouts," Alden said, unabashed.

Dustin and Bodean had found out everything they needed to know, and thanked Alden, departing for Larry's and Gordie's office. Larry was in court, but Dustin was introduced to Gordie, and Gordie was briefed on what the view of the scene revealed. Dustin was not only another witness to Alden's statements but a potential expert as well.

When Bodean called Jamie at the Cooper Ranch, Dustin, Bodean, their wives, and Kate were invited for dinner and horseback riding. The four couples, Kate, Maya, Flossie, and horses whose names go unremembered made the Davies' trip to the mountains all the more memorable. The payback Dustin would not discover until much later would be being called back to testify in Jamie's criminal trial. His visit now, however, would be included in the series of events chronicled in the ordeal.

EXCURSION INTO
THE UNKNOWN

It was seven a.m., a perfect Steamboat September day. Autumn in the air. Children back at school. The fifteenth day of the month, the date scheduled for the motions hearing in the criminal case of *People of the State of Colorado v. James Curtis Cooper a.k.a. Jamie Cooper.*

The defense team was already assembled in their usual lair, coffee mugs conscripted, Verna's fabulous cinnamon rolls claimed, and the blizzard of paperwork unfolding. All were unusually quiet and somewhat somber. Verna, noticing the rolls were virtually untouched, filled their cups and asked, "What? No *joie de vivre?*"

"Just bring us a bucket of Tums," Bodean growled.

"And a hari-kari kit while you're at it," Jamie added.

"I hope this is not the way we feel when we return from court," Larry said. "The fight ain't over till it's over. Where's your optimism? Let's make sure everyone has their assignments. For the most part, we will be governed by the order in which Judge Tibbits takes our motions. Gordie and I are guessing, but this is the order in which we think he will address our motions."

With this, he went over to the now famous flip chart. Already listed were the defense motions: motion for discovery, motion to strike, motion to admit polygraph results, motion for bill of particulars, motion to suppress, and motion for change of venue.

Larry and Gordie figured that the judge would grant the discovery motion and summarily deny the motion to strike and the motion to admit polygraph results. On the motion for bill of particulars, Corbett had already complied and the defense had already filed their notice of alibi. The motion to suppress evidence and motion for change of venue would require the presentation of evidence and legal argument.

Gordie would be handling the motion to suppress. He would call Officer Gary Boyle, who was one of the arresting officers and who advised Jamie of his rights. "We subpoenaed him while we were still thinking of suppressing statements," Gordie said. "He will still be called to establish that Jamie's arrest was unlawful because the authorities had time to get a warrant and didn't. At the time of the warrantless arrest, they searched him and his wallet. The wallet produced Patty's name and telephone number, which triggered the Las Vegas connection and so-called gambling motive." Gordie pointed out that the aim was to suppress all the evidence that was the fruit of that illegal search.

Larry then took the helm. He stated he would be handling the motion for change of venue. He had already filed the copies of the newspaper articles, letters to the editor, Sweeney's editorials, and the eight affidavits. Corbin Sweeney had been subpoenaed to testify and would be waiting at the courthouse when they arrived. Sweeney would testify as to the articles, editorials, and letters to the editor. He would also testify as to the circulation and area of distribution. Bodean would be called to relate some of the TV and radio coverage Jamie's case had received. Corbett had already stipulated that the defense could place the affidavits in evidence without calling affiants.

Larry had also subpoenaed two couples who lived in scattered rural areas surrounding Steamboat to testify as to what they had read and heard and as to their conclusions as to guilt as a result thereof. Their names were Ken and Barbara Chacon and Dale and Shirley Clinger, well respected and well known in the farming and ranching communities and active on the Routt County Fair Board and in 4-H. They also would be waiting in the wings at the courthouse. Bodean had talked to both couples and said they "would not waffle." Gordie said he knew them well and they usually "stuck by their guns and were not swayed by the winds of public opinion."

Jamie commended Larry, Gordie, and Bodean for having done their homework and stated that his spirits had been bolstered. He said he didn't want to watch the Stillwells gloat each time the judge denied their motions. Larry told him not to get his hopes up as, despite popular belief, it is always an uphill battle for the defense. Everything is stacked against them before they even walk into court.

Gordie echoed Larry's remarks. The DA is the representative of the people; his popularity is reflected in the fact that he was elected. He is the epitome of all that is holy, as is the judge. Those uniformed police officers will have their badge and boots spit-shined, uniforms pressed, and looking every bit the part of the Boy Scout. The prosecution side is their side; the defense is the other side. The defendant is considered the blight on society and particularly the defendant's attorneys, who are thought to be paid prostitutes.

Hum, Jamie thought. *I've regressed to what I was when I walked in. Where's my lifeline when I need it?*

═══════════════

At seven forty-five a.m., the defense team was almost last to arrive. Corbett was already seated, with his investigator seated beside him. The coliseum had about the same number of spectators as the last two court appearances—virtually the same faces, with a few new ones. The Stillwells were all in their places with bright shiny faces. The weasel was not there yet, but here came the police officers in parade dress. They would certainly pass inspection. The editor and the two couples Larry subpoenaed were finally spotted, intermingled with the spectators. The weasel walked in and sat in the seat saved for him by the Stillwells.

At eight a.m. sharp, the court was brought to order with the Honorable Clayton Tibbits presiding. In answer to the judge's inquiry, both sides announced they were ready. Almost by script, Judge Tibbits granted the defense's discovery motion and predictably denied the motion to strike, stating that it wasn't prejudicial to list the legal and nicknames of individuals, as almost everyone has a nickname. And predictably, Judge Tibbits denied Jamie's motion to admit polygraph results after first inquiring if Corbett had received a copy of the polygraph results. In denying the motion, the judge said the polygraph was not recognized as being reliable scientific evidence.

Larry asked if he could briefly be heard on the issue. Judge Tibbits said, "Briefly."

"May it please the court, Mr. Corbett. Your Honor, I know that there is still skepticism about the accuracy of polygraph results. I know we can't unscrew the top of someone's head or look into their heart to determine whether or not they're telling the truth. The polygraph is the closest thing we have, and if it weren't accurate, then why are so many law enforcement agencies and employers using it? Jamie has taken and passed the polygraph. Isn't that worth something?"

Corbett rose to counter but was motioned by Judge Tibbits to sit down. "Mr. Whittaker, you make some good points. However, until a greater court mandates me to do so, I will deny your motion."

"Thank you, Your Honor."

"Mr. Corbett, I see where you have complied with Mr. Whittaker's request for a bill of particulars, and that he has filed a notice of alibi pursuant thereto. Mr. Whittaker, are you satisfied with the district attorney's specification?"

"Judge, Mr. Corbett has indicated that the offense occurred sometime within a twelve-hour span between seven p.m. on July 10 and seven a.m. on July 11, 1972. That doesn't really pinpoint it and defeats the purpose of the bill of particulars."

"Mr. Corbett, can't you pinpoint the time of the theft or at least some shorter range?"

"No, Your Honor. Alden Stillwell and another employee counted the money and set the vault time lock for seven a.m. the next day. With people in the bank until seven p.m. on the tenth and people in the bank at seven a.m. the following morning, the theft could only have occurred sometime within that period. We don't have anything more definitive than that."

"Sorry, Mr. Whittaker, you're going to have to live with it. Any other problems with the bill of particulars?"

"No, Your Honor. Nothing other than that."

"Very well, the next matter we will take up is the motion to suppress. Mr. Whittaker or Mr. Brownell, you may proceed."

"Your Honor," Gordie said, "We ask for a sequestration order for all witnesses who will testify in this hearing."

"Any objection, Mr. Corbett?"

"No, Your Honor."

"Very well, all those who have been called as witnesses or anticipate they will be called are asked to wait in the hall. I will leave it up to counsel on both sides to make sure their witnesses are removed; otherwise the witnesses will not be allowed to testify."

With that, all the uniformed officers left the courtroom, along with Corbin Sweeney, Kenneth and Barbara Chacon, Dale and Shirley Clinger, and Bodean.

"Why did he do that?" Jamie whispered to Larry.

"So that they don't hear each other's testimony and come up with the same story," Larry whispered back.

Gordie then called Officer Gary Boyle to the stand. Boyle testified that a call had come into the dispatcher at exactly seven fifteen a.m. on July 11 from Alden Stillwell, who said he found $30,000 missing from the vault. Mr. Stillwell said he obtained a key from the head teller's desk and unlocked the office of one of the bank employees, a Jamie Cooper. He said while searching the office he, Mr. Stillwell, found $1,000 in Mr. Cooper's bottom desk drawer. Mr. Stillwell said he wanted Mr. Cooper arrested and that he expected Mr. Cooper to arrive at work at eight a.m.

Boyle was dispatched along with his partner Lloyd Kensey in one cruiser; Officers Clinton Coleman and Michael Heath arrived in another cruiser. Mr. Cooper was arrested on felony theft charges and transported to the Steamboat Police Station. Mr. Cooper was searched and his wallet confiscated upon his arrest. Mr. Cooper's wallet was searched in Boyle's presence at the police station. A slip of paper that had Las Vegas telephone numbers was retrieved. Officer Coleman tried to reach the two parties whose names and telephone numbers were on the slip but to no avail.

Boyle said Officer Coleman contacted the authorities in Las Vegas and requested that they locate and interview the named persons. Boyle said that they were not aware of any Las Vegas connection up until that time. Boyle testified that he was not told by Mr. Stillwell or anyone else about any Las Vegas connection nor were any of the officers that he knew of so advised, at least not in his presence.

Gordie asked if there had been any discussion about gambling or motive between the police officers prior to finding the Las Vegas addresses in Jamie's wallet, and he answered "No." When asked why he thought the Las Vegas information was important, he answered, "Motive." When asked if Jamie was arrested with an arrest warrant, Boyle said, "No."

Gordie then asked if he was aware as to whether or not County Judge William Dearborn and/or District Judge Clayton Tibbits were in town on either the tenth, eleventh, or twelfth of July and he said, "Yes," that both were in the courthouse on all three days and that he had seen them there because he said he had business there all three days. When asked, he said he was sure because one of his responsibilities was to take and pick up court documents on a daily basis.

When asked how he knew money was missing, Boyle answered, "Because Mr. Stillwell told us that."

When asked how he knew $30,000 was missing, Boyle answered, "Because Mr. Stillwell told us that."

When asked when was the first time he saw the $1,000, he answered, "When Mr. Stillwell brought the money into Mr. Cooper's office and threw it on the desk."

When asked if he saw any money in Mr. Cooper's office, he answered no. When asked whether or not, prior to the arrest, he or any other officer searched Mr. Cooper's office or asked Mr. Cooper his side of the story, he answered no. When asked if he or any other officer that he knew had interviewed anyone other than Mr. Stillwell, he answered no. When asked if he knew or any other officers knew, to his knowledge, Mr. Stillwell, he answered no. When asked if he or any of the other officers, to his knowledge, knew of or had any information concerning Mr. Cooper—other than what he related—he answered no. Gordie told the court he had no other questions of the witness.

Now it was Corbett's turn to cross-examine. He asked Boyle why they arrested Mr. Cooper. Boyle said because they had a citizen's complaint about a possible theft. Corbett then asked why they didn't obtain an arrest warrant. Boyle said because they didn't have time. Why? Because Mr. Stillwell was afraid he would steal more money or get rid of the money he took or leave the country. No further questions.

Gordie only had one question on redirect. Did Boyle or any of the officers know that Jamie was a third-generation resident of Steamboat or bother to even verify what Mr. Stillwell had told them? Boyle answered no before Corbett could object.

Gordie announced he had no other witnesses to call. Corbett said he had none. It was time for argument. Gordie argued that the arrest was made without a warrant. There were no exigent circumstances to eliminate the requirement to obtain a warrant. Two judges were available on the date to issue a warrant. Officers didn't obtain one. The arrest being illegal, the search was illegal. The search being illegal, the evidence obtained as a result thereof was illegal and should be suppressed. Gordie concluded, "This is the fruit of the poisonous tree doctrine, and such evidence was obtained in violation of Mr. Cooper's Fourth Amendment rights. Therefore, our motion to suppress should be granted."

Corbett countered, "Mr. Stillwell had already made a citizen's arrest. The officers were effectuating the arrest. Officers could conduct a search incident to a lawful arrest. Search was legal, seizure of evidence and everything derived therefrom was legal. The fruit was not tainted because the tree was not poisonous, Your Honor. The motion to suppress should be denied."

Judge Tibbits took the matter under advisement and announced he would render his decision by Wednesday of next week.

Now for the change of venue motion. Larry asked the judge to take judicial notice of the attachments to the motion. Larry said he was prepared to call Corbin Sweeney, the editor of the newspaper, who had been subpoenaed and was waiting in the hall. Corbett said that wouldn't be necessary because he would stipulate to authenticity without conceding the allegation as to their prejudicial effect. Sweeney could be excused.

Larry announced he had four witnesses from rural Routt County. He made an offer of proof that they would testify in the same fashion as the affiants in the affidavits filed with the court. "You don't need to call them," Corbett said. "I will stipulate as to the testimony without conceding that the motion should be granted."

"Admitted for that limited purpose," Judge Tibbits said.

Larry argued that the pretrial publicity was so massive and pervasive that it prevented the defendant from receiving a fair trial in Routt County. He said, "The community is so small that the effect is even more pronounced here than it would be in a larger locality. The intensive publicity and misinformation has swayed public opinion against Jamie already as indicated by the affidavits filed with the court. Jamie hasn't even told his side of the story, and he has already been tried in the press and been convicted. It has been a trial by media, not by jury.

"To proceed to trial in Routt County would deprive Jamie of his Sixth Amendment rights. The picture of guilt is so indelibly etched in the minds of the prospective jurors that it can't be erased, no matter the quantum or quality of the evidence to the contrary. Justice cries out for a change in the location of trial. It is the only viable option the court has to prevent a manifest abuse of justice."

Corbett opposed the motion for change of venue because a relocation of the trial would mean all the participants, including the judge, defense attorneys, defendant, witnesses, and prosecutor would be transplanted. The jury would be selected from the new venue. A change of venue would be costly to the citizens of Routt County. All the transplants must be transported, housed, and fed in some distant community. Corbett said, "I have greater faith in the citizens of Routt County to do the right thing than to leave it to strangers who have no vested interest."

Corbett argued that even if the impact of the pretrial publicity was as bleak as that painted by the defense, it could be mitigated or lessened by less drastic alternatives. *Voir dire* (jury selection) would weed out those whose minds were already made up. Corbett continued, "Then there is change of veniremen where Routt County could import jurors from another county, but then that would be expensive too, although not as expensive as a change of venue. Your Honor could delay or continue the trial until the dust settles, but then critical witnesses might become scattered and lost. Your Honor is familiar with the other options, none of which accomplishes what the defense is looking for—jurors who are deaf, dumb, and blind—and I would concede that that doesn't describe the citizenry of our county."

The spectators applauded. After banging the gavel, Judge Tibbits announced, "Any further outbursts and I'll have the bailiff clear the courtroom."

"Any rebuttal, Mr. Whittaker?"

"Thank you, Your Honor. We have a lot of confidence in the jurors in Routt County as well. Jamie is a third-generation resident of this fine community and is one of them. However, we respect the fine citizens of Routt County to the extent that we do not wish to put them in a compromising situation or position. They shouldn't have to walk a tightrope, nor do I think they especially want to pass judgment on one of their own. I know I wouldn't want to sit on the jury in this case, and I have not lived in Routt County as long as have many of them. I'm sorry, but the inconvenience caused to the prosecution by a change of venue is not a violation of the United States Constitution, but *not* changing the place of trial would deprive Mr. Cooper of his Sixth Amendment rights!"

There were audible chuckles.

Judge Tibbits banged the gavel again. "This is the last time I will warn you. This hearing is not a spectacle, and if you want to observe, you have to do so in a respectful and dignified fashion. Gentlemen," Judge Tibbits then said to the attorneys, "I've heard enough argument. I will take this matter under advisement and, like the previous motion, will notify you of my decision by Wednesday of next week. Accordingly, I am setting this matter for a bond return date for next Wednesday at nine a.m., at which time I will announce my rulings. Since this covers all the defense motions and none has been filed by the prosecution, this court stands adjourned."

At nine a.m. on Wednesday, September 20, true to his word, Judge Clayton Tibbits announced his rulings on the defense's motion for suppression of evidence and motion for change of venue. Only about half of the spectators showed. The Stillwells with the weasel, J. Henry Ross, were sitting in the first row in Sunday attire, missing only their hymnals.

Not optimistic, the defense team was not overly disappointed when the rulings were announced. They all had butterflies in the pit of their stomach, in unreasonable anticipation, as Judge Tibbits announced his rulings. He denied both motions. The motion for suppression of evidence was denied because the arrest was based on a citizen's complaint and probable cause was established on the basis of the substantial amount of missing money, some of it having been found in the possession of the defendant. The motion for change of venue was denied on the grounds that any prejudice there be could be mitigated by *voir dire,* admonition to the jury, or sequestration of the jury, or perhaps all three. Change of venue was a drastic remedy for an anecdotal defense claim that, even if true, could be cured by least drastic measures. "Granting a change of venue might be perceived as impugning the integrity of the citizens I serve," the judge stated.

The defense team was not as upset by the ruling as much as the rationale. Larry would later tell Verna that it was "a stupefying display of innocuous legal gibberish." While everyone was there, Judge Tibbits said he wanted to set the matter for trial. While his clerk went to retrieve the court calendar, Judge Tibbits, forgetting that Jamie had already been arraigned, asked Jamie if he was ready to plead. Larry said, "My client is entering a plea of not guilty and requesting a jury of twelve."

Turning to Jamie, the judge asked if that was his plea and request. Jamie answered, "It is, Your Honor."

The matter was set for a jury trial the week of February 12, 1973, with counsel to meet with Judge Tibbits at eight a.m. and jury selection to commence promptly at nine a.m. Larry said that if there were any speedy trial problems depending on when speedy trial commenced to run, that his client would waive it. Without counting the days, Judge Tibbits asked Jamie if that was his wish, and Jamie said, "Yes."

The judge then said, "Very well, your bond will be continued to that date, and this court will stand adjourned."

Jamie asked Larry if he knew for whom the bell tolls, referring, of course, to the outcome of his criminal case. Larry, also being familiar with Hemmingway as well as John Donne, replied, "I hope it tolls *not* for thee." Jamie was not as sure as he had been in the recent past. His hope was fading into the sunset as the darkness of the ordeal was setting in on a community torn apart.

THE CIVIL TRIAL

With the motions hearing in the criminal case behind them and the criminal jury trial not scheduled until February 12, 1973, the defense team was concentrating its efforts on the civil jury trial scheduled for October 16, 1972.

In their pretrial statement, Larry and Gordie certified the following as potential witnesses: Jamie, G. Forrest Cooper, Matthew Thomas Cooper, Jennie Cooper, Ron Skyler, Betty Skyler, Ursula Russell, Alden Stillwell, Brandon Stillwell, Rita Baker, Joseph Michaels, Dustin Davies, Horace Green, Jackie Stiles, Charlie Blankenship, and Officer Gary Boyle.

RD and the weasel, in their pretrial statement, had certified the following as their potential witnesses: Brandon Stillwell, Alden Stillwell, Rita Baker, Mathew T. Cooper, Horace Green, Ranelle Whatley, James Curtis Cooper, Jennie Cooper, and Officer Clinton Coleman.

The parties were also required to certify the exhibits they intended to introduce into evidence at trial. The defendant certified: chit number 72-PD4485 posted at Tobiasis Casino in the name of Patty Cooper in the amount of $1,200; plaintiff's receipt from Tomahawk Cafe on July 10, 1972 in the amount of $5.50; United Airlines purchase receipt in the name of Forrest Cooper; and "any exhibits certified by plaintiffs."

The plaintiffs certified: bank closing checklist dated July 10, 1972; vault balancing journal for July 10, 1972 and July 11, 1972; U.S. currency (twenty fifty-dollar bills); bill strap with Federal Reserve stamp; receipt made out to Jamie Cooper from Tobiasis Casino showing payment of chit number 72-PD4485 in the amount of $1,200; print out of United Airlines ticket issued to Jamie and Jennie Cooper on June 23, 1972; telephone toll records of calls made from James Cooper's home telephone number to numbers in Las Vegas for months of June and July, 1972; and, "any exhibits certified by defendant."

The defense team had met on and off over the past several weeks and felt confident that they had a chance to win the civil case. They didn't feel their hunch was a false reading. They predicted the unfavorable outcome in the motions hearing; now they were predicting a favorable outcome in the civil trial.

It was a typical Steamboat autumn October day, Friday the thirteenth, so far not an unlucky day and hopefully not a bad omen, at least for the defense. The civil jury trial was only a couple of days away. The leaves on the Aspen and Cottonwoods formed a kaleidoscopic pattern of yellows, golds, oranges, pinks, and reds that glistened in the sun and shimmered in the hastening breeze. It would not be long before the leaves would be gone and the snows would bring the hoards to the ski slopes and money into the cash registers of the local businesses.

The defense team assembled in their places at the conference table of Whittaker and Brownell, attorneys at law, may have been mistaken as a rerun if Verna had not known the difference.

Verna was self-abnegating as usual, doting the usual attention on the "knights of the roundtable." But all business these. Lunch having been completed, it was time to get down to business.

Not the flip chart again, they thought as Larry assumed his professorial role with a newly purchased pointer. The "class" was called to order and their attention was drawn to the list of potential witnesses for the plaintiffs.

"At least you could put them in alphabetical order," Bodean had chided.

"They're in the order of the plaintiffs' pretrial statement," Larry said defensively.

Starting with Brandon Stillwell, they speculated he would establish the ownership of the bank; maybe its general layout; who worked for the bank; how the time lock on the vault worked; what the setting was; where Brandon was on July 10 and 11; who was in charge in his absence; who had access to the vault; how the cash drawers were accessed; how much cash was usually kept in the vault and in what dimensions; who had keys and where they were kept; Jamie's employment at the bank; any access Jamie would have to the funds; and location of the various offices in relationship to the vault.

Next, Alden Stillwell, trusted son, heir apparent to the Stillwell fortune and a bank officer. They expected that he would testify that he and Rita Baker constituted the "dual control" team on the evening of July 10, 1972. Both checked out the main vault following a preprinted list requiring a check for each item. All funds were accounted for when they closed the door. The time lock was properly set, preventing the vault door from being opened until seven a.m. the next morning. He arrived at the bank at six forty-five a.m. on July 11, 1972. Jamie was not in the bank. When he went to Jamie's office to retrieve a file, he discovered $1,000 in Jamie's desk. He immediately went to the vault and discovered $30,000 missing. He called the police department. He gave the money he found in the desk drawer to the officers, and the police arrested Jamie.

Next, Rita Baker, head teller for twelve years at the bank and a member of the "dual control" team with Alden. She would likely state that at closing on July 10, 1972, they counted the money in the main vault; all was there. Following procedures that day checked the timer and lock mechanism; all was working and was set to open at seven a.m. next morning. She would say that she arrived at seven fifteen a.m., earlier than normal. Alden was then on the telephone with police when she arrived, and she was advised by Alden of the situation. The vault door was open when she arrived. Alden said he opened it at seven a.m., found $1,000 in Jamie's desk while looking for a file, checked the vault and found $30,000 missing, searched Jamie's office for the rest of the money, and found none.

Next, Matthew Cooper, Jamie's Uncle from Las Vegas. If he is called, he would probably establish the Las Vegas connection i.e., Jamie there June 23 through 26, 1972; paid $1,200 debt to Tobiasis Casino. Not likely plaintiffs would call him.

Next, Horace Green, head bookkeeper and in charge of collections at Tobiasis Casino in Las Vegas. He would produce the receipt showing Jamie's payment of $1,200 to the casino to redeem chit number 72-PD-4485.

Next would be Ranelle Whatley, bookkeeper at United Airlines. If she was called, she would establish purchase of two airline tickets by Forrest Cooper for Jamie and Jennie Cooper.

Next, Jamie as an adverse witness, to establish he was at the bank on the evening of July 10, 1972. He was there on the morning of July 11, 1972, prior to Alden's arrival. He left the car in the parking lot, and he didn't return until eight a.m. He made telephone calls and was in Las Vegas two weeks before the money was stolen.

Next, Jennie, possibly, to establish the Las Vegas connection.

The defense team discussed cross-examination and what questions should be directed and to whom. Larry and Gordie would divide up cross-examination.

Larry flipped to the page listing all the defense witnesses.

They started with Jamie. Jamie would establish: he worked at the bank thirteen years, was first vice president, worked the night of July 10, 1972, until six fifteen p.m. The cleaning service was there when he left. He had a chamber meeting the next morning at six thirty a.m. He was president-elect of the chamber and needed to be there early to prepare. He parked at the end of the parking lot at bank closest to street and Tomahawk Cafe where the meeting was held. He never went inside bank and didn't return to the bank until almost eight a.m. prior to his arrest.

Next, G. Forrest Cooper, Jamie's father. He would testify that his niece, Patty, was having problems paying gambling debts. His brother Matt called and asked if he could borrow $1,200 to pay off one of Patty's debts at Tobiasis. It was urgent because they were threatening criminal prosecution. He asked Jamie if he could deliver the $1,200, as he was not in great health and not up to the flight. He purchased the airline tickets for Jamie and Jennie via a credit card, which he would identify. He gave Jamie the $1,200 plus money for the hotel and other expenses, and he drove Jamie and Jennie to the airport on June 23 and picked them up on June 26, 1972.

Next, Matthew Thomas Cooper, Jamie's uncle from Las Vegas. If not otherwise cross-examined, he would corroborate the testimony of Jamie and Forrest.

Next, Jennie, she would be a corroborating witness.

Next, Ron and/or Betty Skyler from Skyler Cleaning Service. One or both would testify that they arrived at the bank at six p.m. on July 10, 1972. Jamie was working in his office, and he left at six fifteen p.m. They left at seven p.m. Everything appeared in order when they arrived; they didn't see him carry anything out of the bank when he walked out the door, and they locked the door behind him.

Next, Ursula Russell, the owner of Mountain States Abstract and Title Company of Steamboat across the street from the bank. She would testify that on the morning of Jamie's arrest, July 10, 1972, she had arrived at work at six a.m., saw Jamie drive into the parking lot directly across from her office at six thirty a.m., and walked down the street toward the Tomahawk Café. He never went into the bank. She saw Alden Stillwell drive up at approximately six forty-five a.m.; she thought that unusual since he didn't usually arrive until seven thirty a.m. The night before she left work at approximately six thirty p.m. and the only vehicle in the bank parking lot was the Skyler Cleaning Service van.

Next, Jackie Stiles, waitress at the Tomahawk Café. She would testify that she was assigned to service the meeting room at the restaurant where the chamber of commerce held their monthly meetings. Jamie came in shortly after six thirty a.m. and met with Charlie Blankenship, the president of the chamber. The regular meeting started at six thirty a.m. and lasted until about seven fifty-five a.m. Jamie never left the restaurant from the time he arrived until the meeting ended. He paid her for the meal, and she gave him a receipt, which she would identify.

Next, Charlie Blankenship, president of the chamber and a pharmacist would testify that he knew Jamie mainly through the chamber and was with him continuously from six thirty a.m. to approximately seven fifty-five a.m. on June 10, 1972.

Next, Horace Green, head bookkeeper and in charge of collections at Tobiasis Casino in Las Vegas would produce the $1,200 chit signed by Patty Cooper.

Next, is Dustin Davies, banker from Michigan, expert on vault time locks. If needed, he would testify as to SB&T Co.'s time lock system. But it was expected that he would not be needed.

Next, Alden Stillwell, Brandon Stillwell and/or Rita Baker. One or all would testify as to matters defense might be precluded from asking on cross.

Larry and Gordie still had to prepare their opening statement and final argument. Larry was assigned to give defense's opening statement; Gordie the final argument. The defendant's tendered instructions had been included with their pretrial statement. These had all been previously reviewed by the defense team, and each had a copy. As a result of the same requirement for the plaintiffs, the defense team had copies of plaintiffs' tendered instructions, and vice versa. This practice was designed to prevent trials by ambush.

═══════════════

RD had come into town the previous day having flown into the Yampa Valley Regional Airport on a connecting flight from Denver. He had called Larry, and the two, together with the weasel, J. Henry Ross, had met at the weasel's office. They had firmed up their trial stipulations and wanted to finalize them that Friday afternoon. As the defense team was dispersing at three thirty p.m., RD and the weasel appeared, documents in hand, wide smiles both faces. Larry introduced RD to Jamie, Bodean, and Gordie. Saying good-bye for now, Jamie and Bodean departed.

Since the conference room table was laden with books, papers, and typical trial paraphernalia, Larry and Gordie ushered JD and the weasel into the library, where they positioned themselves around a fairly large round oak table with padded chairs.

RD was the first to speak. He pulled a typed, legal-size sheet from his briefcase and set it in front of Larry. Reading over Larry's shoulder, Gordie perused what was entitled, "Trial Stipulation."

"This, I hope represents what we agreed to in the short time we had together yesterday," RD said.

The stipulation, in essence, read that the parties agreed that the following exhibits could be introduced into evidence without objection and without the necessity of laying the proper foundation or calling witnesses:

Plaintiffs' exhibit numbers:

P-1 Bank closing checklist dated July 10, 1972.

P-2 Vault balancing journal for July 10, 1972.

P-3 Vault balancing journal for July 11, 1972.

P-7 Receipt made out to Jamie Cooper from Tobiasis Casino showing payment of chit number 72-PD4485 in the amount of $1,200.

P-8 Printout of United Airlines ticket issued to Jennie and Jamie Cooper on June 23, 1972.

P-9 Telephone toll records of calls made from Jamie Cooper's home telephone number to numbers in Las Vegas for months of June and July, 1972.

P-10 Bill strap and twenty fifty-dollar bills.

Defendant's exhibit numbers:

D-1 Chit number 72-PD4485 posted at Tobiasis Casino in the name of Patty Cooper in the amount of $1,200.

D-2 Receipt from the Tomahawk Café on July 10, 1972, in the amount of $5.50.

D-3 United Airlines purchase receipt by Forrest Cooper for Jamie and Jennie Cooper.

The stipulation also allowed the plaintiffs to introduce into evidence, without objection and without the necessity of laying the proper foundation or calling witnesses, the fact that SCICC, by their insurance contract with SB&T Co., was subrogated in the amount of the claim of loss and that the amount paid on the loss by SCICC was $24,000 and the amount borne by SB&T Co. was $5,000.

"This will save both sides a lot of time and expense," the weasel said while Larry and Gordie read. Gordie would later tell Larry that that was the first profound thing he had ever heard the weasel utter.

Larry and Gordie affixed their signatures to the original and four copies that already contained the original signatures of RD and the weasel. Larry and Gordie looked at each other and saw that one of the signatures was that of J. Henry Ross.

Must be the weasel's alias, they both thought.

Two duplicate originals were retained by Larry and Gordie. The original and two duplicates were returned to RD. RD said he would file the original before the court closed and he did.

─────────────

Jamie and Bodean met at the offices of Whittaker and Brownell, attorneys at law at seven a.m. that October Monday, the sixteenth day of the month. As each arrived, he was quickly ushered into the conference room where Larry and Gordie were buried in work. They were going over the list of potential jurors provided by the clerk late Friday. Each was asked to go over the list and see who they knew, who they wanted, and who they didn't want. Proper notations were made to reflect their comments.

Larry and Gordie estimated that it would take at least three and maybe four hours to pick a jury. They would be meeting with Judge Black at eight a.m., along with RD and the weasel to take care of last-minute items, such as sequestration of witnesses. Larry and Gordie had already decided not to have Bodean sit at the defense table; otherwise, with two attorneys, it would look like they were ganging up on the poor plaintiffs.

When they reached the courthouse a little before eight a.m., they were beginning to experience a little stage fright. A lot was riding on this case, not just on its own merits, but the effect it would have on the criminal case.

All of the prospective jurors on the jury list were seated in court, quiet and reserved. All sixty of them! Maybe some of them were experiencing stage fright as well. After all, this was not a common occurrence.

When they entered the courtroom to organize their books, papers, trial notebook, pleadings, and legal pads, they noticed that the Stillwells, who had been relegated to the back to make room for the general veniremen, were comingling and ingratiating themselves with the jurors. They were shaking hands, patting each other on the back, and exhibiting nervous laughter, which was totally improper. They told RD and the weasel, who had by this time settled in. RD turned and whispered something to the weasel, who in turn reigned in his clients.

"The judge will see you now," the bailiff announced. Larry inquired as to whether he wanted the clients as well, and the bailiff said, "No, just the attorneys."

When they entered the judge's chambers, Judge Cole Black stood and greeted them. The judge was fairly nondescript. His most distinguishing features, however, were his piercing blue eyes and an aura that reflected someone of stature. He radiated a magnetism and mystique that one felt when in the presence of a celebrity or a high-ranking official.

"Judge Black was very accommodating," Gordie would later say. "Instead of feeling you were his servant, he made you feel as though he was yours. Even with the black robe, he was a human just like the rest of us." His manner, knowledge, and eloquence would soon earn the respect his person and position deserved.

He *asked* if his proposed trial schedule was agreeable, as well as the midmorning and midafternoon recesses. He *suggested* that court commence at eight a.m. and adjourn at five p.m. once the jury was selected. That was agreeable to all. He asked if either of the parties was requesting a sequestration of witnesses, and both sides said "yes." He indicated that the clients, even though they might be witnesses, were allowed to sit with counsel at trial.

Judge Black said since the defendant had two attorneys, he would have to restrict tandem or double presentment. In other words, the two attorneys could not split opening statements; only one per side. The same thing was true for final arguments. And only one attorney would be allowed per witness. The plaintiffs would not be so constrained because each counsel represented a different plaintiff. RD told the judge that since their interests were merged, more or less, that they would abide by the same restrictions imposed on defense counsel.

Larry mentioned that he had observed potential witnesses commingling with the jury panel and had spoken to opposing counsel about that, and they had been prompt about rectifying the situation. Judge Black made each side responsible for their respective witnesses, and if there were any improprieties, they should be promptly reported to either him or the bailiff.

Since this was a jury trial, he said he would follow the usual civil process and would call fourteen jurors to the box and each side, starting with the plaintiffs, have four pre-emptories to exercise in an alternate fashion until they ended up with six. He said, "Of course, there would be no restriction on the number of challenges for cause, assuming they are meritorious." He asked how long they estimated the trial would take and was told between three and four days.

"I see from the court file that there are certain stipulations that you have made. I compliment you for making the effort to expedite the proceedings. Are there any other stipulations that I need to be made aware of before we start?"

"No, Your Honor."

"If it looks as though we are taking longer than necessary to pick a jury, I will have to limit your *voir dire*. Try not to be redundant and direct as many questions as you can to the panel as a whole."

With the rules of the game pretty well understood, the attorneys retreated to their respective tables, with the plaintiffs being the closest to the jury box. Brandon Stillwell was already seated at plaintiffs' table, Jamie at the defendant's.

The judge made the usual introductions and preliminary remarks. The entire panel was sworn to "true answers make to all questions of court and counsel." Fourteen potential jurors were called to the box. Judge Black asked general questions to illicit background information. The attorneys, starting with the plaintiffs, asked the usual questions in an effort to make sure the prospective jurors would not be prejudiced against their side. None of the jurors evinced bias or prejudice, and none were challenged for cause. All were customers of SB&T Co., which was expected, since it was the only bank in town. That was not grounds for disqualification.

The bailiff then circulated the list of fourteen jurors among the attorneys. Starting with RD and the weasel, each side took a turn in eliminating four jurors, alternating one at a time. The six who remained constituted the jury. There were four women and two men. Two were in their twenties, two in their thirties, and two in their forties.

The four women were Emily Gould, twenty-three, a sales clerk; Mary Harrington, forty-three, a real estate agent; Hannah Westen, thirty-three, a high school women's basketball and track coach; and Kelsey Bailey, thirty-five, a physical therapist. The two men were Sean Castles, twenty-two, a biologist; and Victor Rougle, forty-five, an accountant.

The jurors then took an oath faithfully to perform their duties in the case before them. The judge then gave them certain admonitions and outlined the format of a civil jury trial.

The attorneys then made opening statements of the things they expected to prove. Since the plaintiffs had the burden of proof, they went first and would do so throughout the trial.

RD made the opening statement for the plaintiffs:

"Ladies and gentlemen of the jury, my name is Richard J. Kuenzi; I represent SCICC in this action. My co-counsel is J. Henry Ross; he represents Steamboat Bank and Trust Co. I will be making an opening statement for both plaintiffs.

"The evidence will show that James Curtis Cooper was an employee of SB&T Co. and had been for a number of years. On the morning of June 11, 1972, Alden Stillwell, the son of the owner of the bank and an employee of the bank, while looking for a file, discovered one thousand dollars in the desk of another of the bank's employees, Jamie Curtis Cooper. Upon opening the main vault, he discovered that thirty thousand dollars were missing. He confiscated the one thousand dollars he found in Mr. Cooper's desk and called the police. The police subsequently responded and arrested Mr. Cooper for theft.

"The evidence will show that Mr. Cooper was working at the bank the evening before the money was found missing. When Alden arrived at work the next morning, Mr. Cooper's car was in the outermost portion of the bank's parking lot. But, there was no sign of Mr. Cooper. In fact, he didn't appear at the bank until eight a.m. on June 11, 1972.

"The evidence will show that Mr. Cooper had a gambling addiction. A secret not even his coworkers or closest friends knew. We will be presenting toll records of numerous telephone calls Mr. Cooper made and a trip he took to Las Vegas in the weeks preceding the discovery of the missing money. To prove our claim, we will be placing in evidence a receipt from Tobiasis Casino in Las Vegas showing that during Mr. Cooper's visit to Las Vegas, he redeemed a gambling chit for twelve hundred dollars. To prove the trip, we will produce a printout of his roundtrip airline ticket.

"When all the evidence is in, you will be convinced by a preponderance of the evidence that Mr. Cooper allowed his gambling propensity to take over his better judgment, resulting in him dipping into his employer's till to the tune of thirty thousand dollars. We will be asking you to return a verdict in favor of the plaintiffs."

"Thank you, Mr. Kuenzi," the judge said. "The defense may now make an opening statement."

Larry then began, "Ladies and gentlemen of the jury, Mr. Brownell and I represent the defendant in this action. First, I want to introduce you to a man who is thirty-four years of age. His lifetime ambition has been to be a banker. It started the summer after his senior year in high school culminating in thirteen years of outstanding service to that same bank, the Steamboat Bank and Trust Co. So stellar was his performance that he rose to the level of first vice president, hopscotching or leapfrogging over everyone at the bank, including the owner's own son, Alden.

"The man that I want you to meet is a third-generation Routt County resident; the president-elect of the Steamboat Chamber of Commerce. This man excelled in sports and was the valedictorian of his high school class. He was a business major and graduated with honors from the University of Colorado. He is married and has two children Max, age twelve, and Collette, age ten.

"On the evening of June 10, 1972, this man was working late, as was his custom. He loved his job and had great responsibilities. He was loyal to his boss, Brandon Stillwell, and wanted to do everything he could to repay Mr. Stillwell for the faith Mr. Stillwell reposed in him. This man left the bank at six fifteen p.m. on the evening of June 10, 1972, leaving only the Skyler Cleaning Service owners, Ron and Betty Skyler, in the bank.

"There was a vault time lock that did not permit admittance to the main vault from the time of closing of the bank until seven a.m. the following morning. The closing of the vault and setting of the time required what is called "dual control"—that is two persons were required to count the money, follow a checklist that Alden was required to initial upon completion of the steps, trigger the timer, and lock the vault door. This procedure was followed by both Rita Baker and Alden. That's the statement, at least, that they gave to the police.

"When the time expired and the vault could be opened with the regular combination having been dialed, guess who dialed the combination? Alden Stillwell. Guess who opened the vault door when the time expired at seven a.m. on June 11, 1972? Alden Stillwell. Guess who was alone in the bank after the vault door was open? Alden Stillwell. Guess who discovered the so-called missing money? Alden Stillwell. Guess who had the $1,000 so-called recovered money in his hands when the police arrived? Alden Stillwell. Guess whose office Alden came out of with the $1,000? Alden Stillwell's.

"Guess who didn't take the so-called missing money or any part thereof? The answer is the man I now want you to meet." With that, Larry went over to the chair where Jamie was sitting and, putting his hand on Jamie's shoulder, said, "This is the man. His name is Jamie Cooper."

After RD had made his opening statement, Gordie noticed that the weasel passed a note to RD via Brandon, who was seated between the two attorneys. RD read the note and leaning past Brandon mouthed "thank you." When RD turned around, Alden gave RD a thumbs-up.

After Larry made his opening statement, there was a deafening hush that pervaded the courtroom. Even Judge Black seemed to be caught up in a moment of reflection. Could it be that the pendulum was swinging back in the right direction? Hopefully, the jury and everyone else were asking, "Why are we here?" Jamie was certainly asking himself that question. No note from the weasel to RD now!

Judge Black, looking at his watch, said, "It's twelve oh five. This is a good place for our noon break." He admonished the jury not to talk about the case among themselves, not to read any newspapers, watch any television, or listen to any radio accounts of the case. He declared the court adjourned until one thirty p.m.

Verna had lunch waiting when the defense team, including Bodean, returned to the office. Everyone seemed to have an appetite, but the conversation centered mostly around cross-examination of Alden and Coleman. They were the key witnesses, and the two who appeared to have an axe to grind. Larry was set to cross-examine Alden, and Gordie was set to cross-examine Coleman.

Jamie sat there in careful reflection. He could see that RD was not a stranger to the courtroom and knew how to go for the jugular. But Larry had impressed him the most. RD was obvious about what he was doing, and Jamie remembered from his logic's class in college a Latin phrase that described RD's approach: *non sequitur* meaning a conclusion that does not follow from the facts. Hopefully, the jury could see through it. Larry, on the other hand, was subtle and appealed to logic and common sense. Rhetoric alone wouldn't cut it.

Almost by the time they left for lunch, it was time to go back. There seemed to be a different tone in the courtroom now. Even many of the spectators were looking in Jamie's direction. Some of the scowls were turning into smiles. Even the Stillwell strut was becoming more of a shuffle.

Brandon was indeed the first witness called by the plaintiffs. After he was sworn in, the weasel questioned him on direct. He testified to basically what the defense had anticipated. Gordie did a good job neutralizing his testimony and eliciting some evidence supporting Jamie's defense.

Cross-examining Brandon, Gordie asked, "Now, Mr. Stillwell, you were gone the whole week of June tenth, is that correct?"

"Yes."

"When you were gone, you said your office was closed. Who had access, if anyone?

"My son, Alden."

"Did anyone else have access?"

"No."

"When the vault time lock was set for the night, that is from seven p.m. until seven a.m. the next morning, could it be overridden or bypassed?"

"No."

"Do you ever know of a time when your vault time lock was overridden or bypassed?"

"I remember a dozen years ago or so we had trouble with the vault time lock and had to call the manufacturer. It seems we were provided with some kind of combination to gain access."

"You don't know if Jamie ever had that combination, do you?"

"No."

"Now, you testified that the cash drawers in the vault were accessed by a key; is that correct?"

"Yes."

"During business hours, were the drawers kept locked?"

"They were required to be locked at all times."

"How many keys did the drawers require in order to gain access?"

"Because they were the old style, they only required one."

"Who had keys to those drawers?"

"Rita Baker, Alden, and myself."

"Did Jamie have a key?"

"No."

"How did you find out that money was missing from the bank?"

"Alden told me."

"By the way, I assume you fired Jamie?"

"Yes."

"Who took his place as first vice president of SB&TCo.?"

"My son, Alden."

"No further questions."

"Very well, Mr. Kuenzi or Mr. Ross, if you have no redirect, you may call your next witness," the judge said.

It was only fitting that the weasel would examine Alden. Alden was sworn in and testified just as the defense anticipated. It was not as if the defense was clairvoyant. After all, they had Alden's statements from the discovery in the criminal case. It would be difficult to change his testimony now. It had already been etched in stone. Though tedious, Gordie thought, the weasel had done a decent job in examining Alden.

It was time for the midafternoon recess. When the court resumed, it was time for Gordie to demonstrate his cross-examination skills.

Gordie asked, "Mr. Stillwell, you're certain the vault door could not be accessed or overridden from seven p.m. on June 10 until seven a.m. on June 11, 1972, aren't you?"

"Yes."

"Is that because you personally tested the vault door to see if it worked?"

"Yes. Oftentimes, after the timer has been set and the door has been closed, I will try the combination just to see. I did test it that night, as I did every night Dad was gone. I didn't want anything to happen on my watch."

"If you and Rita Baker closed the vault door, and the timing device was working as you testified, and you were there at seven a.m. when the timer expired, how do you explain how Jamie or anyone else could have accessed it?"

"You'll have to ask Jamie. I don't know. The money was there when we closed the vault door, and it was gone when I got there at seven a.m. on the eleventh."

"Now, if your father had testified that the vault time lock couldn't be bypassed from seven p.m. until seven a.m., would his testimony have been correct?"

"Yes."

"To your knowledge, has the vault time lock ever been bypassed or overridden?"

"No, not to my knowledge."

"The one thousand dollars that you testified you found in Jamie's drawer, where was it when the police arrived?"

"After I confiscated it from Jamie's desk, I put it in my office for safekeeping until the police arrived."

"Was Jamie's office locked when you arrived that morning?"

"I assume so because I had to get Rita's key to unlock the door."

"And where was the key?"

"In Rita's desk drawer."

"Wasn't her desk drawer locked?"

"Yes, but I had a key."

"Was Jamie's office the only one you searched?"

"Yes, at that time. We searched the rest of the bank later."

"Aren't there three offices in a row perpendicular to the main vault? In other words, wasn't Jamie's office sandwiched between yours and Nan Morris'?"

"Nan Morris retired, but her husband, Gene, still does our appraisals. Annette Carrie took Nan's place, and she is now in Nan's office."

"Did your search Annette's office?

"No."

"Why not?"

"She had customers in with her, and we did not want to disturb them."

"After the police left, did you search Jamie's office more thoroughly?"

"Yes."

"Did you find any other cash or anything you thought suspicious?"

"No."

"Did anyone ever search your office?"

"No, why would they?"

"My question is, Did anyone ever search your office? Yes or no?"

"No."

"No further questions."

Judge Black asked the weasel if he had any redirect, and he answered "no."

The judge, looking at his watch, said that it was getting late in the day and that this would be a good place to break for the day. The jury was admonished once again not to talk about the case with anyone or among themselves and not read any newspaper accounts, watch television, or listen to any radio accounts of the case, and that they were to be in the jury room no later than seven forty-five a.m. the next morning.

Larry, Gordie, and Jamie met up with Bodean, who had been sitting in the hall reviewing case documents and going through the discovery provided in the criminal case and making notes. The defense team headed for the offices of Whittaker and Brownell, attorneys at law.

They critiqued the day's events, re-evaluated the jury, and prepared Jamie and Bodean for direct and cross-examination. They were careful, however, in not discussing Brandon's and Alden's testimony in front of Bodean because Bodean might be called as a witness. They could not and did not violate the sequestration rule and the judge's orders. They all had had a long day and each needed some quiet time alone.

They gathered at the law offices of Whittaker and Brownell at seven thirty a.m. on Tuesday, October 17, and then headed for the Routt County Courthouse and readied themselves for the second day of trial.

Everyone looked more relaxed, and the jury didn't seem to be afraid this day to smile at Larry, Gordie, and Jamie. The Stillwells, of course, had resumed their official seating in the front row of the courtroom on plaintiffs' side. Alden, having been excused as a witness, was among them. The gallery consisted of the regulars, for the most part, but in lesser numbers.

Judge Black called the court to order and, determining that both sides were ready to proceed, asked Kuenzi and Ross to call their next witness.

Plaintiffs then called Rita Baker. She took the usual oath to tell the truth and, in response to questions by the weasel, said that she was the head teller and part of the "dual control" team Alden had described. She had been working at the bank about the same length of time as Jamie. She was certain all the cash was accounted for the night the bank's main vault door was closed and locked and that it couldn't be breached or accessed until seven a.m. the next morning. She, Brandon, Alden, and Jamie all had the regular combination to the safe.

The weasel then had Rita Baker identify the bank closing checklist dated July 10, 1972, which bore exhibit P-4; the vault balancing journal for July 10, 1972, which bore exhibit number P-5; and the vault balancing journal for July 11, 1972, which bore exhibit number P-6. The weasel then offered the items in evidence. Gordie said the defense had no objection. The judge announced, "They're admitted." The weasel's request to have them circulated among the jurors was granted and the bailiff handed them to the first juror who examined them and passed them on each to the next. After all the jurors had examined them, they were returned to the bailiff who handed them to the judge.

The weasel said he had no further questions of the witness. Gordie thereupon cross-examined Rita Baker.

"Ms. Baker, you stated on direct that you, Brandon, Alden, and Jamie all had the regular combination to the main vault.

Now, my question is this, Did the regular combination when dialed allow any of the four of you access to the main vault between the hours of seven p.m. and seven a.m.?"

"No."

"And you are certain of that?"

"Absolutely."

"So, even with the knowledge of the regular combination, Jamie couldn't have possibly gained access to the cash in the bank's main vault from seven p.m. on July 10 to seven a.m. on July 11, 1972. Is that your testimony?"

"Yes, actually the timer was set to begin when we closed and locked the main vault door. That was usually before seven p.m. and normally at five thirty p.m. when the bank closed. That was the last thing we did before we left."

"Then let me understand this, Ms. Baker, that regardless of whatever time you and Alden may have done your count and closed and locked the main vault door, the timer was triggered, and the vault door could not be bypassed or overridden until seven a.m. the following morning. Is that your testimony?"

"Yes."

"When you arrived at the bank at seven fifteen a.m. on July 11, 1972, who, if anyone, was present?"

"Alden Stillwell."

"Who dialed the combination and opened the door of the main vault that morning?"

"Alden said he did."

"Did Alden tell you that he had some of the so-called missing money?"

"Yes, he told me that. He said had found one thousand dollars in Jamie's desk."

"Did you see the one thousand dollars?"

"No, not until after the police arrived."

"Did you assist in the search of the bank for the rest of the missing thirty thousand dollars?"

"Yes, myself and the other employees."

"Did you search or see anyone else search Alden's office?"

"No."

"Did you see the police search Jamie's car?"

"Yes."

"Did you ever see the police or anyone else search Alden's car?"

"No."

"What happened to all of Jamie's personal belongings that were left in his office, if you know?"

"Alden had me box them all up and bring them to him."

"Was Jamie's door then left unlocked?"

"Yes."

"By the way, Ms. Baker, who's office was the closest to the main vault?

"Alden Stillwell's."

"No further questions."

The weasel was asked if he had any redirect. He had none.

RD then called Officer Clinton Coleman to the stand. After he was sworn to tell the truth, he testified that he responded to Alden Stillwell's call to SB&T Co. on July 11, 1972 at eight a.m. He and three other officers, Michael Heath, Lloyd Kinsey, and Gary Boyle, placed Jamie Curtis Cooper under arrest for felony theft. Alden Stillwell came into Mr. Cooper's office while Mr. Cooper was being arrested and threw a bundle of twenty fifty-dollar bills onto Jamie's desk, breaking the strap and scattering the bills. Plaintiffs' exhibit P-10, which was now in a plastic evidence bag, contained the strap and the bills that were given to him by Mr. Stillwell.

The strap was then offered in evidence. Larry then asked if he could question the witness with regard to the proffered exhibit. The request was granted, and he asked, "Officer Coleman, was the strap handed to you by Jamie Cooper?"

"No, I received it from Alden Stillwell."

"Was the strap in Jamie Cooper's office when you and the other officers arrived at the bank?"

"No. Alden Stillwell brought the strap or, I call it a 'band,' and bills in after we arrived."

"Your Honor, we object to the introduction of plaintiffs' exhibit P-10 on the grounds that it is irrelevant, immaterial, and incompetent. There is no nexus to Mr. Cooper. There is a nexus to Alden Stillwell, but not to Mr. Cooper."

"Overruled. Ladies and gentlemen of the jury, you are instructed that the evidence is offered only to show that it was given to the officers at the time of the arrest by Alden Stillwell, not that it was in the possession of Mr. Cooper. Anything else, Mr. Kuenzi?"

"No, Your Honor, we have no other questions of Officer Coleman."

"Mr. Whittaker, before your cross-examination, let's take a midmorning break. Be back in fifteen minutes." The usual admonition was given to the jury.

After the break, Larry began his cross-examination of Officer Coleman.

"Officer Coleman, did you or your fellow officers, if you know, take any money from Jamie Cooper?"

"We took some currency from his wallet, as I recall, thirty-eight dollars. We also took some change he had in his pants pocket. Other than that, no."

"Did you have occasion to search Mr. Cooper's vehicle that was parked in the employee section of the bank parking lot?"

"Yes. Officer Michael Heath was in charge of that."

"To your knowledge, did Officer Heath or anyone find any currency or any items that would tie Mr. Cooper to the theft from the bank?"

"Not to my knowledge."

"Did you or any of the officers ever search Alden Stillwell's vehicle or office?"

"No, we didn't."

"Did you or any other officer search any other employee's vehicle?"

"No."

"How do you know that the one thousand dollars was found in Jamie Cooper's office?"

"Because Alden Stillwell told us it was."

"But you didn't see the money in Mr. Cooper's office until it was brought in there by Alden Stillwell, is that your testimony?"

"Yes."

"No further cross, Your Honor."

"Any redirect Mr. Kuenzi?"

"No, Your Honor."

"Call your next witness."

"Judge, may we have a moment?"

"Yes, but just a moment."

The plaintiffs' team then huddled getting ready for the next play. In a surprise move, RD announced they "rested" their case-in-chief.

"Your Honor, Gordie said, "we have a motion to make outside the ears of the jury."

"Very well. Ladies and gentlemen, the bailiff will escort you to the jury room while the court takes up a matter out of your presence."

The jury was excused, and Gordie moved for a directed verdict in favor of the defendant on the grounds that the quality and quantum of evidence viewed in the light most favorable to the plaintiffs was not sufficient to allow the case to be placed in the hands of the jury. "Because of the insufficiency of the evidence and the groundless nature thereof being evinced by the plaintiffs' case-in-chief," Gordie said, "a judgment should be entered in favor of the defendant on defendant's counterclaim."

Without asking counsel for the plaintiffs to respond, Judge Black said, "Denied." He cited as rationale the testimony of Alden Stillwell to the effect that money was missing and that $1,000 had been recovered from the defendant's desk. That raised an inference that supports plaintiffs' claim and, depending on defendant's evidence, would be a credibility issue and that was for the jury to decide. The motion for directed verdict on the counterclaim was denied on the same basis.

Judge Black announced that he had some other pressing court matters that he had to attend to by telephone and asked if counsel had any objection to releasing the jury until one thirty p.m. That would give the defense time to line up their witnesses. Neither side objected. The bailiff was instructed to so inform the jurors, which he did.

Back at one thirty p.m., the defense was ready to call their first witness: Jamie Cooper. With the criminal case looming, Larry and Gordie were nervous about having Jamie testify. If the strategy of going forward with the civil trial backfired, it would be their fault.

Jamie lived up to their expectations and beyond. Afterward, they would award him a perfect ten. The young women on the jury were particularly attentive, especially Kelsey Bailey, the physical therapist, and Hannah Westen, the high school women's basketball and track coach. Jamie was called to the stand and, after being sworn to tell the truth, was called upon to give the performance of his life—at least up to that point.

When asked about the Las Vegas connection, Jamie testified he was not a gambler. He stated that he indeed made the seven telephone calls in June and the five telephone calls in July to Las Vegas. He also stated that he traveled to Las Vegas to pay off the chit posted at Tobiasis Casino in Las Vegas in the name of Patty Cooper in the amount of $1,200.

Jamie testified as to the purposes of the dozen telephone calls and the trip to Las Vegas and noted from whom he had obtained the $1,200 and travel expenses. He said the airline tickets referred to were paid by credit card by his father, G. Forrest Cooper.

At that point, Larry handed a copy of the chit to Jamie, as well as the receipt from Tomahawk Café, and the United Airlines purchase receipt to Forrest Cooper for Jamie and Jennie Cooper; all of which were offered and admitted in evidence. The defendant's request that these exhibits be circulated among the jurors was granted.

Larry announced he had no further questions of the witness. It was a relief when the weasel rose to cross-examine Jamie. RD would have been much more formidable. The Stillwells thought they picked the right person to conduct the punishing cross-examination; the *coup de grace* needed for a plaintiffs' victory.

Many of the weasel's questions were caustic, demeaning, and condescending. All of Larry's "assuming facts not in evidence" objections were sustained. The weasel was argumentative and succeeded only in reinforcing Jamie's position and in alienating the jury. Several times Larry was on the verge of asking for a mistrial, but felt that Judge Black's admonitions to the weasel and the jurors' awareness were more than ample. Gordie, whispering in Larry's ear, asked, "Do we have to split our fees with the weasel? He's doing such a good job for our side."

Redirect was not necessary; the weasel had already done the defense's job for them. "No redirect," Larry said without being asked.

The weasel had taken so long it was time for the midafternoon break. Judge Black announced that the jury would reconvene at three fifteen p.m.

As the jury filed out of the box, none looked at the plaintiffs table and noticeably avoided eye contact with the gallery of Stillwells. Newfound confidence was swelling as the trial progressed.

"It's strange," Larry told Gordie and Jamie, "how cases either come together or fall apart during trial. This one is coming together."

The court reconvened at three fifteen p.m. Larry called G. Forrest Cooper to the stand. He testified about all the trouble his niece, Patty, was having over some gambling debts and that his brother had asked him to help out financially. His health prevented him from travel. He conscripted his son, Jamie, to deliver the $1,200 to Tobiasis to stave off a civil suit and criminal prosecution. He had provided the funds he had saved from the sale of eggs, chickens, and beef to Jamie and Jennie. He told the jury how sorry he was that he got his son in such trouble.

As hard as he tried, RD was unable to shake the patriarch of the Cooper clan. Not wanting to bury the plaintiffs completely, RD announced he had "no further questions" and tried to mask his displeasure as he retreated to his seat.

Jennie was the next defense witness. She corroborated everything that her husband and father-in-law had testified. Since it would have been like cross-examining Mother Teresa, RD and the weasel opted not to cross-examine her.

Betty Skyler from Skyler Cleaning Service was called as Jamie's next witness. She reaffirmed her and Ron's appearance at the bank from six p.m. to seven p.m. on July 10, 1972, Jamie's presence when they arrived and his departure at six fifteen p.m., their unlocking the door for Jamie and their letting him out, and the fact that the vault door was closed when they arrived. She also testified that they cleaned Jamie's office and noticed no cash or anything out of the ordinary, and when Jamie left, he didn't carry anything out, because if he had, they would have noticed it.

The plaintiffs' team chose not to cross-examine.

Ursula Russell was the defendant's next witness. She testified that she was the owner of Mountain States Abstract and Title Company of Steamboat. Her office was directly across from SB&T Co.; her desk was facing the front window of the building. She arrived at work at six a.m. on July 10, 1972, and observed Jamie drive into the lot of SB&T Co. at approximately six thirty a.m. She watched him park and walk in the direction of the Tomahawk Café. It was the second Tuesday of the month, and she knew he was headed for the chamber meeting that started at six thirty a.m. as she was also a member but could not be there that Tuesday because of a heavy work schedule. She and Jamie were active together in the chamber, and Jamie was its president-elect. At six forty-five a.m. she saw Alden Stillwell drive up and park in the bank parking lot and go inside. She thought that strange because he usually didn't arrive until seven thirty. The night before, she left work at six thirty, and the only vehicle she noticed in the bank's parking lot was the Skyler Cleaning Service van.

RD got nowhere with cross-examination and, being the good trial lawyer he was, just sat down.

Gordie presented the next two witnesses, Jackie Stiles and Charlie Blankenship. Jackie was a waitress at the Tomahawk Café. She confirmed that Jamie was at the chamber meeting from six thirty a.m. until seven fifty-five a.m. on July 11, 1972. She said, "I know because I served him and took his five dollars and fifty cents." Charlie, current president of the chamber, said that he met with Jamie at six thirty a.m. at the Tomahawk Café and sat with him at the meeting until seven fifty-five a.m. on July 11, 1972.

The plaintiffs' team chose not to cross-examine.

The defense had not arranged for Dustin Davies or Matthew Thomas Cooper to testify in the civil trial. Brandon, Alden, and Rita, for all intents and purposes, had been their witnesses, so they didn't need to call them in the defendant's case-in-chief. So why not rest their case-in-chief, which they did. The plaintiffs had no rebuttal, so the case was closed. The defense said they had a motion to make outside the ears of the jury, and the plaintiffs said they had one as well.

Both sides agreed to close the case. With the usual admonitions and instructions, the jury was excused until Wednesday to report at seven thirty a.m. in the jury room, with instruction and final arguments to commence at eight a.m.

Even though it was after five p.m., Judge Black pressed on.

The attorneys made their obligatory motion for directed verdict: the defense on plaintiffs' claim and the plaintiffs on the defendant's counterclaim. Judge Black denied both motions, and all retreated to his chambers. After shedding coats and robe, loosening ties, rolling up sleeves, and filling water glasses, all embarked upon the usual laborious journey of preparing the jury instructions.

In keeping with the way the trial had progressed thus far, it was not surprising, however, that there were few arguments over the instructions. When finalized, there were over twenty-three in number, ranging from the respective parties' claims and defenses to burden of proof to definitions. There were two verdict forms with each having two options. One verdict form was on the plaintiffs' claim with boxes to check for whose favor they found, either for the plaintiffs or for the defendant. The second was on the defendant's counterclaim, again with boxes to check for whose favor they found.

It was almost seven p.m. when the defense team exited the courthouse. Tired but buoyed, they looked forward to the morrow.

━━━━━━━━━━━━━━

Wednesday, October 18, the third day of trial, was a day for instructions and final arguments. The attorneys and their clients were seated, ready for final arguments with instructions appropriately marked and at the ready. Jamie had remarked as they waited for Judge Black that they should probably tip the weasel for his contribution to the anticipated outcome of the case. Larry cautioned Jamie not to be overconfident. "Remember the Alamo," Gordie added, referring to the motions hearing.

The usual spectators were in attendance. Not too much frivolity this day. Concern was written across the faces of everyone except the weasel. He was oblivious to the fact that there was a real possibility that the jury would rule in favor of Jamie and that he would be the scapegoat.

Judge Black read the instructions to the jury and the verdict forms. He gave them instructions on how to complete the verdict forms. He said they would be given the written instructions and the exhibits to take with them to the jury room, where they would elect a foreman. He said only the strap or band would be sent back with them and not the currency. If they wanted to look at the currency, the bailiff would bring it in, and it could be inspected in the bailiff's presence. It wasn't as if they weren't trusted; it was just the way certain evidence such as money was handled.

The plaintiffs had already cleared it through Judge Black that they would divide final argument. The weasel would give the opening, and RD would give the closing.

The weasel, rocking the podium back and forth, began, "Thank you, ladies and gentlemen, for your time and service. We have here a case of a banker gone wild with a gambling addiction and greed. Thirty thousand dollars is a lot of money, especially if it is other people's money. Handling money every day has a desensitizing effect. If Mr. Cooper didn't care about his own self-respect, he should have cared about the effect his actions would have on his family, friends, employer, and the poor depositors who entrusted him and the bank with their hard-earned money.

"The evidence shows here that Alden Stillwell discovered that thirty thousand dollars was missing from a cash drawer in the main vault and searching Mr. Cooper's office found one thousand of it..."

Gordie interposed an objection on the grounds that there was no evidence that the $1,000 was part of the missing money and that the weasel was assuming a fact not in evidence. The judge overruled the objection saying, "This is a final argument, and I will give counsel some leeway in recounting the evidence. The jury will determine whether or not Mr. Ross's recollection is correct."

The weasel continued, "Mr. Cooper was caught with his hand in the cookie jar. If it weren't for Alden Stillwell finding the one thousand in Mr. Cooper's desk and Officer Coleman uncovering the Las Vegas connection, we wouldn't be here. Fortunately, a leopard can't hide its spots—at least not for very long.

"Mr. Cooper had opportunity and motive for taking the money. Even Mr. Cooper can't argue that the money belongs to him or that he had it coming or that he took it by mistake. He has not asserted any of those three excuses. If he did, I didn't hear it, and I've sat here throughout this whole trial.

"Of course Mr. Cooper is going to come into court and say he didn't take the money. I would have thought more of him, and so would you, ladies and gentlemen, if he had come into court like a man and admitted his mistake. I saw no remorse for what he's done to those who trusted him. He's coming in here with hat in hand, begging you to believe him and disbelieve everyone else and to rule in his favor because he's the president-elect of the chamber of commerce. All I can say is the chamber has been duped like the Steamboat Bank and Trust Co. has been duped and like he would like to have you duped. Don't be fooled by that all-American façade. Beware of wolves dressed in sheep's clothing.

"Sympathy should not be a factor in your decision. All of us feel sorry for Mr. Cooper. A promising banking career out the window. The adverse spinoff effect on his family. And the tarnishing of the Cooper reputation and name. Judge the case on its merits and not on emotion. And, if you do that, you will find that you have no choice but to rule in the plaintiffs' favor on their claims and against the defendant on his counterclaim."

"Thank you, Mr. Ross, and now for the defendant's final argument," Judge Black said.

Gordie knew the plaintiffs would have two cracks at final argument on opening and on closing. That was because they carried the burden of proof, at least on their claim. The defendant would be given only one chance, and it had better be good. The pressure was on.

"Ladies and gentlemen, on behalf of my co-council Larry Whitaker, the defendant, Jamie Cooper, and myself, I would like to thank you for your taking time to sit as jurors in this case. Jury duty is not easy, and I would rather be in my role than yours, especially when the case is handed over to you for the all-important verdict.

"Mr. Ross asked that you not be guided by sympathy or emotion, and yet he made an emotional appeal—one that was not based on the evidence presented. To begin with, it is always difficult to prove a negative. How do you prove you didn't do what you've been accused of doing? Normally, all you can say is you didn't do it. Then you are judged on the basis of the likelihood that you did or didn't do it. Jamie has told you under oath that he didn't do it. What's the likelihood that he did or didn't do it based on what you learned in this trial?

"Mr. Ross used the cookie jar analogy, one that is used in virtually every case of this kind. If there are cookies missing, then let's trace the cookie trail in this case. Let's allocate a cookie for every piece of the puzzle dealing with the disappearance of the thirty thousand dollars.

"By everyone's account, all the money was accounted for when the vault door was closed and locked, triggering the running of the vault time lock clock. It couldn't be opened even with a combination until the time on the clock expired, and that was at seven a.m. the following morning. The evidence by all was to the effect that the vault time lock couldn't be bypassed or overridden while the timer was running.

"I'm going to use this flip chart and I'm going to list all the categories and assign a cookie under either Jamie's column or Alden's column to whichever it applies. I will use a black circular sticker with a sad face to represent the cookie."

With that, Gordie asked each question in order and then placed a cookie under whichever column the answer applied.

Who was there when the time lock expired?

Who opened the vault door?

Who was there when Rita arrived at seven fifteen a.m.?

Who was part of the "dual control team" that set the time lock after work the night before?

Who had access to the cash drawers?

Who unlocked the cash drawers?

Who claimed to discover the missing money?

Who claimed he found $1,000 in Jamie's office?

Who was the only person, other than Brandon, who had access to Brandon's office and could have found some secret combination, if any, to override or bypass the vault time lock?

Who had the $1,000 in his possession when the police arrived?

Whose office was not searched?

Whose desk was not searched?

Whose vehicle was not searched?

Whose person was not searched?

Who searched Jamie's office?

Who claimed Jamie stole the money?

Who called the police and had Jamie arrested?

Who is the only one who had a fifteen-minute window to have taken the $30,000?

Who stood to gain the most by Jamie's arrest?

Who replaced Jamie as the bank's first vice president?

"If my addition is correct, that's twenty cookies that were taken from Mr. Ross's imaginary cookie jar. Guess who took all twenty of them? Guess who didn't take any? Mr. Ross is correct in one respect; the thief who stole the cookies is likely the thief who stole the thirty thousand dollars, but that was not Jamie.

"The plaintiffs introduced a receipt in evidence issued to Jamie showing payment of a chit in the amount of twelve hundred dollars to Tobiasis Casino in Las Vegas. But they told you only part of the story—a misleading one at that. It took the defense to produce the rest of the story. The actual chit Jamie redeemed was incurred by Jamie's cousin, Patty. The gambling was Patty's, not Jamie's. If they were fair and honest, the plaintiffs would have told you that the Las Vegas connection, as Mr.

Ross terms it, is only a figment of his imagination. It never existed, and it doesn't exist. Try as they might, there are no dots to connect—at least not to Jamie.

"It is difficult to defend a case like this. As I said, 'How do you prove a negative?' I only hope Mr. Whittaker and I effectively communicated Jamie's lack of culpability in seeking justice for him. But our duties are over, and we're placing Jamie's fate in your hands to seek and administer justice. In doing so, we hope you rule in his favor on the plaintiffs' claim for relief because the plaintiffs have wholly failed to meet their burden of proof by a preponderance of the evidence. We also hope you rule in defendant's favor on the counterclaim because he has met his burden. Thank you."

"The court will take a short midmorning break to allow the jury to stretch. The court is in recess for fifteen minutes," said Judge Black.

When the jury came back, RD was standing at the podium ready for plaintiffs' closing argument.

"Ladies and gentlemen, I too thank you for your service and attention. I will be brief. Mr. Ross has already outlined the evidence, but there are a few impressions I need to clarify in Mr. Brownell's recollection of the facts and his interpretation thereof.

"First, despite whether Mr. Cooper paid for Cousin Patty's gambling debts or his own is immaterial. He used cash to redeem the one chit, and we don't know how many others ..."

"Objection, Your Honor," Gordie interposed, "that calls for speculation. There's no evidence that there were other chits."

"Overruled. Mr. Kuenzi, you may proceed."

"Regardless, we do know that all the expenses of that trip were paid by cash. It is the plaintiffs' contention that that money belonged to the bank and was taken without authorization.

"Second, Mr. Brownell in his eloquent illustration connecting the cookies forgot about a misplaced cookie, a cookie larger than all the rest. That jumbo cookie, the dot that connects Mr. Cooper, is the fact that one thousand of the missing thirty thousand was found in his locked office in a drawer in his desk. I refer your attention to the evidence consisting of the Federal Reserve band and the twenty fifty-dollar bills. That is the 'smoking gun' in this case.

"Third, and final, the defendant wants you to believe that it was Alden Stillwell who was responsible for taking the thirty thousand dollars. My only question to you is this: Why would Alden take the money? It would be like stealing from himself, since he was the sole heir of his father's estate."

"Objection, Your Honor." Gordie was livid. "There is absolutely no evidence that Alden was the sole heir. We object on the grounds that Mr. Kuenzi is assuming a fact not in evidence."

"Sustained. The jury will be instructed to disregard the 'sole heir' reference. Mr. Kuenzi, refrain from any such further references."

"I apologize. Thank you, Your Honor. Ladies and gentlemen, I appeal to your logic and not your emotions in asking you to return a verdict in favor of the plaintiffs as to both plaintiffs' claim and defendant's counterclaim. We too ask that you dispense justice. Justice is marking a simple x in the box opposite plaintiffs in both verdict forms. Thank you."

"Thank you, Mr. Kuenzi," the judge said. "Ladies and gentlemen of the jury, the bailiff will now escort you to the jury room along with the written jury instructions and exhibits. Lunch will be waiting for you. You will elect a foreman and deliberate. If you need anything, the bailiff, Ron Scott, will be right outside your door. Knock, and he will come to your service. After you have reached a verdict, you will be brought back into the courtroom to announce your verdict. Now go and remember the admonitions I have previously given you. The rest of you please remain standing until the jury has left the courtroom."

The jury left. The judge asked that the attorneys let his clerk know where they could be reached in the event the jury had a question or were ready to return a verdict. The judge left for his chambers. The defense team gathered and walked the half block to the offices of Whittaker and Brownell, attorneys at law.

Relaxed, enjoying Verna's hot spaghetti and meatballs, French bread, tossed greens with vinaigrette, and assorted beverages, the defense team ate like wild wolves.

"I'm glad you've regained your usual voracious appetites," Verna said. "For a while, I thought I would be fired as the chief cook."

The defense replayed the mental trial tape, recounting the key testimony mainly for Bodean's benefit since the exclusion of witness rule kept him out of the courtroom. They also did it for their own benefit because they wanted to bask in the sunshine of their anticipated victory.

Jamie complemented and thanked them all for the superb job of defending him in the civil trial. He asked if any of them would in retrospect have done anything differently. After careful reflection, they said, "No, not a thing!" They also complemented him on his great job on the witness stand.

Again, he said, "It's easy when you're telling the truth."

Bodean said the defense team had been working together too long; they were beginning to think alike. They all felt Jamie would prevail on the main claim, but that the counterclaim was in jeopardy. Larry said they had included it more for the psychological effect than anything. He said he felt the plaintiffs' claims were frivolous, but he didn't think the jury would buy it. Gordie said he thought juries liked compromise verdicts.

"They liked to give something to each side."

"I would certainly trade losing the counterclaim for winning the main claim," Larry said. They all agreed.

With regard to how long the jury would be out, the defense team was not in agreement. Jamie said he didn't want to speculate. Bodean said since he did not hear the testimony and could only go on what they had told him, maybe two hours. Gordie fudged and said between one and a half and two and one half hours. Larry guessed three. When Verna was asked to speculate, she wrote five different numbers on separate pieces of paper, turned them over and picked one. It was four.

If the jury went back to the jury room at twelve thirty, had lunch until one thirty, went over jury instructions until two, and deliberated for four hours, they would come back with a verdict around six thirty. "If they stall long enough, they will get a free dinner at one of the restaurants, usually the Crazy Cat down in the next block," Gordie said. "When my wife had jury duty, that's where they were taken."

Because they didn't know when the jury would return, they all thought they should stick around. Larry and Gordie went to their respective offices to process their mail and do work that had piled up in their absence. Bodean ran an errand. Jamie called his wife and browsed in the firm's law library.

The hours were going by slowly, and Verna was kept busy answering "Have you heard anything yet?" When the clock on the town hall chimed five, five thirty, and then six, the defense team was beginning to feel the "jitters," as Bodean would say. Bodean ran over to the courthouse and confirmed that the jury had been taken to dinner at the Crazy Cat. They had left about six fifteen. The defense team went to the Tomahawk Café, returning to the office about seven fifteen. About eight thirty, they received a telephone call from the bailiff announcing that the jury had reached a verdict and that the judge wanted them ASAP.

The defense team arrived first. RD and the weasel, J. Henry Ross, arrived next with Brandon, Alden, and the rest of the Stillwells close behind. Apparently, the plaintiffs had a different read on the outcome of the trial; they were all gloating. The defense team was now rethinking their strategy and wondering what they should have done differently. They were in an anomalous situation. Panic was setting in, and Larry tried to dispel it. "I see the weasel is his usual inimitable self," he said to Jamie and Gordie.

"You knock him down, and he keeps getting up asking for more," Gordie said.

"I wonder how he will feel after the verdict is read," Jamie quipped.

Less than half of the usual onlookers showed up. Hardly a fitting tribute for the story of the year. *The vultures must have found other prey,* Gordie thought. Just then, the jury came in escorted by the bailiff. Verdict forms were in the hands of Sean Castles. "I thought for sure Victor Rougle would have been the foreman," Larry whispered to Jamie.

"Me too," he whispered back.

Judge Black entered and called the court to order. "You may be seated. Mr. Foreman, have you reached a verdict?"

"We have, Your Honor," Mr. Castles said.

"Please hand the forms to the bailiff." Sean Castles complied, and the bailiff approached the bench and handed them to the judge.

Judge Black looked at the first verdict form and then the second, nodding in apparent agreement. He then read the verdict forms aloud. "We the jury duly impaneled and sworn in the above entitled cause as to plaintiffs' claim for relief do find for...defendant." Those in the courtroom let out a collective "Ooh." Turning to the second verdict form, he read, "We, the jury, duly impaneled and sworn in the above entitle cause as to defendant's counterclaim do find for...plaintiffs." Not much reaction.

"Was and are these your verdicts, Mr. Foreman?"

"They are, Your Honor."

"So say all you, ladies and gentlemen of the jury."

"We do," they all responded.

"Do you wish the jury polled?"

RD said, "Yes, Your Honor. Plaintiffs do."

Judge Black then asked each of the jurors, "Was and are these your verdicts?" Each responded in the affirmative. When Kelsey Bailey and Hannah Westen responded, both looked and smiled at Jamie.

"We have a motion to make outside the ears of the jury," RD said.

"Ladies and gentlemen, we have a matter to take up outside your presence. We thank you for your valuable service. You can wait in the hall or leave if you wish. You can say as much or as little as you want to the attorneys or nothing at all. Should they or anyone criticize you for your verdict, please report it to me. Again, thank you. You are excused."

As the jurors filed out, all made eye contact with Jamie. RD made a motion for a directed verdict *non obstante veredicto,* meaning a judgment in plaintiffs' favor, notwithstanding the jury's verdict as to the plaintiffs' claim. Larry made the same motion with respect to the defendant's counterclaim. Both motions were denied on the grounds that the jury had spoken and there was sufficient evidence, if believed, to support the verdicts.

This was not the place to celebrate, but the defense team having been joined by Bodean and Verna, who they didn't know were in the courtroom, exchanged handshakes, hugs, and whispers of congratulations. "I knew it," they said, and to Jamie, "You deserved it," and "We've been praying for you."

RD came over and shook everyone's hand, including Jamie's. When he shook Larry's hand, it was with the secret Sigma Chi handshake. No enemies we. The weasel did not join in the congratulatory ceremony, but instead went to where the Stillwells were standing and commiserated with them in somber resignation over the incredulous verdict.

The jurors all were in waiting. They greeted Jamie with handshakes and smiles, several of the ladies with hugs. They said they had reached a verdict on the plaintiffs' claim on the very first vote but had trouble reaching a decision with respect to defendant's counterclaim because of the way the instructions were worded.

RD smiled, shook hands with, and thanked the jurors. None of the others from the plaintiffs' table or side of the courtroom did. Judge Black came out into the hall after shedding his robe and after visiting briefly with everyone, rode off into the sunset. His part in the ordeal had been fulfilled.

When they returned to the offices of Whittaker and Brownell, attorneys at law, the conference room had been decorated with crepe paper and had the trappings of a New Year's party. A large cake with "Congratulations, Jamie" was in the middle of the table along with plastic plates, plastic spoons and forks, napkins, plastic glasses, several bottles of bubbly in ice buckets, and a large punch bowl. There were two trays of cold cuts and assorted cheeses, diced fruit, and breads and crackers of all sizes, shapes, and kinds.

The defense team was greeted by relatives, friends, and well-wishers. Jennie, Max, and Collette were the first to meet the victorious defendant. Next were his mom and dad, Forrest and Bessie. Among the five hanging, hugging, and holding, the others had to fight just to touch him. Many of Jamie's church families were there, along with the pastor, Reverend Joseph Langley. There were many chamber friends also, as well as workout friends, skiing friends, bank customers, childhood friends, and even Corbin Sweeney, the newspaper editor.

The law offices were filled beyond capacity. "I just hope the fire department doesn't take a head count," Bodean was heard to say.

Larry whispered to Verna, "Thank you for planning this party, but didn't you take a calculated risk? How did you know Jamie was going to prevail?"

"I just did." With her hands pressed together in prayerful pose and while looking heavenward, she said, "Didn't we?"

In the next day's edition of the newspaper was a front-page article with a headline that read, "Local Boy Makes Good." Although the defense didn't notice a reporter present, all twenty of the cookie points Gordie made in his final argument, together with the sad-faced cookies were printed in graphic form. The paper quoted him extensively, including where the cookie trail led. The editorial with the caption "The Cream Always Rises to the Top," was the only one the Coopers would clip out and save.

Just as Judge Cole Black rode off into the sunset, so did the civil trial phase of the ordeal.

MY FAIR LADY

Thanksgiving at the Cooper Ranch was always a memorable time, this year especially. The defense team and their families were now adopted members of the Cooper Family. Reverend Joseph Langley, who was there with his wife, Ruth, son, Colby, and daughter, Michelle, said the grace while all joined hands. There were two tables, and there was a unity that not even the ordeal could break. Even Jennie's parents, Dr. Millard and Fran Carpenter, were there to join in this special day of thanksgiving.

Christmas 1972, was a special one in the Cooper household. The chamber gala Christmas celebration was held in the banquet room of the Broken-Bow Hotel, an old but elegant hotel in Steamboat, on Friday, December 29, 1972. It was at this event that the outgoing president would turn the presidential reins over to president-elect Jamie Cooper.

For a Christmas present, Larry's wife, Bonnie, had given Jennie what Bonnie called for lack of a better description, a French, sea-blue satin party dress, which the Whittakers had brought back from their Paris trip. Bonnie had obtained Jennie's size before leaving for Paris, hoping to find just such a dress. With Jennie in it, Bonnie thought, it would be even more stunning.

Jennie had just turned thirty-four in September, but she had the looks and shape of a twenty-four-year-old. She had penetrating blue eyes about the color of the dress, Bonnie thought. She had a peach complexion and facial features of a China doll. Her hair was a natural golden blonde, reflecting the Nordic side of the family. White perfect teeth were always on display, even during these difficult times. Her shoulders straight, she graced the streets of Steamboat and made heads turn in the grocery stores.

Jennie, much to her embarrassment, was described by her parents as a "perfect child," and they were not talking about the outside; they were talking about the inside. An accomplished piano player, she had taken classical piano lessons since she was five years of age.

She was an honor student in high school as well as in college. She had spent a semester abroad when she was a junior in college and loved to travel. She spoke French and Spanish fluently and a little German. She had been a cheerleader and captain both her senior year in high school as well as college. She also ran track in both high school and college.

Jennie and Jamie had been in love as long as they could remember. Described as the perfect couple, they treated each other with the utmost respect and love that each needed and deserved. They were very family-oriented, and their adult lives were centered around Max and Collette. All four grandparents

wyer's ook deal

$30,000, as told from the viewpoint of his son, Max.

In "Justice Denied," good vs. evil is a theme, and characters seek guidance through prayer, but otherwise the Christian influence is not overt, and the plot compares to other legal dramas in which fate can be flipped by a convincing argument or piece of circumstantial evidence.

Ultimately, justice is an attainable goal, Multz said, but the legal road there is filled with twists and turns, and not everyone gets timely or full justice.

That "championing the cause of the underdog, of the innocent," is what compelled Multz through his legal career and now provides plot complications.

"I've always had a feeling that I needed to turn windmills right side up, and I was offended by injustice," Multz said.

Multz's second novel, "It's You Who I see," is expected to be released in mid-2011.

GRETEL DAUGHERTY/The Daily Sentinel

"JUSTICE DENIED" by Carroll Multz will be released Nov. 30, but is now available at www.tatepublishing.com for $23.99.

BOO

Own career fodder for GJ l
'Justice Denied,' first of five

By LAURENA MAYNE DAVIS
Laurena.Davis@gjsentinel.com

Carroll Multz didn't have to look far for inspiration for his first novel, "Justice Denied." He had only to reflect on his own storied career.

Multz, a retired Grand Junction trial attorney, has been a district attorney and adjunct professor, and was one of the drafters of the Colorado Criminal Code. In 1992, he was appointed by President George H.W. Bush to chair the Upper Colorado River Commission.

His successful defense of Roberta Young, who was charged with shooting and killing her husband after enduring a decade of brutal abuse, brought "battered woman syndrome" into national awareness.

In 1969, he argued a case before the U.S. Supreme Court.

But not all of Multz's endeavors had the same gravitas.

After meeting the sister of teen idol Troy Donahue at a social event in Flagstaff, Ariz., a young Multz was hired to be a stunt horse rider for "A Distant Trumpet," the 1964 Western that Donahue was filming in the Painted Desert nearby.

That one brief flirtation with Hollywood aside, the Montana-born Multz made a 40-year career in the courtroom. And now those courtroom "war stories" and expanded classroom lessons fill the pages of novels.

"Justice Denied" is the first of five suspenseful legal novels Multz has been contracted to write for Tate Publishing & Enterprises, a Christian-based imprint in which authors invest in publication.

The transition from attorney

"JUSTICE DENIED"
by Carroll Multz
officially will be
released Nov. 30 but
is now available at
www.tatepublishing.
com for $23.99.

---

and teacher to author was a
less one, Multz said, describi
his fiction as "textbooks, dis
guised as novels."

"I'm really interested in tr
ing judges, lawyers, law stud
and my students," said Mult
teaches business law and me
law at Mesa State College. "I
a lot of satisfaction out of do
that. Originally, I started out
guess, feeling a duty, a payba
for some very gifted professo
had."

Multz also has authored o
co-authored eight nonfiction
books and technical manual
published several articles in
journals.

"Justice Denied" is set in
Steamboat Springs, a town M
knows well from his two ter
district attorney for the 14th
cial District, which covers G
Moffat and Routt counties. T
plot revolves around the fra
of upright bank official Jam
Cooper, charged with embez

were very much a part of their lives as well, and with Jennie's parents having moved to Florida, there was a longing that she felt every day. Jamie's parents had been almost as much a part of her life as her biological parents, having known her as long as she had known Jamie. Forrest and Bessie loved Jennie as much as she loved them.

Things had been difficult since Jamie had been arrested. Jennie had been shunned by many she thought were her friends but not as it turned out by what Jamie called her *real* friends. She had resigned from several boards and organizations because she felt ostracized by some and barely tolerated by others. She still was active in her Bible study group and church activities, and she believed she "couldn't have made it without their love, prayers, support, and understanding." She and Jamie also had started having financial problems because he had been the sole provider. Both sets of parents had been helping, and Jamie was receiving some income by working at the Cooper Ranch.

The spinoff of the ordeal also was having a deleterious effect on Max and Collette. Although they were not whiners, Collette was heard to cry, and that hurt worse than anything. Max and Collette were treated by some of their classmates and a few teachers as if they "had leprosy," the way Max had described it. Max was able to express his feelings and emotions. Collette, on the other hand, was keeping it inside and refused to talk about it.

Collette became so withdrawn that it was not long before she was under the care of a child psychologist. She was diagnosed as agoraphobic (fear of being in public places), anhedonic (unable to express pleasure), and psychotic (losing contact with reality). No one, except Collette, would know how cruel her classmates had been.

The verdict in favor of Jamie in the civil jury trial had eased the situation somewhat, but with the shadow of the criminal jury trial looming over them; both children were still experiencing anxiety and depression.

Whether the district attorney would dismiss the criminal case was something they could only pray for. With Chief Hammerville, the driving force in his personal quest for revenge, the DA, they speculated, might be more determined than ever to obtain a conviction. So far, the prosecution was not bending. For now, the Coopers must live their lives as if the ordeal were nothing more than a bad dream.

It was five p.m. on that cold wintery December Friday. It had been snowing all day, and the crystal flakes had frozen as they fell, reminding Max and Collette of the designs that they had cut out of folded white paper in school. Snow deep and piled above the fence, it hid even the bushes. Jamie had shoveled out the driveway leading to the plowed street but could find no space for the newly fallen snow.

Jamie showered in the guest room and put on the starched white shirt Jennie had laid out for him and the dark suit she had earlier pressed. While he was getting ready, Jennie was fitting herself into her new party dress in the master bedroom. Jamie finished dressing first and was reading the previous day's edition of the newspaper when this angelic vision appeared in the room. Jennie indeed looked like an angel in her sea-blue satin dress, her blonde hair in a tight bun exposing the full lines of her fine face, a gold necklace and earrings to match, and blue Cinderella high heels. *What a vision to behold, and she's mine,* Jamie thought.

"Am I dreaming, or did I die and go to heaven. Did God send you to meet me? You look absolutely stunning!" Jamie exclaimed.

"You look pretty handsome yourself. I'm going to hang onto you so the young ones don't get their hands on you."

They slid into each other's arms, holding each other so tight that neither could breathe.

"I love you."

"I love you too." Neither wanted to let go.

When they walked into the banquet room, everything seemed to stop. Even the orchestra quit playing for that brief moment. It wasn't just Cinderella shoes that walked into the banquet room, it was Cinderella herself! Every eye was riveted on the handsome prince leading Cinderella into their midst. "Don't leave after midnight. Your carriage will turn into a pumpkin," Charlie Blankenship, the chamber president, chided.

"And your horses into mice," an unidentified voice added.

After the rare prime rib and roasted chicken had been consumed, the pastries relished, and the dishes cleared, Charlie called the annual meeting to order. It was brief, and the slate of officers was unanimously approved for the coming year. Charlie presented Jamie with the gavel, and Jamie in turn presented Charlie with a plaque acknowledging Charlie's valuable service to the chamber as its president. As his first order of business, Jamie declared the meeting adjourned. "Let the dancing begin," he proclaimed.

As was the custom, the new president and the first lady were to dance a few bars and then be joined by the members and their spouses. Tonight was different. Those who were watching became mesmerized by the magic of this Steamboat Camelot. The music ran out before the men could ask their partners to dance. The name of the song: "The Impossible Dream."

Jennie was the belle of the ball. The chamber group was as cordial and caring as their church group. It was as if a moratorium had been declared, and if anyone had the power to declare so, tonight it would be the Steamboat Springs Chamber of Commerce. The armistice was a welcome respite, especially during the blessed Christmas season and in the wake of the absolution brought about by the verdict in the Cooper civil case.

Jamie and Jennie danced well into the night. Caught up in the fairy tale themselves, the ordeal lost its stranglehold, at least for those few precious hours. Max and Collette were at the Whittakers' until the next day. Jamie and Jennie could continue to be lost in the deep throes of love and ecstasy until the star-filled sky was interrupted by the day's dawn, and before long, the noonday's sun.

THE PASSING OF THE SEASONS

Seasons come and go, as do good times and bad. The ordeal had been like a tennis match. First in one court, and then in another. It was match point, and Jamie was not serving.

Corbett, no doubt because of Hammerville's influence and pressure, refused to dismiss the criminal case. Both Larry and Gordie had tried to persuade Corbett to take another look at the case, and if Corbett wanted Jamie to take another polygraph, he would do so. Corbett didn't believe in polygraphs. If Jamie prevailed in a case where the burden of proof was less than in the criminal case, how did Corbett expect to obtain a conviction? "Different jury—different issues," said Corbett.

On January 12, 1973, Corbett deposited an additional page of discovery into Whittaker and Brownell's drop box at the courthouse. It was a report of Officer Clinton Coleman dated January 10, 1973. The report read, "This reporting officer received a telephone call from Alden Stillwell, First Vice President of SB&T Co., regarding the James Curtis Cooper theft case. On January 10, 1973, at ten thirty a.m., Mr. Stillwell reported that while sorting through some of Mr. Cooper's personal effects that had been sitting in his office since Mr. Cooper's arrest, he found a vault combination slip in his father's handwriting that did not match the current combination to the main vault. When he checked with his father, his father confirmed that the numbers and letters were in his handwriting.

"Alden Stillwell reported that his father then went on to relate that approximately twelve years ago, about the time Mr. Cooper first came to work at the bank, the bank had trouble with the bank time lock and had to call the manufacturer to get the bypass combination. The combination was tested by him and his father at eight p.m. and found to be the bypass combination. That meant that Jamie must have come back to the bank at some time between seven p.m. on June 10 and seven a.m. on June 11, 1972, when no one was there, and, using the bypass combination, overrode the bank vault time lock and stole the thirty thousand dollars.

"For obvious reasons they didn't want to let anyone have that combination. However, this reporting officer did confirm with Alden's father, Brandon Stillwell, that all that his son had reported was true."

When Verna brought the additional discovery into Larry's office, along with other court documents, Larry read in utter disbelief. "I wondered when the other shoe was going to drop," he said to himself. The usual imperturbable Gordie was flabbergasted when he saw Coleman's report. "This could be the 'smoking gun' the prosecution has been looking for," he said dejectedly. They both just shook their heads and wondered if the Cooper curse was indeed more than just a fable.

Larry had asked Verna to call and set up an appointment with Jamie and Bodean. They were scheduled for an appointment at one thirty p.m. that afternoon.

When they all assembled in the conference room, they were reminded of the victory celebration that took place there following the verdict in the civil case back in October. That was now becoming a faded memory in light of the so-called newly discovered evidence. Although they had taken one giant step forward, it appeared they had taken two giant steps backward.

For the most part, the defense team had prepared for the criminal trial when they prepared for the civil trial. Now a whole new challenge faced them. How could they contend with this new devastating twist, and were there other dragons out there that would be rearing their ugly heads?

It was decided they could not take Alden's word for it. They had to confirm that the so-called override combo was legitimate. Number one, did it override the bank vault time lock? Two, when was the override combo written? Was it of recent vintage and thus contrived? Or was it written as suggested twelve or thirteen years ago? Three, was it found in Jamie's personal belongings as claimed, or was it placed there by Alden? Was that how Alden had accessed the vault? Had he found it in his father's desk when he was looking for something else? Or was it father-son collusion and contrived?

The defense team knew the answers to these questions were key to the defense. But who would be allowed to inspect the override combo and try it? The entrustment of that override combo just to anyone would be a breach of security and an invitation for the unsavory.

It was decided that Larry or Gordie should immediately contact Corbett and arrange for an independent evaluation.

They knew that the bank wouldn't allow Bodean or anyone of the defense's choosing to perform the task. It was Larry, the one closest to the conference room telephone, who called Corbett. Corbett was sympathetic to Larry's concern, and after some discussion, it was decided that a local locksmith and antique dealer by the name of Kaiser Elliott, who was bonded and a third-generation Steamboat resident, would be a likely candidate. Plus, he was on the sheriff's posse and would be trusted by law enforcement. Corbett agreed to contact Brandon Stillwell and get the green light. He would call right back, one way or the other.

Within minutes Corbett called back, saying Brandon wanted to check with the insurance company first, and if they were agreeable, the bank would be also. Corbett would call Larry as soon as he heard back from Brandon. In about half an hour, the defense's request was granted. Corbett would contact Kaiser Elliott, and the two would meet with Kaiser and detail the assignment.

At three thirty p.m. Larry, Gordie, and Bodean met at Corbett's office, joined almost simultaneously by Kaiser Elliott. Kaiser would arrange that day, if possible, to inspect the paper on which the override combo was written to determine its antiquity and try the combo while the timer was running to see if the bank vault time lock could be bypassed. Kaiser was then to contact both Corbett and either Larry or Gordie and report his findings. Kaiser was also to record his findings and provide Corbett and Larry or Gordie with signed copies of his report. Even though Kaiser wasn't an expert, the defense had faith in him.

The defense team then spent the next several hours reviewing the discovery, the trial prep documents in the old civil case, witnesses' statements, a tentative set of criminal jury instructions, and research memoranda. They discussed trial strategy,

focusing primarily on how they would counter the newly discovered evidence in the event it proved valid.

Gordie called Jamie and then Bodean with the bad news. He
had Kaiser's report sitting on his desk. Kaiser had met Brandon
and Alden at the bank at approximately seven thirty p.m. In his
presence while confirming the numbers, the turns and directions on the dial with those on Brandon's slip of paper, the bank
vault time lock was overridden. His report indicated the timer
was operational at the time. In his opinion, because of the condition of the paper and faded ink, it was at least a dozen years old.
Kaiser, however, had made it clear when he spoke with Gordie
that he was not an expert in dating documents.

Dennis Hinton, Corbett's investigator, had sat in on the civil
trial, hearing most of the testimony of witnesses and final arguments. He was known as a thorough note taker. Both Larry
and Gordie wished that he had been their note taker as they sat
through their law school classes. Apparently, Dennis had taken
typing and shorthand in high school.

As a result of what Dennis had learned in the trial and the
outcome of the case, Corbett decided not to pursue the Las
Vegas connection aspect in the criminal case. He told Larry that
he had made the decision based on his concern that because of
the bogus nature of the so-called gambling motive, which the
defense would negate, the jury would end up throwing the good
evidence out with bad, much like what they did in the civil case.
He said he didn't want the jury in the criminal case to throw

the baby out with the bathwater. He also noted that he had won many a case where the defense shot-gunned the jury, throwing everything in their arsenal at them, and the valid got lost with the bogus. Corbett believed there was also the ethical or moral issue. The district attorney's office had conducted a thorough investigation and found absolutely no evidence of gambling on Jamie's part. Also, his office was convinced that Forrest Cooper was telling the truth when he testified the cash used in Las Vegas came from him.

Corbett was asked to and did provide Larry with a letter to that effect. The defense was now free of the worry over the Las Vegas connection. Larry and Gordie felt that was a wise strategy decision on the part of Corbett. And they also respected him for his ethics. Besides, with the newly discovered evidence, Corbett didn't need to take any cheap shots.

═══════════════

It was a sunny Monday February 5, a good day to test the slopes. There was a foot of fresh powder on the top of the hill, and the Ski Steamboat Corporation's reduced Monday fare was beckoning them. It was not to be, at least for this forenoon. The defense team was snuggled in for their long winter trial prep. With the Las Vegas connection no longer a part of the equation, it would be a shootout at the O.K. Corral between Alden and Jamie. It would boil down to whom to believe: Alden or Jamie. Alden was the lynchpin to conviction if any there be.

It was agreed that it would be a simple, straightforward trial. The prosecution would call Brandon Stillwell, Alden Stillwell, Rita Baker, Kaiser Elliott, and Officer Clinton Coleman. The only exhibits they would introduce would be the bill strap with the Federal Reserve stamp and the twenty fifty-dollar bills. They could not introduce the slip of paper with the override combo because of the security risk.

The defense would call Jamie, Betty Skyler, Ursula Russell, Jackie Stiles, Charlie Blankenship, and Jennie Cooper. The only exhibit would be the receipt from the Tomahawk Café on July 10, 1972, in the amount of $5.50.

Larry summarized the evidence of the prosecution using his flip chart. Through their witnesses they would prove:

1. Venue: the offense took place in the county of Routt, state of Colorado.

2. Identity: Brandon, Alden, Rita, and Coleman would identify Jamie.

3. Joint access: Jamie had access to the main vault with his generic combo between seven a.m. to five thirty p.m. (depending on when the vault door was closed, locked, and the timer set)

4. Exclusive access: According to the latest discovery, Jamie was the only one, presumably, to have the override combo, and therefore access from five thirty p.m. (depending on when the vault door was closed, locked, and the timer set) to seven a.m. the following day.

5. Cookie crumbs: Jamie's car was found in the parking lot when Alden arrived at six forty-five a.m. on July 10, 1972. Alden discovered $1,000 in twenty fifty-dollar bills with a strap or band bearing the Federal Reserve Bank stamp similar to those in the cash drawer of the main vault hidden in Jamie's desk drawer in his locked office. Alden discovered $30,000 missing from the vault.

The money had been there the night before. The money was taken sometime between closing time on July 10 and six forty-five a.m. on July 11, 1972, when Alden arrived at the bank.

6. Conclusion: Since no one besides Jamie had access to the vault when the timer was running and money that was there when the timer was set and was not there when the timer expired, Jamie must have taken it.

Gordie summarized the evidence of the defense, using the flip chart now recognized as a valuable tool for trial preparation. Through their witnesses, they would prove or attempt to prove:

1. Joint access: Brandon, Alden, and Jamie all had the regular combination and access when the timer was not set.

2. No access: While the timer was running, no one, without the override combination, could bypass the bank vault time lock.

3. Override combo: Jamie never saw one, never had one, and didn't know Brandon had one.

4. Alibi: Jamie left the bank at six fifteen p.m. on July 10, was at home with his family from minutes of that time until six thirty a.m. the following morning when he attended a chamber meeting at the Tomahawk Café at the Broken-Bow Hotel. He was there until seven fifty-five a.m., at which time he walked to the bank, arriving in his office at eight a.m.

5. Corroboration: Jennie can verify that Jamie arrived at home at approximately six twenty p.m. on July 10, 1972, and stayed home the whole night with her and the chil-

dren until approximately six twenty-five a.m. the following morning. Jackie Stiles and Charlie Blankenship can
verify that Jamie was attended a breakfast meeting of the
chamber at the Tomahawk Café from six thirty a.m. to
seven fifty-five a.m. on July 11, 1972.

6. Defense: Jamie didn't do it. There were no eyewitnesses
   but only Alden's word. Jamie had an alibi.

7. Alternate suspect: Alden Stillwell. (Another cookie to
   add to the Alden column. Number twenty-one: who
   provided the override combo?)

The prosecution's witnesses had been endorsed on the second page of the charge form. Witnesses not so endorsed could
not be called, with the exception of rebuttal witnesses. Corbett
had already endorsed Kaiser Elliott as an additional and "recently
discovered" witness.

Bodean confirmed that Betty Skyler, Ursula Russell, Jackie
Stiles, and Charlie Blankenship had all been served with defense
subpoenas and had been provided the required witness fees. He
had spoken with each of them and informed them what information was sought to be elicited. Since they had already had
a dress rehearsal in the civil case, they were prepared for what
awaited them.

Jamie seemed to be holding up pretty well in light of the
latest setback. He said that the outcome of the civil case had
accomplished a number of things. Other than the obvious, it
had let the air out of the Stillwell balloon, changed the public
mood, and resulted in elimination of the Las Vegas connection.
The drawback, he speculated, was that since the plaintiffs' feath-
ers had been ruffled by the adverse verdict, the Stillwells had to

come up with some way to stack the deck. The resurrection of the override combo was their answer.

Bodean surmised that Alden found the override combo in his father's drawer. Curious, he tried it after hours and found it worked. On the night of July 10, he removed $30,000 and planted $1,000 in Jamie's desk so as to detract attention from him. Or he might have planted it to even the score for all those years he had been cheated out of his perceived just desserts. Gordie said he thought Alden took the money between seven a.m. when he opened the vault and seven fifteen a.m. when Rita arrived. Regardless, he was $29,000 richer but couldn't spend it without arousing suspicion. He was in one heck of a predicament.

The jury list probably wouldn't be provided by the court clerk until Thursday or Friday. The profile of the ideal juror had to be along the lines of the jurors in the civil trial, Gordie proffered. Young and preferably women. No schoolteachers—they were too technical and strict. No senior citizens—they were too judgmental and inflexible. No middle aged or older men because they were unsympathetic. No businessmen who have been victims of embezzlement or theft. No bankers or ex-bankers.

"That doesn't leave room for many to choose from does it." Larry noted.

All agreed it was just luck of the draw in the civil case. Even the rejected jurors were not bad and would probably have come up with the same result. Leaving Jamie's fate in the hands of chance didn't seem to be the proper way of dispensing justice. Jury selection was like a lottery; one never knew whose number might come up or whose name might be drawn. In the civil case, Jamie had been accused of gambling, and in the criminal case, he would be risking his life on the gaming tables of the ordeal.

THE CRIMINAL TRIAL

The day that was the center of all his nightmares since his July arrest and a day that Jamie had dreaded was now at hand. The drab gloomy day of reckoning, Monday, February, 12, 1973, would wait no more.

Jamie was again seated in the courtroom whose every inch had been scoured and indelibly etched in his memory. He was seated between his guardian angels, Larry on his left and Gordie on his right. Bodean, who was designated as defendant's advisory witness, was seated to Gordie's right. That meant that even though the advisory witness rule was in effect, Bodean could still testify, even if he sat through the whole trial. The same thing would be true of the prosecution's advisory witness.

Across from Larry was the prosecution's table, formerly occupied by the plaintiffs' team, RD, Brandon, and the weasel. Only this time, Corbett sat in the chair to the right and his investigator, Dennis Hinton, sat in the chair to the left. The chair formerly occupied by Brandon had been removed. Dennis was the prosecution's advisory witness.

What a difference a season makes, Jamie had commented to his guardian angels. During the civil trial, there were warm autumn days, windows open, and the rustling of the crisp leaves vibrating in the breeze. Today, the windows were tight against their frames, frost covering the outsides and some even on the insides. The riveting action of the old-fashioned hot water radiators announcing their functioning had the attention of several of the prospective jurors. They were trying to warm their frozen hands but were careful not to touch the piping-hot, silver-colored radiators. Some of the prospective jurors were still wearing their heavy winter coats and scarves, others were shedding their snow boots and shaking off the snow from their mittens, and still others were just sitting there with red noses and faces—all in nervous anticipation.

"Didn't the county pay the heat bill?" Bodean asked Gordie.

"Don't know, but they must have just turned it on before we came in," Gordie said.

"Things will heat up soon enough," Jamie said.

Conspicuous from their absence in the courtroom were the Stillwells. Corbett must have warned them to stay away, at least during *voir dire*. No cajoling and insincere handshakes here. No ingratiating smiles or winks of endearment or platitudes. Why risk mistrial or reversal in event of a conviction?

When Judge Tibbits was about to enter, Ron Scott, the bailiff in this and the civil case, banged the gavel, commanding all to stand, and announced, "This court is now in session. Call the case of *People of the State of Colorado, versus James Curtis Cooper also known as Jamie Cooper, defendant*," Judge Tibbits announced.

Asking if everyone was ready and greeting the jury, he had all the jurors stand, raise their right hands, and take the oath to truthfully answer all questions propounded by the court or counsel. He then told them they could sit down.

Judge Tibbits read from a script. It was not flowery and was geared to the uninitiated. The jury was introduced to the participants in this criminal case. The charge was read to them, and they were advised that Mr. Cooper had entered a not guilty plea. He outlined the phases of a criminal jury trial and explained that at the conclusion of the case, they would be instructed as to the law that they would be required to follow.

The veniremen were advised that fourteen would be called to the jury box. The first twelve selected would be the jury *per se,* and jurors thirteen and fourteen would be alternates, who would deliberate with the others only if one of the original twelve, for one reason or another, could not continue to serve.

The bailiff assisted the clerk in drawing and recording the names of the first fourteen. The bailiff directed the seating arrangement much like a traffic cop. He placed juror thirteen in the seventh chair in the front row, juror fourteen in the fourteenth chair in the back row.

The attorneys at both tables were given a revised alphabetical list with the names opposite the sequential numbers that went from one to one hundred. The judge and the attorneys were keyed to the announcement of the number then followed by the name. The attorneys' lists contained the name, age, address, occupation, place of employment, length of residency in Routt County, and native state for each prospective juror.

The attorneys had been given the unrevised list on the preceding Thursday, and there were a number of substituted names that Gordie was having Bodean review and write comments. Beforehand, the judge had instructed the attorneys that they would have seven pre-emptory challenges per side—the normal five, plus one for each alternate.

Pre-emptory challenges were limited because no reason was required to be given upon issuance of the challenge. Challenges for cause, on the other hand, were unlimited. Reasons for challenges for cause included absence of a qualification to be a juror; relationship to the defendant, or any attorney engaged in the trial; being a witness to any matter related to the crime charged; or the existence of a state of mind indicating dislike or bias toward one side or the other. The last, obviously, was the most nebulous.

Fourteen prospective jurors were called to the box. The judge asked some general questions of the panel as a whole, such as whether any had ever served as a juror before, ever been a witness in any kind of court proceedings, or knew the defendant or any of the attorneys. If a juror raised a hand, he or she would be asked to explain as to whether that would in any way affect their decision. The jurors were then read the names of the witnesses who were to be called by each side and asked whether they knew any of them. Would that cause them to be swayed one way or the other?

When asked if they had read, seen, or heard anything through the print or electronic media, all raised their hands. Without telling the judge what they read, saw, or heard, had they made up their minds as to the innocence or guilt of the defendant? If they said yes, they promised they would set aside their preconceived notions and judge the case solely on the evidence presented. Their answers were postured in such a way that there would be no challenge for cause. However, the defense team noted who said yes, as well as who admitted to knowing prosecution witnesses. It was difficult to determine which way the prospective jurors were leaning. They masked their biases, if any they had, remarkably well.

When it was time for the attorneys to *voir dire*, Corbett went first. That was because the prosecution had the burden of proof. Corbett was most ingratiating. He, of course, "just wanted to make sure the laws of the state of Colorado were being enforced." He acknowledged that the prosecution had the burden of proving Mr. Cooper guilty beyond a reasonable doubt but pointed out that that was not proof beyond *all* doubt "as that would be an impossible burden."

Corbett made sure that they understood that if he met his burden and proved Mr. Cooper's guilt beyond a reasonable doubt, they were bound by law to return a guilty verdict. Did they all understand that? And if he were to prove each and every one of the elements of the crime charged, could they and would they do that?

He also asked if any of the jurors banked at SB&T Co. They all raised their hands. Since the bank was the named victim in the case, he asked whether that would in any way affect their verdict. All said no. This was the same question Corbett was to ask all replacement jurors.

Gordie turned to Bodean and remarked: "Corbett is pretty foxy. Knowing we would be asking the question, he jumped the gun."

"Just taking the wind out of our sails," Bodean replied. "Besides, he wants the jury to marvel at his fairness."

Overhearing their conversation, Larry whispered, "I call it 'gilding the lily.'"

Corbett concluded by asking them personal questions about their background and whether there was anything that he should have asked and didn't that might evince bias or prejudice one way or the other. All shook their heads and answered no. Corbett then passed the jurors for cause, which meant he had no legal basis for disqualification.

It was Larry's turn to *voir dire*. He walked to the podium without a list of the jurors' names and no papers of any kind. He had memorized their names—all fourteen—during Corbett's *voir dire*.

Larry told the jurors that this was the opportunity for the attorneys to ask questions in an effort to ascertain whether they could be fair, "not just to one side or the other, but to both sides." He remembered the jurors who had raised their hands, acknowledging prior jury service, knowing a witness, or being exposed to pretrial publicity, and asked each by name the follow-up questions. He asked them if they realized there were two sides to every story and that they hadn't heard Jamie's side yet. Would they keep an open mind and not judge the case until they had heard all the evidence?

Corbett had postured the questions concerning presumption of innocence, burden of proof, and reasonable doubt to suit the prosecution. Now it was Larry's turn to posture but in a vein favorable to the defense. Since these concepts were the essence of a criminal prosecution and the attorneys could only ask questions and not make statements, Larry was cautious and deliberate.

"Do you realize that every person charged with a crime is presumed to be innocent? Do you realize that the presumption of innocence remains with the defendant throughout the whole trial and should be given effect by you unless, after considering all of the evidence, you are then convinced that the defendant is guilty beyond a reasonable doubt?

"Do you realize that the burden of proof is upon the prosecution to prove to your satisfaction beyond a reasonable doubt the existence of all of the elements necessary to constitute the crime charged? Do you realize that Jamie does not have to prove anything, that that is the prosecution's job? Do you realize that Jamie does not have to testify and that if he doesn't it can't be held against him?

"Do you realize that the gauge in this case is not whether Jamie is guilty or innocent but whether he is guilty or not guilty? In other words, whether Jamie is innocent is irrelevant if the prosecution fails to prove any one or more of the elements of the crime charged, then you are bound by law to return a not guilty verdict. Do you understand that?

"Do you realize," Larry continued, "that the proof in a criminal case is different than the proof in a civil case. In a civil case, it's just the greater weight of the evidence, which means that the side to which the scale of justice tips, even slightly, wins. In a criminal case, on the other hand, the burden of proof imposed on the prosecution is greater. The burden of proof imposed on the prosecution is proof beyond a reasonable doubt. Do you understand that? If the prosecution fails to meet its burden of proof, what would your verdict be?

"Mr. Corbett has attempted to give you his definition of 'reasonable doubt.' Do you realize that the court will instruct you that 'reasonable doubt' means a doubt based on reason and common sense that arises from the fair and rational consideration of all of the evidence or the lack of evidence in the case. It is a doubt that is not a vague, speculative, or imaginary doubt, but such a doubt as would cause reasonable people to hesitate to act in matters of importance to themselves. If you were given such an instruction, would you follow it?"

Larry said he passed the jury for cause, without waiving his continuing objection with reference to the court's failure to grant defense's motion for change of venue.

Corbett then exercised the first of his seven pre-emptory challenges without having to state a reason. "Your Honor, the prosecution would exercise its first pre-emptory challenge to juror number seventeen seated in seat one, Mr. Flannigan."

"Mr. Flannigan, you are excused.

"Would the bailiff please choose another name?"

"Juror number three, Edith Alder."

Corbett then asked her the general background questions, followed by questions concerning circumstantial evidence. "Did she realize that few cases involve eyewitnesses, and that 'circumstantial evidence' meant that if the finger of guilt pointed to an accused and the jury was convinced of that person's guilt beyond a reasonable doubt, the jury must find that person guilty?" She gave all the *right* answers. Corbett passed Mrs. Alder for cause.

It was Larry's turn to *voir dire* Mrs. Alder. He asked a series of questions also: Had she heard the questions proposed to the other prospective jurors? Would she have answered the questions substantially different? Had she ever served on a jury before? Was that a civil or a criminal case? Was she satisfied with the verdict? Did she realize that the burden of proof in a criminal case was different than in a civil case? Had she read, seen, or heard anything about this case other than what she had heard so far in this courtroom? Could she set aside any opinions she may have as a result of the pretrial exposure and decide this case solely on the merits? Could she be fair to both sides? Again, she gave all the *right* answers. Larry passed Mrs. Alder for cause.

Larry exercised his first pre-emptory challenge as against juror number twenty-three, Calvin Fredericks. He was replaced by Arlene Richardson. The same routine was repeated with Mrs. Richardson but with different questions being asked.

No challenges were exercised for cause. Corbett exercised five pre-emptory challenges; Larry exercised six of his. Both said they accepted the panel "as presently impaneled and constituted." Larry had added "subject, of course, to our continuing objection." With that, the jury that would hear the Cooper criminal jury case had been selected.

They had taken the usual midmorning recess in between selection of jurors, and now it was 12:10 p.m. The jurors who had not been called to the box were excused. The jurors who were selected were sworn to faithfully perform their duties as jurors. They were then instructed to follow the bailiff to the jury room and would be allowed to call their family members and advise them of their selection. The bailiff would then take them to lunch, and court would resume again at two p.m. Upon discharge, they were given the same admonitions that Judge Black had given the jurors in the civil case.

The defense was not happy with the jury that was selected. It seemed as though the replacement jurors were less desirable than the ones who had been challenged and excused. Larry and Gordie held back the last pre-emptory challenge just in case they needed it. They didn't like Dennis Rawles, the last juror selected, in seat twelve (now designated by seat number) but were afraid if they used their last challenge, they might end up with someone far worse. It was not the perfect jury they had hoped for and certainly not like the one they'd had in the civil case. Worry spread as Gordie said he observed one juror, number ten, Irene Stapleton, nod and smile at Corbett as the jurors filed out at the lunch break.

Back at the offices of Whittaker and Brownell, the defense team analyzed the jury they would have to live with for the remainder of the trial. When they received the jury list on Thursday, they went through the list meticulously. Between the four of them, they knew or knew of most of them. The ones that they didn't know, Verna did. They had put a blue plus mark adjacent to the desired, a red minus sign next to "definitely didn't want," and a green question mark for those they weren't sure of. There was some type of mark for everyone.

After they received the revised list of jurors the morning of trial, they noticed that many of the blue plus jurors' names had been removed, and after Gordie and Bodean evaluated the dozen or so additions, most were in the red minus sign category. When the bailiff had handed Larry the revised list that morning, he said the judge had excused the ones who had been crossed out at their request because of personal hardships, and the clerk had to scurry around for replacements.

The defense team opined that the dozen or so, most of whom Jamie knew and thought would be favorable, bailed out because they thought they might be biased in Jamie's favor. Unfortunately, their bailing resulted in stacking the deck for the other side.

Juror number one Edith Alder, sixty-four, was a retired nurse and a Routt County native; juror number two, James Branch, thirty-nine, was a high school counselor, a resident of the county for twelve years, and a Michigan native; juror number three, Ronald Gross, forty-two, was a rancher and a Routt County native; juror number four, Cheryl Taylor, fifty, was a store clerk for a hardware store, a resident of the county for four years, and a Colorado native; juror number five, Bernard Johnson, fifty-seven, was a pharmacist, a resident of the county for twenty-six years, and a California native; and completing the front row was juror number six, Arlene Richardson, forty-nine, a dental assistant and a Routt County native.

In the back row was juror number seven, Dolores Norton, forty-nine, a housewife married to a rancher and a Routt County native; juror number eight, Reneé Moore, forty-two, was a civil engineer, a resident of the county for nine years, and a Colorado native; juror number nine, Benjamin Creaton, fifty-six, was a postal worker, a resident of the county twelve years, and an Iowa native; juror number ten, Irene Stapleton, sixty-one, was a retired school teacher, a resident of the county for thirty-eight years, and a Wyoming native; juror number eleven, Carrie Jenkins, sixty-nine, was a widower, husband was a rancher, a Routt County native; and juror number twelve, Dennis Rawles, seventy, was a retired bus driver and a Routt County native.

The alternate jurors were juror number thirteen, Claxton Moss, eighty-one, retired rancher and Routt County native, and juror number fourteen, Ruth Painter, fifty-one, artist and Routt County native.

The jury was composed of seven women and five men. Mrs. Alder was the only one with prior jury service. Mr. Creaton had some traffic citations and a fish and game violation. Mr. Gross, Mrs. Taylor, and Mr. Johnson had each been the victim of a crime. All were customers of SB&T Co. but had indicated on *voir dire* that that would not affect their decision in this case one way or the other. The pretrial publicity was something they could disregard. All had indicated that they were the type of jurors they would want if they were either the prosecution or the defense.

As the jury was being sworn in, Gordie scribbled a note on his yellow legal pad and slid it in Larry's direction. It read: "If you believe the jury can and will disregard what they've heard and read outside the courtroom and won't be affected by being customers of SB&T Co., then I have some swamp land in Florida to sell you."

━━━━━━━━━━

Back in the courtroom, with familiar faces in the gallery, the court was called in session. Corbett was about to give his opening statement.

Corbett began his opening statement by recounting the discovery of the missing bank funds and uncovering of the strapped stack of twenty $50 bills totaling $1,000 in one of Jamie's desk drawers. After stating that the Steamboat Springs Police Department was notified of the missing funds that pointed in Jamie's direction, Corbett stated, "Alden Stillwell will testify that when he arrived at work on July 11, 1972, Mr. Cooper's car was in the bank parking lot, but Mr. Cooper was nowhere to be found. He will testify that Mr. Cooper arrived at eight a.m. about the same time as Officer Clinton Coleman and three other police officers. Alden Stillwell gave the police the one thousand that he had confiscated and they placed it in evidence. That same one thousand, plus its strap with a discernable Federal Reserve stamp, will be introduced in evidence in this case.

"Mr. Cooper, of course, was discharged from the bank, and his personal effects were boxed and stored. In preparation for this trial, Alden Stillwell went through Mr. Cooper's personal belongings and found a suspicious-looking paper with his father's handwriting that appeared to have a vault combination written on it. He tried it on the vault door, and it didn't work. After closing that night and after the bank vault timer was set, he tried it again. Bingo! It opened. It was the combination bypass that could override the time lock. No one knew or at least remembered that anyone at the bank knew the override combo.

"Brandon Stillwell will testify that he vaguely remembered a problem with the time lock some years ago when Mr. Cooper had first come to work and that the manufacturer had provided some type of combination that allowed access to rectify the problem. He recognized his handwriting on the slip of paper Alden Stillwell found in Mr. Cooper's belongings, but he will testify that he doesn't know where it had been all these years.

"When the evidence is all in, you will be convinced beyond a reasonable doubt that James Curtis Cooper, also known as Jamie Cooper, is guilty of the theft with which he has been charged. We will be asking you to return a guilty verdict. Thank you."

The defense attorneys in a criminal case have three options with respect to the opening statement. They could either give their opening statement now, wait until the prosecution attorneys had completed their case, or they could waive it altogether. The timing depended on a number of factors. There was some school of thought that if you gave it now you alerted the prosecution to your theory and allowed them to counter it in their case-in-chief, thus nullifying the sting. Another theory was to let the jury know there was another side of the story so that they didn't make up their minds until they had heard all the evidence. The defense attorneys opted to give their opening statement now. It was delivered by Larry.

After advising the jury that even though the defense was not required to present evidence and the defendant was not required to testify, Larry stated that the defense would nonetheless be presenting evidence to refute the charges and that Jamie would in fact be testifying in his own behalf.

Larry said the evidence would show that Jamie first began working for SB&T Co. while he was still in high school and that the bank had a job waiting for him upon his graduation from college in 1959. Jamie, Larry would state, had worked for SB&T Co. since that time rising in the ranks to first vice president and was second in command only to the bank's owner and president, Brandon Stillwell.

Larry then outlined the order in which the defense witnesses would be called together with a brief summary of their anticipated testimony. He then concluded by stating, "Jamie will categorically deny having taken the missing money. He will testify under oath that he was not at the bank from the time he left the night before until he returned to the bank at eight a.m. the next morning. Again, under oath, he will testify the first he heard of the override combo was when, months after his arrest, Alden Stillwell claimed he found it in Jamie's belongings left at the bank. Jamie will testify he never had it in his possession or ever saw the slip of paper on which the override combo was written. He will state that at this very moment he has not seen or had in his possession the override combo.

"If the evidence is as the defense anticipates, we will have no hesitancy whatsoever at the conclusion of the trial in asking you to return a not guilty verdict."

Brandon Stillwell was the first witness to be called. He took the oath to tell the truth. His testimony was similar to that in the civil trial. The only difference was with respect to the slip of paper on what was written the override combo. He identified his handwriting. He vaguely remembered the incident involving the vault malfunction that occurred about the time Jamie had first been hired.

On cross-examination, Gordie established that Brandon didn't know where the override combo slip was found, other than what Alden had told him. He said he didn't know where it had been stored all those years and had no knowledge that it had ever been in Jamie's possession. Brandon also stated that he had no independent knowledge that the $1,000 that Alden found came from Jamie's desk drawer, and he admitted that Alden could have made up the stories about where he found the override combo and the $1,000, but he didn't think so. When asked who had replaced Jamie as first vice president of SB&T Co., he responded that his son, Alden, had taken over.

It was time for the midafternoon break. After the break, Alden Stillwell was the prosecution's second witness. He was sworn in and testified in the manner and fashion as in the civil trial, but he was more prepared. With regard to the slip of paper identified as being that of his father's, he testified that he stumbled on it totally by accident while preparing for trial and re-examining Jamie's personal belongings that had been stored in a box Rita had brought to his office after Jamie's arrest. He knew it was an override combo because he tried it both when the timer was on and when it wasn't, and it only worked while the timer was running. Alden identified the strap and the twenty fifty-dollar bills as being identical to the strapped bills turned over to Officer Clinton Coleman. He also testified that the slip with the override combo was the same one he turned over to Kaiser Elliott to obtain access to the vault while the timer was running. Alden then identified Jamie.

On cross-examination, Gordie realized that the dress rehearsal of the civil trial had been of benefit to the prosecution as well. Alden was now a formidable force to be reckoned with. *Forewarned is forearmed*, Gordie thought. No surprises for him. Gordie followed almost identically his cross in the civil case. Regarding the override combo slip, Gordie realized that that might be the defense's Achilles' heel. Alden's explanation of the last-minute discovery of the slip was that he decided to inspect Jamie's personal belongings in prep for trial. It was only then that he discovered it. He admitted no one was with him at the time and he could have made the whole thing up but he said he didn't because he wouldn't want to commit perjury. The same thing was true of the discovery of the $1,000.

Rita Baker was sworn in and testified as she had in the civil trial with the exception of the override combo slip. She testi- fied that she was there when the locksmith, Kaiser Elliott, per- formed the experiment. She said that even though she did not read the slip, she watched Scott dial from the slip two times. The first time was before the vault time lock was set, and the second time was when the vault time lock was on. The vault door did not open the first time; it did on the second. Rita also identified Jamie.

Cross-examination mirrored the cross-examination in the civil trial with the exception of the adjustment now required by the override combo testimony. Ms. Baker admitted she had never seen or heard about the existence of the override combo slip until Alden produced it. She had never seen it in Jamie's possession or ever heard him talk about it. She had not inspected Jamie's belongings at or during the time she boxed them up or at any time since. Certainly it could have been possible that while the boxes sat unsealed in Alden's office someone could have planted the slip. Alden brought the slip out to her. She never saw Alden remove it from Jamie's belongings and didn't think anyone else did.

Kaiser Elliott was sworn in and testified that he was a locksmith. He had done maintenance work on the mechanisms on the main vault door, including the timer for the bank on various occasions. He had tried the override combo both before the time was set and while the timer was on. The override combo only worked when the timer was on. On cross-examination by Gordie, he admitted he didn't know where Alden had obtained the override combo slip. It was always in Alden's hands. He never saw Jamie with it or anyone else.

It was time to break for the day. The jury was excused to seven thirty a.m. the next day, at which time they were to report in the jury room. The customary admonitions were given to the jury. They were excused. After they departed, the court was adjourned to eight the following morning.

The only witness the defense team thought the prosecution had left to call was Officer Clinton Coleman, through whom they would introduce the torn Federal Reserve strap and the twenty fifty-dollar bills. They thought Corbett was wise in streamlining the trial and not muddying the waters. It was a pretty clean trial so far, they thought. Corbett didn't want to risk a reversal on appeal. Jamie thought that might be another reason why Corbett aborted the Las Vegas connection. If no evidence was used that was illegally obtained, then any error in Judge Tibbits's denial of the motion to suppress was moot.

Larry took Jamie through another dry run on his testimony. Gordie as he had done on similar such occasions mimicked the cross. Not much worry here. Jamie was implacable.

Bodean touched base with the defense witnesses and told them to be prepared to testify around ten a.m. There was a witness room in the courthouse to meet in, but they were not to discuss their testimony with each other or to enter the courtroom. He would be watching for them.

At eight a.m. on February 13, the criminal case of *People of the State of Colorado v. James Curtis Cooper a.k.a. Jamie Cooper* entered its second day. There were a few less spectators than the previous day. Corbett was asked to call his next witness, Officer Clinton Coleman.

Officer Coleman was unabashed in relating his police training, years with the Steamboat Police Department, his certifications, and recertifications. After he was sworn, he testified as he had in the civil trial, with the exception of the evidence connected to the Las Vegas connection and the new evidence relative to the discovery of the override combo. In fact, none of the witnesses made any reference to the Las Vegas connection. Prosecution exhibits of the band and the twenty fifty-dollar bills were offered in evidence and, over the defendant's objection, were admitted. Officer Coleman also established venue, i.e., that the offense occurred in the county of Routt, state of Colorado.

Gordie, on cross-examination, followed his previous script, with the exception of the modifications dictated by the direct-examination. Coleman admitted that all he knew was what had been told by Alden Stillwell. He neither saw the belongings from whence the override combo slip came, nor was he present when it was removed. Until Alden called him seven months after Jamie's arrest, he had no idea that such lock combination existed, and, to his knowledge, neither did any of his fellow officers.

Corbett rested the prosecution's case-in-chief.

After the jury was excused to take up matters outside their presence, Larry made a motion for judgment of acquittal.

"If Your Honor please, pursuant to the rules, the defendant moves the court for an order entering a judgment of acquittal of the offense charged on the grounds that the evidence is insufficient to sustain a conviction.

"The relevant admissible evidence presented in this case, when viewed in the light most favorable to the prosecution, is insufficient to support a conclusion by a reasonable mind that the defendant is guilty of the charge beyond a reasonable doubt."

Corbett argued that the evidence was more than ample to allow the case to go to the jury, and to grant such a motion would be to contravene the province of the jury and a complete nullification of the role of the jury in our whole justice system.

The judge ruled, "Defense motion is denied. The court finds that there is more than ample evidence, viewing it in the light most favorable to the prosecution, to allow the case to go to the jury. Do you intend to call witnesses, Mr. Whittaker?"

"We do, Your Honor."

"Very well. Be prepared to call your first witness after the break. The court is adjourned for fifteen minutes."

Before the jury was brought in, Larry advised Judge Tibbits that he was going to call Jamie as his first witness. The judge then inquired of Jamie if that was his decision. Jamie said it was. The judge then advised him of something similar to the Miranda rights, saying that he was not required to testify and that if he testified his statements could be used against him. He made sure that Jamie's waiver was knowingly, intelligently, and voluntarily made.

After the break, Larry announced, "The defense calls the defendant, Jamie Cooper."

Jamie could not have been more effective or impressive. He certainly came off as a man's man. There was quite a contrast between Jamie and his nemesis. Alden had never been competition, and today was no different. In comparing the two, it was obvious why Alden was no match. Unless one had blinders on, it was easy to tell which one was telling the truth and which one had an axe to grind.

Excluding the testimony regarding the Las Vegas connection, one couldn't tell his testimony in the civil trial from this trial. With regard to the override combo slip, Jamie testified he had never seen it; didn't know it even existed. As far as he knew, it wasn't included in the items taken from his office and was certainly not among the items that belonged to him. He testified that he had inherited certain files and folders from the retired loan officer who had occupied his office before him and never had occasion to sort through those files. The slip could have been in one of those files, but he also said he doubted it. He never accessed the vault as the testimony suggested, never took the missing money or any part thereof, and never put the $1,000 in his desk drawer. The first time he saw the money was when Alden threw it on his desk.

The breakfast receipt from the Tomahawk Café was offered by the defense and then admitted into evidence.

When it was Corbett's turn to cross-examine, Corbett committed the unpardonable sin. He asked one or maybe two too many questions, "Do you know who put the one thousand in your desk drawer?"

"Yes."

"Who?"

"Alden Stillwell."

Even Judge Tibbits had to keep from bursting into laughter. It was indeed hilarious. Corbett needed to go wash his mouth out with soap, with so much riding on the line with a case like this and this being an election year. "How could I be so stupid?" Corbett must have asked himself as he announced, "I have no further questions."

Jennie Cooper was sworn in as the second defense witness. It, indeed, was Cinderella, but this was not make-believe; it was part of a drama that could change her life and the life of her family forever. Jennie was radiant, despite the occasion. She was articulate and straightforward. When she answered, she looked at the jurors, each and every one, in the eye. No deception here.

Jennie testified that Jamie had come home his usual time, which was about six fifteen or six twenty p.m. on Monday July 10, 1972. Dinner was waiting, and after dinner, while she washed the dishes, Jamie played with Max, Collette, and Maya, the dog. They were playing catch with an old football of Jamie's, and the kids were joined by the two neighbor boys across the street, as well as one of Collette's friends who had eaten dinner with them and was going to spend the night. Jamie and all of the kids decided to scrimmage. It was Jamie and the two girls on one team and the three boys on the other. When Jennie had finished the dishes, she was conscripted to be on the girls' team. She remembered because Jamie was arrested the following day, and that was the last time they had a day and night free of worry.

She testified they lived in the middle of town several blocks from SB&T Co. She was not a sound sleeper and hadn't been since Max and Collette had been born. If Jamie had gotten up in the middle of the night and left the house, she would have heard him. The cars were in the garage adjoining the house, and if Jamie had used one of them, she would again have heard him. She related Jamie left home at approximately six twenty-five a.m. the next morning to attend a chamber meeting and from there onto work.

She further testified that she saw no extra cash and that Jamie had not acted suspicious. Jamie liked SB&T Co. and was very satisfied there. He took pride in his position as first vice president and was loyal to his boss, Brandon Stillwell. She believed there was no way Jamie would take money from the bank.

Although Corbett was still reeling from his previous cross-examination, he was still going to give it the law school try.

"Mrs. Cooper, you love your husband, don't you?"

"Yes."

"And you would do anything to help him, wouldn't you?"

"If you're inferring that I would lie for him, the answer is no. I love him too much to do that."

"No further questions."

This was probably an ideal place to break. Corbett was not about to object. He needed a hole to crawl into. The jury was excused with the usual admonitions. Court was adjourned until eight the following morning, the fourteenth day of February, 1973.

It was Valentine's Day. The timing was uncanny. Jamie said they would go out to dinner when he returned from court. The hiatus in the middle of trial was just what the doctor ordered. It would give them time to put everything on hold and just focus on each other. Jamie had smuggled in heart-shaped boxes of chocolates for Jennie, Max, and Collette. It was now only a matter of days before the bad memories would fade away and the ordeal would be no more. At least, that's what they prayed.

As the trial resumed, Betty Skyler testified as to the events on the night of July 10, 1972. Same direct as in the civil trial. The cross-examination, however, was more accusatory and caustic. She was asked, "You don't know what Mr. Cooper put in his pockets, do you?" and "You don't know what he might have put in his car before you arrived, do you?"

Ursula Russell testified as per the civil trial script. Same ineffective cross-examination.

Jackie Styles and Charlie Blankenship established Jamie's alibi from six thirty a.m. to seven fifty-five a.m. on July 11, 1972. The cross-examination was crass. "You don't know what Mr. Cooper did before the meeting or what he did afterward, do you?"

Great try, the defense team thought.

Larry announced that the defense rested. Corbett said the prosecution had no rebuttal witnesses. Larry said he had a motion to make outside the ears of the jury. The jury was informed that the evidence on both sides had been closed, that he and the attorneys would be working on instructions, and that they would be excused until one forty-five p.m., at which time they were to meet in the jury room to be escorted to the courtroom. The judge gave them the usual admonitions.

Outside the presence of the jury, Larry renewed the defense's motion for judgment of acquittal. Without argument, the judge denied it, stating there was sufficient evidence to go to the jury, and any factual issues there be were for the jury's consideration and not his.

Larry and Gordie had debated objecting to the charges having been brought under the general theft statute instead of the specific embezzlement statute under the banking code. Since jeopardy had attached, now that the trial had commenced and Jamie couldn't be retried in the event of a dismissal, they thought this would have been the place to do it. Both agreed it was not a matter of jurisdiction, and the charge form did state an offense. Therefore, it would be deemed to lack merit and be untimely as well. If they had made it before, the prosecution could have amended anyway.

The attorneys went back in chambers with Judge Tibbits, and since each side had been required to tender their instructions in advance, Judge Tibbits had the ones he planned to give organized and sitting in a pile for each side. If the attorneys wanted to make an objection on any of the proposed instructions, now was the time, and if they had any to present, they must do it now or forever hold their peace. All three of the attorneys had been there before; so had the judge. What was sometimes a tedious task, especially with inexperienced counsel or trial judge, was a piece of cake with these experienced professionals. Corbett for the prosecution and Larry for the defense announced that they "had read and studied the instructions, did not object to them, and had no additional instructions to tender."

After the court convened at two p.m. and the jury had been brought in, Judge Tibbits instructed them as to the law that they were required to follow. Part of the oath that they took was to uphold the law. They were instructed as to the nature of the charges, the elements that had to be proven, the fact that the charges were mere allegations and not evidence, the presumption of innocence, the burden of proof, the legal definition of reasonable doubt, the acceptance of circumstantial evidence, and the culpable mental state required to be proven in addition to an act, and assessment of credibility of witnesses. The jury was also given a verdict form on which they were to check either "not guilty" or "guilty" and have it signed by the foreman.

After the instructions were read, the attorneys gave their final arguments. Since the prosecution had the burden of proof, Corbett went first and would go last.

In his opening argument, Corbett outlined what he said the prosecution said they would prove in their opening statement and what they ultimately proved. "The prosecution kept its word," Corbett argued. "Alden Stillwell while searching for a file found a strap of twenty fifty-dollar bills in Mr. Cooper's desk drawer. The strap had the same Federal Reserve stamp as the other stacks of bills in the vault. Alden Stillwell became suspicious and checked the cash drawer in the vault and found thirty thousand dollars was missing. When Alden and Rita Baker had left the night before, they counted the money and set the timer on the vault door so that it couldn't be opened until seven the following morning. The vault door could not be opened until seven a.m. with the regular combination in the possession of Brandon, Alden, and Mr. Cooper.

"If the money was in the safe when the timer was set and couldn't be accessed until the timer expired by the regular combination, then how did the thief gain access? I didn't hear any testimony that it had been blown open, did you? The only way that the thief could have had access was knowledge of the manufacture override combo. The mystery was solved when Alden Stillwell found the override combo in Mr. Cooper's belongings left at the bank.

"It is clear that the road of guilt leads to Mr. Cooper. No matter how you slice it, it was Mr. Cooper who took the money. Neither Brandon Stillwell nor Alden Stillwell had the ability to access the vault while the timer was running. The only one who did was Mr. Cooper. We're asking you to return a verdict of guilty to the charge. Thank you."

Gordie had a daunting task. Corbett's argument was persuasive. One plus one equals two. Corbett's cookie trail led to the defendant, at least by Corbett's assessment.

"Ladies and gentlemen of the jury," Gordie began. "Thank you for your unselfish service. Mr. Corbett has put everything in a nice neat little package and tied it with a bow and now wants you to buy it. If you follow his directions, you'll get lost. The road of guilt doesn't lead to Jamie. It leads to someone else. When Mr. Corbett says the one thousand dollars was found in Jamie's desk drawer, he forgot to tell you that that's what Alden said. When he says the override combo was found in Jamie's belongings, he forgot to tell you that that was also what Alden said. He didn't mention in his final argument that the override combo was not in Jamie's handwriting but in Brandon's handwriting. Nor did he mention that Jamie didn't have access to Brandon's office and desk but his son Alden did. The likelihood is greater that Brandon's handwritten slip came from Brandon's desk than Jamie's belongings that supposedly sat in Alden's office several months before they were examined. By Mr. Corbett's calculations, one and one doesn't equal two. They equal four or maybe six or eight."

Gordie then asked the twenty rhetorical questions he had asked the jury in the civil case, plus one more just for this jury.

1. Who was there when the time lock expired?
2. Who opened the vault door?
3. Who was there when Rita arrived at seven fifteen a.m.?
4. Who was part of the "dual control team" that set the time lock after work the night before?
5. Who had access to the cash drawers?
6. Who unlocked the cash drawers?
7. Who claimed he discovered the money missing?
8. Who claimed he found $1,000 in Jamie's office?
9. Who was the only person, other than Brandon, who had access to Brandon's office and could have found some secret combination, if any, to override or bypass the vault time lock?
10. Who had the $1,000 in his possession when the police arrived?
11. Whose office was not searched?
12. Whose desk was not searched?
13. Whose vehicle was not searched?
14. Whose person was not searched?
15. Who searched Jamie's office?
16. Who claimed Jamie stole the money?

17. Who called the police and had Jamie arrested?

18. Who is the only one who had a fifteen-minute window to have taken the $30,000?

19. Who stood to gain the most by Jamie's arrest?

20. Who replaced Jamie as the bank's first vice president?

21. Who claims he found the override combo in Jamie's belongings some seven months after Jamie's arrest?

"If you answered Alden Stillwell to each and every one of those questions, then that road of guilt leads to someone other than Jamie," Gordie stated. "Not only has the prosecution failed to prove Jamie's guilt beyond a reasonable doubt, but the defense has done something we're not required to do, and that is prove that Jamie is not the one who committed the theft in this case. In fact, the evidence points the finger of guilt at the most likely suspect, the one who stood the most to gain from Jamie's prosecution.

"After three days of trial, everything boils down as to who to believe: Jamie or Alden Stillwell. It also boils down to motive. Who had the most to gain by eliminating Jamie? Certainly not Jamie. His being a bank officer was the realization of almost a lifelong dream that started when he first worked for SB&T Co. while still in high school. Alden Stillwell, on the other hand, couldn't stand to be in third place behind a non-Stillwell. And guess who is now the bank's first vice president? Alden Stillwell.

"During the defense's opening statement, we promised that if the evidence adduced during the trial was as we anticipated, we would have no hesitancy at the end of the trial in asking you to return a not guilty verdict. We're keeping our promise. We're not asking you to find Jamie innocent; we're just asking you to find him not guilty.

"It is not easy for an attorney to represent someone where you have to prove a negative—where you have to prove your client didn't do it. Although, remember, a defendant doesn't have to prove anything. However, Mr. Whittaker's and my job in seeing that justice is done is over. And now, ladies and gentlemen of the jury, we're putting Jamie in your hands to see that justice is done. And in doing so, we beg and pray that you return a verdict of not guilty. Thank you."

Corbett now had the last opportunity to sway the jurors. Theoretically, he could only respond to the defendant's final argument.

Corbett began, "I'll be brief. The defense had the opportunity to attempt to refute my opening argument. Now I have the opportunity to refute theirs.

"To attempt to imply that Alden Stilwell stole the thirty thousand, and not Jamie, defies all logic. To deflect guilt away from his own client is one thing, but for Mr. Brownell to suggest that Alden would in essence steal from himself is to insult the intelligence of all of you, good ladies and gentlemen. I've heard a sucker is born every minute, but I have greater faith in you that you will not fall for Mr. Brownell's and the defense's sleight of hand trick. He who commits theft must pay the price. Don't let Mr. Cooper off because Mr. Brownell says you should. Return a guilty verdict because Mr. Cooper is guilty. Thank you."

Judge Tibbits said, "Ladies and gentlemen, the bailiff will now lead you to the jury room for your deliberation. These jury instructions are yours; they will be going back to the jury room with you as well as the exhibits, with the exception of the actual cash. Let the bailiff, who will be seated outside the jury room, know when you reach a verdict or if you need something. Please follow him, keeping in mind the admonitions I've given you."

After the jury left, the attorneys were instructed to leave their telephone numbers with Judge Tibbits's clerk so that they could be available when a verdict was reached or they were otherwise needed.

The defense team went their separate ways, leaving their telephone numbers with Verna and promising to keep her informed if they were to be at a different number. Larry and Gordie said they thought it would be a long night. Little did they know that a verdict would not be rendered until late Friday.

On that Thursday afternoon at five thirty p.m. when the jury had still not been able to reach a decision, Judge Tibbits gave them a modified version of what trial attorneys alternatively refer to as *the Allen Charge, a.k.a. the Dynamite Charge, a.k.a. the Alamo Instruction, a.k.a. the Shotgun Instruction.* Simply, it meant they were to go back and try again to reach a decision. The instruction Judge Tibbits gave the jury read in part, "It is your duty as jurors to consult one another and to deliberate with a view to reaching a verdict, if you can do so without violence to individual judgment. Each of you must judge the case for yourself but do so only after impartial consideration of the evidence with your fellow jurors."

The jurors were not locked up for the night or kept together. Each was allowed to go home and return the next day. Judge Tibbits told the attorneys that if the jury had not reached a verdict by five p.m. Friday, he was going to declare a mistrial and there would be a retrial.

Larry had advised Jamie that, if Jamie was convicted, his father would be needed to agree in open court to continue the bond or Jamie would be incarcerated. So Forrest and Bessie stayed in town Thursday night with Jamie and Jennie and were prepared to do so again on Friday if necessary. In the event of a conviction, Jamie would be sentenced at a later date. They would be asking for a bond pending an appeal because certainly they would appeal any conviction.

Jamie said to Larry, "Things don't seem to be too promising, do they?"

"I can't read this jury," Larry responded, "but we need to prepare for the worst just in case."

It was colder than usual on that February Friday, and at four p.m., night was trying to assert itself. Everyone would rather be home with family in front of a warm crackling fire, snuggled in their favorite comforter. But that was not for those cast in various roles in the Cooper criminal jury trial. The Stillwells were in their usual place on the prosecution side behind the railing that separated the participants from the spectators awaiting the much-anticipated verdict. So were the usual dedicated group of curious. For the first time seated in the front row on the defense side, Jennie, Forrest, and Bessie were there to hear the good tidings, but they were prepared to be there beside their husband and son. Just in case a verdict was unfavorable, Max and Collette were staying with Larry's wife, Bonnie.

It was fingernail-biting time, and although the jury had been brought in, Judge Tibbits had not yet made his appearance. Gordie asked Larry if he noticed who had the verdict form in hand. Larry nodded. Dennis Rawles, the juror they didn't like but had to keep, was the foreman. A bad omen. Two of the female jurors, Cheryl Taylor and Arlene Richardson, were wiping tears from their eyes, and Benjamin Creaton sat shaking his head with his eyes fixed on the floor. Larry and Gordie didn't like what they saw.

While they were waiting, Jamie prayed quietly, "Heart of love, I place my trust in you. Though I fear all things from my weakness, I hope all things from your goodness."

"Judge Tibbits is taking his sweet time," Gordie whispered to Larry.

"Wonder why the delay," Larry whispered back. The longer Judge Tibbits delayed, the greater the suspense and the anxiety being experienced by the defense team especially Jamie. Clutched in Jamie's hand was a note passed to him by Jennie when she arrived in court. It read: "Regardless of the verdict, you are innocent. Whatever they do to you they do to me. Wherever you go I will be there also. Trust in God and his plan for you. Continue to give him glory regardless of the outcome. Question not his wisdom. Know you are in my heart and soul and will always be. Love, Jennie."

From the moment Judge Tibbits entered the courtroom, there was an eerie silence. Even for Larry and Gordie, it was stomach-churning time. They were representing an innocent defendant, and he had placed his future and the future of his family in their hands. They only hoped they had created enough reasonable doubt to produce a not guilty verdict. They were asking the jury to return only a *not guilty* verdict, not a verdict of *innocence*—even though the latter was warranted.

Larry's hands were clammy, and he could feel the beads of sweat drip from his underarms. He could not have been more nervous if he had been the one on trial. Trial attorneys were supposed to be dispassionate but not this time: not for him or Gordie, especially not for a defendant like Jamie. He wondered if he was the only one who could hear the pounding of his heart. If he felt that way, what about poor Jamie, his wife, and his parents? What must they be feeling?

When Judge Tibbits asked if the jury had reached the verdict, Dennis Rawles stood and announced they had. The jury foreman was then instructed to hand the verdict form to the bailiff, and he immediately complied. The bailiff, in turn, delivered it to the judge. Judge Tibbits then asked Jamie to stand. After a longer pause than usual, Judge Tibbits read from the verdict form.

"We the jury duly impaneled and sworn in the above entitled cause do find defendant, James Curtis Cooper, a.k.a. Jamie Cooper … guilty of felony theft, to wit: embezzlement of bank funds."

While the verdict was being read, Larry and Gordie had stood on each side of Jamie. When the word *guilty* was announced, Jamie sagged, and it was as if life left him at that very moment. He was assisted to the closest chair, and the court took a short recess. Jennie, in the interim, was being assisted to by Jamie's parents and was soon joined by Bodean, who removed the three to the conference room just outside the main doors of the courtroom. To Judge Tibbit's credit, he allowed Jamie, accompanied by two uniformed sheriff's deputies who had been called to be present at the announcement of the verdict, to go to be with Jennie.

In his head, Larry could still hear the ring of the word *guilty*. A word no defense counsel wants to hear as well as Jennie's heart-wrenching sobs as she was being lead from the courtroom.

He also replayed the looks exchanged between Jamie, Jennie, and Jamie's parents just prior to the reading of the verdict. As strong as Jamie had been throughout the whole ordeal, the guilty verdict was more than even he could bear. Jamie and his family were now on a collision course with destiny.

Except for the Stillwells and their faithful, those who remained in the courtroom sat in stunned silence. Even Corbin Sweeney, who remained in the courtroom after the verdict was announced with one of his reporters, sat shaking his head in disbelief. The only Stillwell not taking a curtain call was Debbie, Alden's wife. She sat as still as a block of salt as the other Stillwells congratulated each other. The Stillwells had set out to bury Jamie, and at long last they had, at least for the moment, succeeded.

Verna, who had been summoned by Bodean, helped calm Jennie and Jamie's parents and ushered Jennie and Jamie's mother from the court house to the law offices of Whitaker and Brownell. Jamie's father returned back to the courtroom to be with his son. Jamie was still paralyzed by the verdict but did manage to signal to his father that he was all right and received a signal back from his father that all was well on that end. Jamie was much more concerned about his family than himself and was feeling pangs of guilt about all he was putting them through.

The rest was a blur for Jamie, but he vaguely remembered that after the court reconvened, the jury was brought back into the courtroom and polled at Larry's request. The jury was given the stock discharge instruction. They were discharged with Judge Tibbit's thanks. The defense made its obligatory motion for judgment of acquittal, notwithstanding the verdict. It was denied. Jamie's bond was doubled. His father agreed to stay on the bond. Sentencing was now continued to February 22, Washington's Birthday, at ten a.m. Bodean had followed the jury out so that he could speak with the various jurors if they were so disposed.

—————————————————

The defense team together with Jamie and his father retired to the law offices of Whittaker and Brownell. There they would try to regroup and reassess the situation as dispassionately as they could. No one was able to hide his or her feelings, and no one tried.

Although the outcome was predictable, it was still a tremendous letdown. Even when things look dismal, there was always that glimmer of hope that against all odds Jamie would emerge victorious.

Bodean came in fresh from having interviewed three of the jurors. They told him the first vote was split six and six, pretty much along gender lines. Edith Alder (number one) and five of the male jurors voted for conviction; Mr. Creaton and the other five women voted for acquittal. They were pretty much deadlocked until there were nine for conviction and three for acquittal. When they received the modified Allen charge, the two women, Cheryl Taylor and Arlene Richardson became circumspect and voted with the majority. Benjamin Creaton held out, but when he determined it was futile, voted for conviction.

The jurors, Bodean related, felt that the case hinged on the credibility of Jamie and Alden. Even though Alden had something to gain, they thought it unlikely that he would steal from his own father and ultimately himself. They thought if he had taken the money, it most likely would have magically reappeared. The claim of the $1,000 was not as important as the finding of the override combo in Jamie's belongings. Without that, one juror said, they probably would have acquitted.

The three men, led by Dennis Rawles, who was selected foreman, said Jamie had a "motive" as they called it, and that was some kind of gambling problem Jamie was having in Las Vegas at the time. The three holdouts had told Rawles that that information was not in evidence and that it was improper to even consider it. Rawles mentioned gambling only one other time after that. Bodean asked the three holdouts if they would be willing to sign an affidavit stating what they had just told him, and they said they would.

"I don't believe it," Gordie said in indignation. "The jurors were *voir dired* on that point and said they could set aside what they read, saw, and/or heard and judge the case *solely* on the evidence presented at trial. After they were impaneled, Judge Tibbits instructed them on numerous occasions not to consider anything other than the evidence presented in the courtroom. His admonitions obviously fell on deaf ears."

Larry, who had been unusually quiet and numbed by and since the verdict, said, "Tibbits's so-called alternatives to a change of venue didn't work, did they? That shows it was error to have denied our change of venue motion in the first place. The trial from the beginning was tainted by the massive and pervasive pretrial publicity. The jurors had already made up their minds and Tibbits's so-called trial-level remedies (i.e., *voir dire* and admonitions) worked about as well as tossing a bag of cement to a drowning victim."

"Failing to change the place of trial is certainly a great appellate issue that should result in a reversal of Jamie's conviction," Gordie added, feeling it was little consolation.

POST-CONVICTION PHASE

The law firm of Whittaker and Brownell filed a motion for new trial, motion for a mistrial, motion to set aside verdict and motion for stay of sentencing. In their motion for new trial, the defense claimed that the court had erred prior to trial and at trial in not granting defendant's motion for change of venue; not striking the SB&T Co.'s customers from the jury panel; in admitting the band and twenty fifty-dollar bills in evidence; and, in not granting defendant's motion for judgment of acquittal and motion for judgment of acquittal *non obstante veredicto*.

In support of the defendant's assertion that the court erred in not granting their motion for change of venue, the affidavits of three jurors were attached, confirming that the jury in its deliberations considered pretrial evidence that had not been introduced at the criminal trial, the jury was prejudiced by such evidence, and *voir dire* and admonitions to the jury had been totally ineffective.

In the alternative, because of juror misconduct, primarily the improprieties of Dennis Rawles in interjecting the gambling motive, the defense argued that the court should vacate the verdict, not enter judgment thereon, and grant a mistrial.

The defendant's motion also asked that the court vacate the sentencing and dedicate the sentencing date to a hearing on the defendant's motion for new trial and his other post-trial motions.

Corbett opposed defendant's motion for new trial and other motions and conceded that the sentencing date should be postponed and that a hearing be held on defendant's post-trial motions.

Judge Tibbits vacated the sentencing date and set the hearing on the motion for new trial and other post-trial motions in its place. At the hearing on the motion for new trial and post-trial motions, the defense called the three jurors whose affidavits had been submitted to the court. Each reaffirmed what was in their respective affidavits and testified that they were swayed by gambling references in their deliberations, if not consciously, certainly subconsciously. Judge Tibbits denied the motion for new trial as well as the other post-trial motions on the grounds that the jury had spoken, and if there was error, it was not so serious as to deprive Jamie of a fair trial. He then entered a judgment of conviction based on the guilty verdict. So much for that. Sentencing was continued until Wednesday, February 28 at ten a.m.

Prior to sentencing, Gordie had filed a notice of appeal with the Colorado Court of Appeals. He was the firm's appellate expert. He also filed a motion to stay sentencing pending appeal. By minute order, Judge Tibbits denied the motion. Sentencing would take place on February 28, 1973, at ten a.m. The case had been referred to the probation department when sentencing was first set. They interviewed Jamie and the victim, SB&T Co. Alden had been the spokesman for the bank. Alden said the bank recommended prison time, but he didn't say how much. The bank opposed probation. The probation officer submitted a presentence investigative report (PSIR) to Judge Tibbits recommending probation for two years, one hundred hours of community service, and $4,000 restitution to the bank. It was not recommended that Jamie reimburse the insurance company for their payout to the bank because that matter had been litigated in the civil trial.

At the sentencing hearing, Corbett said he would leave the matter totally within the court's discretion and when asked by the court, said he didn't disagree with the probation department's recommendations. He cited Jamie's otherwise clean criminal record, the fact that this was not a case involving a violent crime, and considering the circumstantial nature of the case, no eyewitnesses.

Corbett had upstaged Larry somewhat, but Larry stressed that Jamie was a good candidate for probation; that he had been a productive member of society; that he would not be a threat to society, that the financial support of his wife and family was dependent upon him; that his children were young and needed a father; that society would not benefit if he were incarcerated, not only because of the removal of a productive member, but the expense attendant to incarceration; and that the ends of justice would better be served by placing Jamie on probation. Brandon Stillwell, along with Alden, was in the courtroom. Judge Tibbits asked Brandon if he would have any objection to the granting of probation. Brandon stated that he and his son Alden had a disagreement on that point, but that he, Brandon, had no objection to probation.

Despite the PSIR report, the recommendation of the probation officer and Corbett's and Brandon's statements, Judge Tibbits sentenced Jamie to the maximum, ten years in prison and a fine of $5,000, plus costs of prosecution. Jennie, who was in the courtroom with Jamie's parents, fainted, and a recess was taken while she was revived and taken out of the courtroom.

Judge Tibbits did agree to stay execution of the sentence pending appeal and also agreed to Jamie continuing to stay out on bond, assuming Forrest had no objection. He didn't. Judge Tibbits made it clear that Jamie would be wasting his time to file a motion for reconsideration of sentence. Even if Judge Tibbits hadn't stayed the sentence of imprisonment, it became automatic upon Jamie's filing of his notice of appeal.

IN THE WAKE OF UTTER
DISASTER: UTTER DESPAIR

From the time of Jamie's arrest, the Coopers' lives had been turned upside down. Nothing would ever be the same, but they hadn't realized just how much.

They were already in the throes of financial ruin, and to pay a $5,000 fine, the court costs, and the attorney fees, past and present, meant they would have to sell their home. Ultimately, that's what they did, moving in with Jamie's parents until they could renovate the house that had formerly been occupied by his grandparents. Max and Collette, being closer to the Hayden School system, transferred there. One good thing, at least, they were closer to their church, which had not abandoned them.

Jamie resigned his chamber post before he was asked to do so. The house sold quickly. The snows had melted somewhat, but moving was still a hassle, especially when they left the county road and turned into the Cooper Ranch. They had a lot of help that last weekend in March with the rest of the defense team and their wives, Charlie Blankenship, Corbin Sweeney, and their church friends. Life could have been worse, but Jamie and Jennie didn't know how.

The appeal took about ten months, and Jamie's conviction was affirmed by the Colorado Court of Appeals the Friday after Christmas, December 28, 1973. The Colorado Supreme Court refused to hear the case. Jamie turned himself in to the Routt County Jail and was delivered to the Colorado State Penitentiary in Canon City to begin his ten-year sentence on January 4, 1974. With good time—earned time, Jamie would be released in about five years and could be eligible for parole even sooner. Whittaker and Brownell even tried to get Jamie's case heard before the United States Supreme Court, but the high court declined to issue a *writ of certiorari*.

Outwardly, he appeared very brave as he said his good-byes to Jennie, Max, Collette, and his parents and told them that time would go by quickly and they would all be back together soon. Inwardly, he felt as though his heart and soul had been snatched from him. He felt hollow inside. Unable to sleep at all the previous night, he was still haunted by the thought of his conviction and having to leave his family behind. As he was led from the sheriff's office to the unmarked cruiser that would transport him across the expanse of Colorado to the Colorado State Penitentiary, he took one last look at Jennie, Max, Collette, and his parents, and he also caught his last glimpse of freedom. Coming to grips with uncertainties, he would learn, would become a dauntless task.

Jamie did the best he could in prison, taking whatever courses they offered. He even became the assistant chaplain and helped his fellow prisoners cope with their birdcage life and having nothing but time on their hands. He read incessantly and started writing poetry. He was helping inmates draft *habeas corpus* petitions and told Larry during visits to get an office ready for him because he would be ready to practice law when he was released.

Jennie was frantic without her Jamie. Forrest and Bessie started to suspect she was sampling the "sauce." Max and Collette were coping, but that was about all. Even after they moved into the renovated Cooper cottage, they still missed their home and their friends. Nothing was the same without their daddy. Even Maya tired of running to the door whenever she heard a car drive into the Cooper Ranch. One day she just disappeared and never came back.

Jamie had barely served two and a half years in the Colorado State Penitentiary when he was stabbed in the chest by a homemade knife while trying to break up a fight in the prison's exercise area. The wound was serious, the knife having pierced one of the valves in his heart. Told Jamie was not expected to live, Jennie, Max, and Collette, accompanied by Larry and Bonnie, were at his side in the prison infirmary. Jamie told Max to go to law school like Uncle Larry and Uncle Gordie and fight for all those poor innocent souls who had no one to fight for them.

He told Max and Collette, "I had all these great things I was going to tell you, and now I can't remember them. When I see you, all I can think of is how much I love you and thank God he put you in my life. I can't imagine how empty it would have been without you. But I won't be that far away, and I will be watching you every day. When you look at the sky, smile and never frown, otherwise I will think you're upset with me. When you think you're alone, God will be on one side of you, and I will be on the other. Please promise me that you will live your life in such a way that we all end up in the same place, together someday. I would not want to spend eternity without you."

Wearing the religious medal and chain that Larry had given him at the start of his legal journey, and with his two hands extended and holding Larry's two hands in one and Bonnie's two hands in another, Jamie said, "Take care of these three like you took care of me." Looking into Larry's eyes, he said, "See you in the big court in the sky."

Even though his injury theoretically prevented him from sitting up, he sat erect, and reaching for Jennie said, "What are you doing up here? I didn't know they would let you wear that sea-blue satin dress here. You look gorgeous, my fair lady." Pulling her close, their eyes reflecting their undying love for each other, Jamie left to be with the Lord. Jennie's heart went with him.

Life was pretty difficult without a husband, a father, and a son, but somehow Jennie, Max, and Collette and Jamie's parents survived. Max and then Collette finished school. Max went on to college. But just before Collette's high school graduation, Max received a letter from Larry saying that Collette had run away. That was May of 1981 when Collette was eighteen years old. Max had not heard from his mother in quite some time and depended upon Larry, Bonnie, and his grandparents for news from home.

With her husband's death, Collette's disappearance and Max away at school, Jennie's constant companion became the bottle. In short order, Jennie was fighting acute alcoholism and in and out of rehab. A DUI conviction resulted in her losing her privilege to drive, and she ultimately was forced to sell her car to pay for her daily supply of coping power.

It was not long before Max received word that his mother was frequenting the local cowboy taverns and bars and would bring a cowboy home now and then. The news from his grand-parents was so distressing that Max started throwing away their letters without reading them.

Max worked the summers in Boulder and came back home very seldom. It was not really home, and ever since his father's conviction, he was made to feel like a stranger in his own town. Wherever he went, he was held up to ridicule and scorn and introduced as the son of the con or bank embezzler or some other pejorative reference. It was so depressing when he went home that it took weeks to work out of the depression.

The year Max graduated law school, he received word that his mother had passed away. That was on September 16, 1985, the day after her forty-seventh birthday. The death certificate recorded the cause of death as acute alcoholism and heart failure. Max told the county coroner that the cause was not heart failure but a broken heart.

It wasn't too many years later that Max's grandfather and then grandmother passed away. The Cooper Ranch was sold. Half of the proceeds went to Max, and the other half was put in trust for Collette, if and when she returned.

The ordeal had played itself out. There were no more Coopers in Routt County, and the ranch was no longer referred to as the Cooper Ranch. All traces had been erased, and now every-one could go on with their lives and live as though the Coopers never existed.

PART THREE:
THE ORDEAL IS OVER

THE END OF AN ERA

When the plane touched down at Yampa Valley Regional Airport shortly after ten p.m., Max had regained his composure. With the coffee intake, the adrenaline pumping and an air of confidence, he was preparing for whatever awaited him. Mr. Whittaker or Uncle Larry, as Max fondly referred to him, was there to meet him. They hadn't seen each other for a number of years, and Max wasn't sure they would recognize each other. Time and space, as it turned out, had not been an impediment. They gravitated toward each other as if drawn by a magnet. "Uncle Larry!" Max shouted.

"Max!" he echoed back. They shook hands, embraced, cried, laughed, and patted each other on the back all at the same time. While they embraced, Larry whispered in Max's ear, "Max, the ordeal is over."

Taking Uncle Larry aside, Max said, "The suspense is so overwhelming that I can't contain myself. What was the 'development' in my father's case that caused you to summon me?" Larry stood there beaming, trying to find words to respond.

"You said I needed to drop everything I was doing for the next several days and book an immediate flight for Steamboat!"

Still trying to find words, Larry finally said, "Max, it's about time you just called me Larry. You've earned that with your law degree and all. The reason for the urgency, to cut to the chase, is that our nemesis, Alden Stillwell, before he died, made a deathbed confession admitting that it was he who embezzled the bank's funds and that your dad was innocent. He admitted to framing your father and said he had lived with his sin too long and wanted to make peace with those he wronged and especially his Maker."

As Max stood there speechless and in shock, Larry continued, "Alden was able to describe where the money had been stashed, that the bank remodel had prevented its retrieval, and that he was afraid of getting caught if he ever attempted to remove it."

Incredulously, Max asked, "Larry, did they recover the money? Was it in the place Alden said it was?"

"No, to your first question," Larry replied. "In answer to your second question, the recovery process is being formulated as we speak."

When Max asked Larry if he had any idea what Alden had said about the location of the money, he said that Alden's wife and one of their daughters contacted him with the news last Saturday. Alden had told them that back in 1972 there was a trapdoor in his office covered by a throw rug with a large oak roll-top desk that had been atop the throw rug for years.

The trapdoor, which was undetectable, led to a cellar where some old metal file cabinets containing early bank records were stored. His grandfather, the late Wellington D. Stillwell, had conscripted Alden for help in moving the roll-top desk to gain access to these records. Alden was only twelve or thirteen years old at the time, and the grandfather and grandson were the only ones at the bank. The grandfather made Alden promise he would never divulge the existence or location of what he called their "secret hideaway."

The trapdoor and oak desk were located in a storeroom accessible only by what later would become Alden's office. In 1972, Alden, who was then thirty-four years of age and an employee of the bank, had somehow obtained an override combination to the main vault, whereby he could access the vault while the timer was running. He was the only one who had the override combination, which ordinarily the manufacturer solely possessed.

Alden then requisitioned, without authority, $30,000 in various strapped bills each containing $1,000 bearing the stamp of the Federal Reserve Bank of Denver. He then placed $1,000 of strapped fifty-dollar bills in the bottom drawer of Max's father's desk (without Max's father's knowledge). The remaining $29,000 was put in the drawers of one of the file cabinets stored in the "secret hideaway."

When Alden went to a banking conference in Salt Lake City, Utah, in early 1973, his father, Brandon Stillwell, still president of Steamboat Bank and Trust Co. surprised his son upon the latter's return with a newly remodeled office. The remodel included new floors. Since no one made mention of the trap door and it couldn't easily be seen, it was covered over. Alden never gained access and was never able to retrieve the $29,000.00 without raising a red flag.

"The look of shock on Alden's face when he returned to find the 'secret hideaway' sealed was no doubt construed as an expression of surprise and joy," said Larry with a chuckle.

"No doubt," Max muttered.

"Alden's widow and daughter recorded the deathbed confession and have allowed me to copy it. Would you like to listen to it?"

"Not right now. Does the Steamboat Police Department have the tape?"

"They have the tape as well as a written statement from the two of them. They also have given written permission to have the flooring removed to expose the trapdoor."

"Can we be there to witness the recovery?"

"They've included me in the recovery process, and I assume they'll have no problem if you tag along."

"Did Alden say anything about the slip of paper with the override combination written on it?"

"He told his wife and daughter that while his father was at a conference in Salt Lake City, and while looking in his father's desk, he accidently stumbled upon the strange combination. Suspecting it might be an override combo, he tried it while the bank vault timer was on, and it worked. He said that's how he accessed the cash when no one was around."

"How did it end up in my father's belongings?"

"Alden said he planted it there to draw attention to your father."

"So Alden planted $1,000 that he took from the vault in Dad's desk drawer and placed the vault's time lock override combo in Dad's belongings to make it look as though Dad sneaked in after hours, accessed the vault, and stole the money?"

"Exactly."

"If everything pans out as expected, what do you think our chances are of having my father's conviction vacated and his record expunged?"

"With the cooperation of everyone, including the district attorney's office, the police department, and SB&T Co., it's a slam dunk!"

"I hope you're right. Only then will justice truly be done."

THE LAST GOOD-BYES

When Larry and Max arrived at the Steamboat Bank and Trust Co. that snowy February day, the carpet layer was busy peeling the carpet away from the east wall of the annex to Alden's old office. The large oak rolltop desk originally belonging to Alden's grandfather had been moved to the opposite wall. It was not long before the hidden trap door was exposed and opened. A Steamboat Police Department Detective and the investigator from the district attorney's office descended into the darkness below with spotlights, returning with a musty money bag bearing SB&T Co. on the outside. Inside was the $29,000 Max's father had been accused of taking.

"All roads did lead to Alden," Larry said, barely audible.

"What did you say?" Max asked.

"Twenty-seven years ago almost to the day, Gordie argued to the jury in your father's case that the road of guilt led to Alden Stillwell, not to your father."

"I wonder what the jury would say today, if they were here to witness this recovery," Max said.

"They would find your father not guilty and join us in having your father's conviction vacated posthumously and beg for mercy for having bet on the wrong horse."

"I hope the police department and D.A.'s office issue a joint press release, and I hope the headlines reach from end to end on that front page proclaiming 'Cooper Vindicated in Death,'" Max said.

Larry met with the new district attorney, and together they drafted a motion in arrest of judgment/motion to vacate judgment of conviction/motion to dismiss with prejudice/motion to expunge records. It was immediately presented to Judge Tibbits's successor, the Honorable Horace T. L. Casey. Judge Casey knew about the famous case of *People v. Cooper*. He even had read the file and a copy of the court transcript. He readily signed every place his signature was required.

"The court will make sure that everything is erased, even his incarceration in the Colorado State Penitentiary."

"Thank you, Judge," Max said.

"Mr. Whittaker, would you like my clerk to issue a press release on the ruling?"

"Yes, thank you Judge."

"Larry?"

"Yes."

"Would you drive me to the Hayden Memorial Cemetery so I can visit my parents' graves, maybe for the last time?"

"Absolutely."

Both knew where the graves were because they had been there many times. But it had been a number of years since Max had been there. He was surprised when he saw that a small evergreen had been placed there. "You and Bonnie?" Max asked.

"Yes."

Max and Larry brushed the snow off the large granite head-stone that was shaped like the Roman arch that had spanned the two windows of Max's father's office at the bank. Along the curve was chiseled "Inseparable in Life—Inseparable in Death." Near the peak of the semicircle in the middle were two angels holding hands. Facing the stone, one side of the gravestone was inscribed:

James Curtis Cooper
"Jamie"
Born July 15, 1938
Died July 4, 1976
The other side of the gravestone was inscribed:
Jennie Mae Cooper
Born September 15, 1938
Died September 16, 1985

Max and Larry also visited the graves of Max's grandparents and great-grandparents.

On the way back to Steamboat Springs, Larry said he had a confession to make. Slowly and haltingly, Larry revealed that Collette hadn't run off. She had been institutionalized. She was in a private sanitarium near Steamboat. Larry, Bonnie, his mother, and grandparents hadn't told Max for fear that he too, with all that he had been through, would go off the deep end. They wanted to spare him the anguish.

Larry asked Max if he wanted to see her and give her the wonderful news.

"Will she recognize me?"

"I don't know. She recognizes Bonnie and me."

"Will she understand what I'm telling her?"

"Hard to say. Sometimes she appears to understand; other times not."

"I would like to see her!"

At Strawberry Park Enrichment Center, Inc., one of the attendants led Larry and Max into a wing that reminded Max of a college dormitory. The room had a door with wire-inlaid glass. Through the window Max could see a surprisingly attractive slim woman in a white flower-patterned gown. She had medium-length auburn hair and was wearing white stockings, no jewelry, and no makeup. She appeared to be reading a book in her lap, but there was no book. "She's been like that ever since she was admitted," Larry said sadly.

Before they arrived, Larry had told Max that Collette had not uttered a word since she was institutionalized. "Outwardly she manifests no emotional reaction and has no facial expression. Be prepared."

The attendant opened the unlocked door for the two men then departed. Collette did not look up when Larry and Max entered. They positioned themselves in front of the motionless figure sitting on the rocker. When Larry asked how she was doing, she looked up; a faint glint appeared in her eyes. He took her hand and said, "I have a surprise for you. I brought someone you haven't seen in a long time."

When Larry said, "This is your brother," she looked with expressionless eyes at Max, and several tears appeared on her cheeks. She appeared to smile as she stared at Max and him at her. Max, eyes watering, couldn't utter a word.

It seemed like forever, but Max finally regained some composure. In a shaky voice he said, "Our father has been completely vindicated of the theft charges for which he had been wrongfully convicted those many years ago. He has been completely exonerated and cleared of the charge! Alden Stillwell confessed to the theft and to setting Dad up. You can now rest in peace knowing Dad was innocent. We can all rest in peace."

Collette just stared and said nothing. Larry and Max talked softly together. Max recounted some of the memorable times they had as children when they were with their parents and grandparents. Max spoke to Collette about his wife and children and what he did for a living. He thought he detected some recognition and some reaction, but he couldn't be sure. As they were leaving and closing the door, Max turned back and, hesitating for a moment, stared in amazement as a faint smile appeared upon Collette's face as she looked heavenward and clasped her hands as if in prayer.

After her brother's visit, Collette's psychotherapist determined that her cognition was returning, and within six weeks she was starting to utter words and then whole sentences. Within fifteen weeks, Collette was diagnosed as having overcome her psychotic disorder. Her mental competence having been restored, she was soon released. Collette moved to Chicago to live with Max and his wife. And, after receiving her share of the proceeds from her grandparents' estate, which amounted to $1.4 million with accumulated interest, she purchased a house next to Max and Pam's. She enrolled in college and graduated with honors with a degree in psychology. Collette would go on to write a book in her field, entitled *Shedding the Old to Make Room for the New*. The period from her father's arrest until Max's visit, some thirty-six years, had been completely erased from her mind. Collette's psychotherapist described this as selective psychogenic amnesia, which he indicated occurs in a dissociative state. Max never spoke of the ordeal with Collette again. If he had, she would have had no idea what he was talking about.

With the ordeal behind him and all that he had recently experienced, he would be the type of father to his children, grandfather to his grandchildren, and if God willing, great-grandfather to his great-grandchildren that they all deserved.

Whether freeman or prisoner, everyone entering the Jamie Cooper Memorial Chapel at the Colorado State Penitentiary in Canon City, Colorado, passes a large brass plaque with the engraved inscription:

> Welcome to the Jamie Cooper Memorial Chapel dedicated to the man who was unable to cheat destiny but was cheated by destiny instead. Not vindicated in life, he was vindicated in death. His legacy lives on for laying down his life for a fellow inmate—not caring if he were innocent or guilty. *Greater love has no one than this that he laid down his life for his friends.*

Max and Collette would not have been aware of the plaque if they had not been invited to partake in the dedication of the extensive remodel of the chapel and library complex, made possible thanks to the generous contribution of a benefactor known only by the initials L.W.